The Virus

By Steven A. Spellman

DEER HAWK
PUBLICATIONS

THE VIRUS is published by:
Deer Hawk Publishing, an imprint of
Deer Hawk Enterprises
www.deerhawkpublications.com

This is a work of fiction. Names, characters,
places, brands, media and incidents portrayed in this book
are either the product of the author's imagination or are
used fictitiously.

Cover design by:
Ray Polizzi

Layout by:
Aurelia Sands

Library of Congress Control Number:
2013948604

Printed in the United States of America

For my wife, the only reason I've made it thus far...

Chapter 1

"I need a heart monitor in here stat!" the doctor yelled.

"Get me an oxygen machine!" another demanded.

The scene was chaotic: Nurses and assistants rushing to and fro, struggling to gather machines and medical materials that were being demanded much more quickly than they could be produced. Everyone was wearing thoroughly-sanitized, impeccably clean white hospital gear. With the bright lights and ubiquitous stainless steel surfaces, the scene was unreal; a blur of cloudy movements against a backdrop of colorless walls and glistening instruments. All the chaos was because a single female patient had complained of minor shortness of breath. But this was not just any medical facility, and this was not just any patient. This was *the* patient, the only woman left who could save mankind.

Chapter 2

The United States Space Quest Program was something completely new to the nation's wealthy elite. Russia had been sending civilians, for a very hefty fee that is, to the International Space Station orbiting Earth for nearly a year now. Just as with the Sputnik crisis, the U.S. was scrambling to catch up. Sure, there was a U.S. startup company that could broker a private trip into the great beyond for an American at a cost of a miniscule 25 to 30 million dollars but, like all private space trips at the time, transport was handled solely by a Russian government agency, the Russian Space Alliance, and thus all flights launched from Russian soil...not very patriotic.

Then, a massive break for the U.S. came in the form of a shrewd political maneuver on the part of the Russian Federation. Russia's human presence on the International Space Station was of paramount importance to the Federation. When the Russian men on the space station informed their home country that they needed more men and additional provisions, Russia was quick to act. Unfortunately for the Federation, however, this meant that private flights to the International Space Station would have to be temporarily halted, as all available space on flights, private or otherwise, would be needed to carry Russian astronauts and supplies. With so many private entities more than willing to foot the bill to say that they had ventured into space, this halt, even temporary as it was, could represent hundreds of millions of dollars in lost revenue for Russia. With America being the only other country with the technology and money to send ordinary civilians into space, what could they do? Would they be willing to lose their stranglehold on the extremely lucrative fledgling space tourism industry, and, to, of all countries, *America*? Absolutely not, was the cumulative Russian cry.

The stalemate seemed impossible, until some of the Federation's top officials came up with an ingenious plan. Through a series of secret meetings, the United States government was presented with an interesting opportunity. The Russian Space Alliance would temporarily concede its monopoly on the space tourism business to the U.S., allowing private companies in the U.S. to host flights from American soil, but with two conditions: America would announce publicly that the flights were still *Russian* endeavors, and pay the Russian government a sizeable 25 percent of the proceeds. With returns of over 150 percent, 25 percent was more than reasonable, even though American companies would have to pay 100 percent of the bill, and so, the U.S. eventually agreed to the terms. It would seem that, at least sometimes, American patriotism extended only to where the product ended up...not from whence it originated.

As soon as the word spread that private flights were leaving from American soil, the already lengthy waiting list grew tenfold. To be the very first in outer space was everyone's great desire, but, it would only be awarded to one. The lucky participant—*lucky* being a very subjective word, considering the fact that the participant paid close to 60 million dollars for the privilege—was a successful American entrepreneur named Lenard Hanson. He was the well-known founder of the largest luxury hotel and spa chain in the world, Hanson Hotels. A billionaire in his mid-seventies, Lenard Hanson saw a trip into outer space as one of the final accomplishments he could hope to enjoy before his life drew to an inevitable end. He had been on the waiting list for a number of years, and never expected the possibility of actually taking off from his own country. Now that such an opportunity had unexpectedly arisen, he was happy to pay a few extra million dollars to be secretly moved up the list, and thus, Lenard Hanson secured the glorious privilege of being the very first non-astronaut American to be launched into space from his native soil.

But, for all the excitement, the milestone was not to be reached, at least not by the elder Mr. Hanson. He had been on the waiting list for more than a few years (twelve and a half to be exact) and back when he had first signed up, he was in much better shape. Now, he was an old man, not capable of handling the particular rigors and stresses associated with being blasted through Earth's atmosphere, as was clearly shown by the fact that he could no longer endure the months of intense preparations and tests that were required of any participant before space flight. Of course, Mr. Hanson was greatly disappointed to say the least, but there was still an option left: His daughter, his only child. She was still young, only twenty-two and a half at the time, and so, she could still endure what her father could not. She could still make it possible for the Hanson name to be the first to take advantage of this great privilege. The only thing that remained for Lenard was to convince his privileged daughter that this was an opportunity, as risk ridden as it was, that she would want to take advantage of. Only time would tell if his powers of persuasion were as capable as his business savvy.

Chapter 3

Delilah Hanson was an exceptionally beautiful young lady. Her creamy shade of coppered skin always glistened as if freshly polished. Her hair was always freshly pressed or curled into the most up-to-date styles available, and her face had the high, perfect cheekbones and enviable symmetry of a supermodel. If a book *could* be judged by its cover, then this one would certainly not disappoint. Delilah was every bit as spoiled and superior as her fabulously good looks suggested. Her face was gorgeous, all the more so when she flashed those well-choreographed smiles of hers, and her body...well, suffice it to say, she was a complete knockout in every respect. Just as she had been born with exceptionally beautiful looks, so she had also been birthed into the great privilege that comes with ridiculous wealth. Since the day she was born, her father saw to it that she had anything she asked for, as well as a great many things that she hadn't asked for. The few things his money could not purchase for her—and which, consequently, she didn't desire—were discipline and substance of character. But who needs such trivial things? It wasn't like intrinsic worth was nearly as important as high limit credit cards.

Delilah had been named so by her mother. Her father, who didn't often oppose the wishes of his wife, did, however, protest at this. Such a name, he reasoned, came with undoubtedly negative connotations, and besides, the name Delilah meant 'impoverished', which the Hansons most emphatically were *not*. Lenard's wife, however, was the very personification of a strong-willed woman and the fact that her husband told her no on something signified to her that it was the right move to make. Later, when Delilah was teased in school and wanted to know why she had been named thus, her mother kindly and patiently informed her that her namesake embodied strength.

"The world is meant to be ruled by women, My Darling." said her mother, "The strongest man who ever lived was conquered by a woman, and I named you Delilah because I want you to remember that there is no man so strong that you cannot conquer."

From that point on, Delilah was proud of her name. It was a faithful reminder that she was the rightful ruler of the world. There was nothing she could not possess and no one who could deny her whatever her pompous heart desired. Thereafter, whenever she was teased by the other girls about her name, she would proudly explain to them that they were weak and frail, destined to be ruled over by men even more weak and frail than they, and that she alone was worthy to be called woman. Any of her female peers who listened to her long enough, would usually end up feeling inferior for not being taught as she was, to know their rightful place of being able to subvert any man. Since the Hanson's money made Delilah very popular wherever she went, she was sure to turn the tide in her favor among the other impressionable youths in whatever private school she happened to be. As time went on, she began to see arrogance not as a vice but as an extreme virtue that everyone save the elite were just too misled to properly appreciate. When her mother died, she knew that she had to appreciate the virtue doubly so.

Delilah's mother had smoked expensive cigarettes in the same long, elaborately-engraved, and polished ivory cigarette holder for as long as anyone could remember. The sight of such fashion accessories were extremely rare in modern society and whenever anyone would inquire about the practice, she would kindly inform them that she was a woman of uncommon class, like Marilyn Monroe and the debutantes of old, who also practiced such extravagances, and that such class never went out of style. She believed herself so resolutely that it was difficult for anyone else to not believe, or at least not admire her as well. It was this 'high fashion' that brought on the throat cancer that spelled her demise a few years before her husband was medically rejected for his scheduled space flight. As per her ardent demand, she was buried with her cigarette holder and custom-made silk gloves with which she always used to hold it.

One of her mottos was that she had "Lived by my own damn rules, and will damn well die by them too." And so, even in her coffin, she was dressed to the hilt and accompanied by some of her closest and truest friends: Her dazzling gloves and her expensive cigarettes.

Initially, she was supposed to have accompanied her husband into outer space (or rather, it was *he* who was doing the accompanying, if you had asked her) and it was not too long after her passing that Lenard began trying to convince his daughter to take her place. Now that he found out that he could not go either, convincing his daughter to assume the torch, so to speak, was doubly important. For one thing, the newly-forged American space tourism project was just getting off the ground—literally—and a strict no refund policy was instituted, which meant that if Delilah didn't take the trip, Lenard would simply be out of tens of millions of dollars. Even more important than the money though, was Lenard's reputation. How could he ever face the guys at the country club once word got out that he had forked over a fortune for an opportunity that he was now too old and out of shape to take advantage of? It was already a sensational back alley truth among his peers that it was his wife who had worn the pants in the Hanson household, and now, with her gone and him unable to complete this trip, it would certainly look like he wasn't man enough to do *anything* without her.

Having his daughter take their place wouldn't ease the sting of what Lenard knew to be public perception of him much, but it was better than rock bottom. The only problem was that Delilah wanted nothing to do with it. She was young, rich, and free of concern. She saw no reason to be cooped up in some spacecraft just because it was a 'historical opportunity'. The space suit she would wear wouldn't even be a designer label! Outrageous! It was only when her father drew attention to the fact that she would be the youngest person to ever make the trip—something none of her friends could boast—that she began to come around. He told her she could expect to receive considerable press before she left and especially upon her safe return. Lenard painted a picture for his daughter that he knew she would understand: One of flashing cameras, eagerly awaiting throngs of admirers, and most of all—most of all—the envy of anybody who was somebody in the world of privilege.

Much to his satisfaction, his daughter eventually agreed to the endeavor. With that, he had saved a measure of face among his elite associates. During the months of rigorous exercises and tests that Delilah was subjected to, she wanted to quit many times, but even the overly-privileged have *something* for which they will fight, well beyond their precious comfort zones. For Delilah, that something was the promise of being the recipient of jealousy and envy on an epic scale. The applause of many who she knew would secretly hate her being the youngest and first American tourist in space, was enough for her to subject herself to that which no other motive would—discipline. She completed the course, which was, by no means, an easy feat, and within a few months, was blasted off into the black recesses of outer space. At her beckoning, her father had paid an extra five million dollars for her to be able to take a guided two and a half hour long 'spacewalk' on the space station (more for her peers to be envious of) and by all accounts, the trip was a success. That is, except for a single, unexplained phenomenon that took place just before the cramped Soyuz spacecraft housing Delilah and two certified astronauts, exited Earth's atmosphere.

Delilah couldn't see anything from the module she was in, but shortly after takeoff, she heard muffled voices. From her long months of training, she understood them to be Mission Control. They told the astronauts in an absurdly calm tone, that there may be a problem. It would seem that a small meteor had entered Earth's atmosphere a little over a mile from where the spacecraft was. This meteor was unusual in more than a few ways: First, it had not been seen by any of Mission Control's extensive launch window apparatuses, and in addition, it had not showed up on any of their state-of-the-art tracking devices until it actually entered the atmosphere, which was completely unheard of. The attending astronauts in the spacecraft stood by to initiate the craft's emergency landing mechanisms, but, like magic, the meteor exited Earth's atmosphere as suddenly and unexpectedly as it had come. The only sign that it even existed was a pale bluish substance that comprised its tail. This mysterious substance filled the entire skyline, and dissipated into the open air, being carried in every direction by the strong winds of the upper atmosphere. It was gone in a matter of minutes.

It was all very odd, but as there seemed to be nothing more happening and all was again clear, the flight continued as normal. The craft eventually arrived at the International Space Station orbiting the planet, conducted its space tourist on her tour, and reentered Earth's atmosphere. The descent module of the craft touched down in the Mojave Desert, exactly six days after its initial takeoff. A rescue craft was there to gather the crew, put them through the necessary reentry procedures, and with that, the ride of a lifetime was over.

But, as Delilah and the rest of the world would soon find out, the ride had only just begun. What the astronauts didn't know was that the 'meteor' they were warned about had reentered Earth's atmosphere again…and then again, some 220 times, at varying points around the globe, until it had circumvented the entire planet, leaving behind the same disappearing faint bluish substance. Nothing, not a planetary aircraft, a meteor, *anything* could do that, but that didn't stop this 'meteor' from performing such an impossible feat. What nobody knew at the moment was that interplanetary warfare had been initiated, and Earth had been struck with the first—and maybe the last—blow.

Chapter 4

A blinding cloud of flashing cameras, hot studio lights, and envious smiles: It was all for Delilah, and she bathed in it as happily and naturally as if it was the expensive heated infinity edge pool back at her home. The last seven to eight months had been the most physically and mentally exhausting time of Delilah's entire life, and it had all been for this. As far as she was concerned, it was well worth it. Her itinerary was quickly filled with so many interviews; photo shoots for magazine covers; and meetings for possible book deals, that she barely had any time to breathe. And she wouldn't have had it any other way. With the help of her father, Delilah secured a personal body guard, and with her new security man-slash-chauffer always within arm's reach, she set about the country, staying in only the most fabulous hotels, milking her time in the limelight for all it was worth.

Meanwhile, many thousands of miles away, in the barren recesses of Antarctica, a team of scientists were being drawn to the observation decks of their massively-domed research station by what appeared to be the most awesome display of southern lights any of them had ever seen. It was the proper season for the southern lights, so a dazzling display of colors in the open sky was not unusual. What *was* odd was that this display was predominantly green with some blue interspersed, which was very rare for the phenomena. To a layperson looking on, this would've been a trivial, if even noticed, deviation in what the Aurora Australis usually were, but the scientists watching it just now recognized the absolute significance of it.

Among these scientists, a young intern was standing near his superior.

"Wow!" observed the intern, staring up through the thick, specially-insulated glass geodesic dome above him, as the heaven bound curtains of vibrant colors passed by overhead. Antarctica was currently experiencing one of its polar nights, where the sun does not rise above the horizon for months at a time, and so, even though it was mid-morning, the sky was dark enough to render this spectacle even more fantastic.

The intern's superior asked, "Now, did you notice anything *out of the way* about this display, Geoffrey?" One of the scientist's many quirks was that he never said *odd* or *unusual*, but only *out of the way.*

"It's spectacular." answered Geoffrey, absently, unable to summon his gaze away from the brilliant colors. He had read about the phenomena many times, but actually witnessing it firsthand now…well, the lengthy book descriptions just didn't do it justice.

The scientist—his name was Arnold though he insisted he be addressed as Mr. Reynolds—scoffed at the intern's childlike awe. He was an extremely practical person who prided himself on never being taken off guard for any reason. He had long forgotten the non-book oriented passion and curiosity that drew him into the field of astronomy in the first place. His appearance certainly suggested as much. He had a tall, lanky frame with long, thin limbs and a face that looked as if it had been sucked dry by the very vacuum of space which he was paid to study. His head was covered by a full mane of curly dull, black hair that matched the simple goatee he kept meticulously trimmed. His eyes were slightly recessed into his drawn face, but were still as penetrative as if they were a pair of black binoculars bulging out of his head. The centerpiece of this facial mosaic was the thick glasses the scientist wore even though there was absolutely nothing wrong with his vision. He fancied that they helped him notice things that perhaps he would not have otherwise.

He was the only black person stationed at the research facility, and, excluding his young intern, he was the youngest there at just thirty-nine years old. He usually assumed an air of snobbery (he would call it *confidence*), as he was assuming just now, but for all stuck up appearances, he was, in fact, a brilliant scientist.

Already, a chemical nuclear reaction and a certain type of cosmic radiation that he had discovered, were named after him, and some believed—most ardently, he, himself—that it was only a matter of time before he was a proud (in the truest sense of the word) recipient of the Nobel Prize in Physics. He had been at this particular research station for a total of six months now, and saw it as a prestigious, albeit *cold*, assignment. He always assumed that his brilliance had been the deciding factor that earned him the right to be here, considering that he was a minority and much younger than the other scientists, but in reality, it was the simple fact that no one else wanted to deal with the 'young upstart who knew everything except how to keep his damn mouth closed', that had gotten him here. It was just as well. He would certainly prefer his own rendition of things anyhow.

The glasses Mr. Reynolds wore were the modern half rim design that were normally assigned as prescription glasses. He steadied these upon his semi-flat nose now, as he scoffed at his youthful assistant. "Yes, I grant it, it is a worthy sight," he said, speaking of the curtains of lights in the sky, though his tone would imply that he was too mature to be taken aback by such trivial emotions as wonder, "but if you intend to be any kind of a scientist worth your salt, you're going to have to learn to move past the mere aesthetic properties of observation and

17

teach yourself to find the scientific value, if there be any, of those observations."

It was Geoffrey's turn to scoff now, though he was not so foolish as to do it loud enough for his lofty, and unfortunately, influential, mentor to hear. "I thought that's what I was here for, so you could teach me to pinpoint 'scientific value' where I would have otherwise missed it." observed Geoffrey, still without looking away from the sky above (it could not be deduced by his tone whether or not he was being sarcastic, but Mr. Reynolds's excessive store of pomp was such that he could fairly well interpret anything as a well-deserved compliment). The platform where the intern, Mr. Reynolds, and the other scientists stood, had been raised high into the huge domed structure for just such observation. In addition, there were sets of large steps by which a person could elevate themselves even further into the dome, and telescopes of varying size and power were scattered strategically for the same purpose.

With great grandeur, Mr. Reynolds stepped up two or three of these steps and positioned himself in front of one of the telescopes. For such a practical man, it didn't matter that the southern lights in the sky were so close that using this or any of the observatory's telescopes was completely unnecessary. In Mr. Reynolds's mind, positioning himself just so made him look sophisticated.

"Quite right." He answered his assistant. "And if you intend to learn anything worth learning, you've come to the right person. But no one, not even I, can *teach* you how to be a scientist. You have to be born with a special something already in place. I can only teach you science itself..." It looked as if Mr. Reynolds was about to open into a lengthy treatise of some sort, as no doubt he likely would have, had it not been that Geoffrey was suddenly taken over with an aptly-timed bout of suspiciously insatiable curiosity.

"Mr. Reynolds, you were saying that something was strange about these lights. What did you mean?" interrupted the intern.

"Not strange, Geoffrey, out of the way." Corrected the scientist.

"Okay, Mr. Reynolds, out of the way, but what was it?"

"Come up here, Geoffrey." The scientist instructed. Once Geoffrey made it up the steps and stood beside him, he pointed a finger at one of the predominantly green curtains that was in the process of waving by. "Now, do you see that?" he asked. Of course Geoffrey did, but that also didn't seem to matter. "Now, I take it that you've never seen an aurora before?" Geoffrey shook his head that he hadn't. "Well, that is truly unfortunate, because if you had seen an extensive amount of them—as I have—then you would know that that greenish hue you're seeing now is highly out of the way for auroras. Highly out of the way…"

Geoffrey worked quickly to avoid yet another meaningless lecture. "How so? What exactly is…out of the way about it?" he asked humbly, scratching his head in intimation that he knew nothing without Mr. Reynolds's significant expertise.

The scientist went on to explain to the decidedly-ignorant Geoffrey that the southern lights, like their northern counterparts, were the results of great amounts of radiation from solar winds bathing and interacting with Earth's atmosphere. He continued on to explain that the outermost layers of the atmosphere were sparsely propagated with a much higher percentage of pure oxygen than was the rest of the layers. Through a highly-complicated series of cosmic radioactive interactions, that saturation of oxygen was the catalyst that made the pure green lights possible. The only problem was that the reaction should be happening where the oxygen was, on the outermost layer of Earth's protective coating, not, as it were, so close and in plain view.

After this explanation, Geoffrey asked the question that most non-experts would've asked at this point; namely, what was the difference between that oxygen and the stuff humans depended on to live every day, to which, Mr. Reynolds awarded his intern with a look that said clearly, 'My poor, ignorant, and totally inept Geoffrey. How very much you have to learn. Thank God in heaven that you met me', etc…etc…, before informing him that oxygen was a highly reactive substance, one of the most reactive substances in the universe, in fact, and that the oxygen that caused the green reaction of which he spoke was so pure that it could actually kill humans from acute oxygen toxicity if breathed for any extended period of time. So, seeing the southern lights so green was therefore highly *out of the way* because it would suggest that a saturation pure oxygen was in the breathable part of Earth's atmosphere…which would mean that shortly, everyone breathing it would soon be dead.

If Geoffrey hadn't been paying attention to such a confusing and complicated explanation, he was all ears at the mention of the possible demise of all people.

"But, since none of us seem to be falling over dead at the moment, I'd say something else was happening." said Mr. Reynolds, noticing the alarmed look on his apprentice's face.

"*What* else?" asked Geoffrey, cautiously.

"Well, as scientists, and *aspiring* scientist, in your case my dear Geoffrey, that's what we're here to find out, isn't it now?" Mr. Reynolds's observation had obviously scared the intern, and he (Mr. Reynolds) was enjoying every moment of it. Unfortunately for the proud scientist, his observations were much closer to the truth than he could've imagined: He and everyone else around him were, indeed, breathing in highly toxic substances. It just wasn't the kind he had in mind.

Meanwhile, as the lights subsided, Geoffrey gazed out onto the unbroken white of compacted ice that surrounded the station in all directions. Though his eyes were steady upon the hypnotizing lack of color that was the Antarctic tundra, his mind was far removed. Even in the short time that he had known Mr. Reynolds, he knew him to be a consummate asshole, but he also knew another thing: Mr. Reynolds's observations were usually dead on. What bothered Geoffrey was that in this, Mr. Reynolds's latest observation, *dead on* may very well be taken literally. As much as he wanted to, he didn't press the scientist to elaborate. He knew he didn't want to die out here, away from his family and friends, in this frozen wasteland.

Now, he looked out from the lightly-tinted glass dome, at the unforgiving habitat surrounding it, in earnest. Though he tried to block them out, images of his body dotting an otherwise monotonous ice sheet dominated his vision. He imagined himself fighting for precious life against some fucking *oxygen toxicity*…and losing. He saw himself gasping for air and being choked to eternal stillness by the very substance his body needed. He stood, staring at the imagined dots of him on the frozen surface for so long that he began to believe he actually saw a dot on the horizon. He shook his head hard to get rid of the hallucination, but it was still there. He moved up a few steps to get a better look and to prove to his shaken psyche that the dot was no more than his unfounded fears preying upon his mind, but still, the dot remained.

Reluctantly, he called one of the other scientists in the room to his aid. He tried not to arouse the attention of Mr. Reynolds, as he was sure he would make more out of this than was necessary. One of the other scientists came to find out what was the problem.

Geoffrey pointed into the distance. "Do you see anything there?" he asked timidly. He hoped like hell that the scientist didn't see it so he could assure himself that it was all in his head, but the other guy *did* see it. The scientist went to one of the telescopes to get a better look at the dot. He stood with his face in the goggle mask-like apparatus of the telescope for a few moments. When Geoffrey next saw his face, there was a confused and meditative look on it that promised not to bode well. The scientist returned his face to the telescope's mask for a few more long moments, then did the very thing that Geoffrey least wanted. He called loudly to Mr. Reynolds. Mr. Reynolds and a few of the other scientists came to see what the fuss was about. Each in their turn looked out through the telescope and they, too, shared the same strange look.

As they stood by, talking amongst themselves, Geoffrey took the opportunity to look through the telescope himself. Really, he didn't want to see what was out there—he had called for help in the first place to debunk the frightening hallucination, not verify it—but as no one seemed to be paying his repeated questions any mind, the only thing left to do was see it (whatever *it* was) for himself. When he did feed his face into the mask, he saw what looked remarkably like a small meteorite fragment. The fragment seemed to be about the size of a small beach ball and permeated completely with small craters. Staring intently at the fragment, Geoffrey's eyes widened. The meteorite seemed to be glowing, but glowing wasn't the proper description for what it was doing. There was a light or perhaps some faint radiation, emanating from the fragment, but it illumined it like nothing Geoffrey had ever seen before. The fragment was nearly two miles away but the faint 'light' surrounding it made it appear like it was no more than a few feet from Geoffrey's eyes.

It was nothing like any natural or artificial light on Earth. In fact, it basically defied any description at all. The luminance didn't seem to wane even though a decent distance separated it from the viewers. Furthermore, it seemed to pulsate with some equally mysterious power. Whatever it was, it promised to be the very first of its kind, even an alien artifact perhaps. Eager to have yet another discovery named after him, Mr. Reynolds suggested, and all the other scientists agreed, that it should be checked out. Of course, Mr. Reynolds was at the head of the expedition, as everyone mounted up on special snowmobiles that had been fabricated specifically for scientific discovery in the coldest weather on the planet. Once everyone had gained a few extra pounds in protective clothing, the voyage began.

There aren't many life forms in Antarctica and virtually no animals, so, except for the cold, no one feared venturing out into the open tundra. Even beneath myriad layers of thick, double-insulated fabric, the biting frost could still cut to the quick, and so, it was with shivering limbs and chattering teeth, that a reluctant Geoffrey and the group of ambitious scientists (Mr. Reynolds always foremost) arrived at the fragment. Everyone was interested to see what new thing they had stumbled upon. Even though they were closing in on the thing, the 'light' coming from it did not grow brighter. Whether from the observatory two miles back, or right up on it, the unnatural glow gave off a clear luminance as if the observer was always very near to it.

Gathering around it now, everyone dismounted their dual track snowmobiles and drew cautiously closer. It was truly fascinating. The luminescence covering the fragment made it difficult to see exactly what it was, but it was not creviced as it initially appeared. Rather, the assumed craters were minute variations in the light surrounding the fragment. What lay beneath the light looked like some kind of transparent, perfectly round rock. It was *impossibly* perfect. Everyone's snow mobile was equipped with a decent-sized storage bin that contained, among other things, large tongs for just such an event, whereby an unusual specimen might be handled. Mr. Reynolds was the first to get his out. Another scientist produced a plastic container that looked large enough to hold the glowing meteor.

Mr. Reynolds closed in on the fragment, tongs outstretched, as the others looked on. They all wanted to be the first to handle the thing and thereby take more credit for its discovery, but being so close to it now, without the thick, glass dome to protect them, the fragment looked suddenly more ominous and threatening. It was only sheer pride and ambition that led Mr. Reynolds to move where the others hesitated. In reality, he was just as scared as they (perhaps more), but as strong as his fear was, his thirst for recognition was that much more. The tongs he held were intended to collect smaller specimens, approximately the size of a soccer ball, and it soon became apparent that they would not suffice to pick up this strange artifact. Mr. Reynolds asked if anyone had anything larger that may be of better use. Everyone looked in their storage bins, but no one had anything.

Geoffrey cleared his throat, "I have a shovel…"

"That won't help," snapped Mr. Reynolds, uncharacteristically agitated, "The ground is too hard to dig around it and I don't want to damage it. It could be fragile." Exasperated, Mr. Reynolds slumped his shoulders. "Somebody needs to go get something bigger that we can put this in."

Geoffrey moved toward his snowmobile. "Not you," the scientist snapped, and Geoffrey froze where he was standing, "You'd probably bring something useless back," he waved his hands impatiently at the other scientists who were looking around nervously and shifting side to side, "Someone go get something we can pick this up with. Hurry, off with you!"

The other scientists left to get more supplies, while Mr. Reynolds and Geoffrey stayed. Once they were alone, Mr. Reynolds adjusted the glasses just above his scarf, and stepped closer to the object.

"That might not be a good idea, Sir," advised Geoffrey, as the scientist pulled his scarf away from his face and knelt down beside the fragment so close that his prescription grade glasses nearly touched it.

"Who's the professional here, Son?" Mr. Reynolds asked, coolly. He reached out, not really intending to touch the thing. He removed his gloves and raised both hands over it to see if any heat was coming from it, when the fragment pulled his hands onto itself. It all happened so quickly that Geoffrey hardly had time to react. In a split second, Mr. Reynolds had gone from hovering over this thing, to grasping it, both hands clasped upon it by some irresistible force, and clinging to it for dear life, quite against his will. With the fragment firmly in his hands, he began to shake violently. His mouth hung open and his eyes rolled back in his head until nothing but the whites showed. He head began to bulge slightly as if some creature was filling it, and his shaking grew ever more violent and erratic.

If Geoffrey didn't do something—and *now*—Mr. Reynolds would be shaken to death. Already, Geoffrey saw the spittle flying from Mr. Reynolds's mouth while his teeth and jaws were being rattled loose from their sockets. Geoffrey grabbed the shovel and slammed Mr. Reynolds's shoulder with it as hard as he could. Thankfully, the hit knocked the scientist and the fragment loose from each other. The scientist flew in one direction and the fragment in another. Geoffrey dropped the shovel and checked on the overly ambitious astronomer. He was still shaking, but not nearly as much. His irises were still nowhere to be found, but he was breathing.

Geoffrey looked back at the fragment, and noticed that the 'light' coming from it had dimmed considerably. It was also here that he noticed that the 'light' was actually separating the fragment from the ice beneath it. The light wasn't coming from it, but *encasing* it like a shield. From what Geoffrey could see, the light had a physical presence. As far as he could tell the 'light' was solid matter! He turned back to look at Mr. Reynolds's hands, and just as he suspected, the light, though also noticeably dimmer, was covering them like a glove...and being sucked into them with every passing second. In the course of a few brief minutes, Mr. Reynolds's hands absorbed the light like a sponge would a syrupy liquid. Then, Mr. Reynolds's hands stopped glowing and his body ceased its shaking, but still he showed no signs of consciousness.

The others are definitely not going to believe this! Geoffrey thought as he waited anxiously for their return.

Chapter 5

Lenard Hanson was well used to spoiling the women in his life, partly because he loved them, but mostly because they would accept nothing less. His wife had demanded every convenience and luxury his money offered from day one and had taught his daughter to do likewise. Delilah was used to driving or being chauffeured in the most expensive cars, and, when she didn't fly private jets, flying only first class. Now, she was right at home as she traveled across the nation under only the best accommodations to receive all the press and attention lavished upon her for being the first non-astronaut American to journey into space from American soil. Extra attention was given her, as her father had predicted, for being the youngest person to venture into outer space at all.

There were welcome parties waiting for her at every airport and hotel; security officials at every place in between. Thousands upon thousands of people were eager to catch a glimpse of what it looked like to be young and ultra-privileged, even if it was only from behind a camera or a restraining rope guarded by armed men that, for all appearances, knew only how to shout, "Stay back, you!" Nothing—absolutely nothing—was going to threaten Delilah's time in the spotlight. She intended to keep the eyes of the nation glued upon her, and only her, for as long as humanly possible. Imagine her indignation and shock when talk of a possible global epidemic drew everyone's attention away from her story. She was in New York City when the agent her father had hired called her room to inform her that her interview—the one for which she came to the Big Apple in the first place—the one that was scheduled for the next morning, had been cancelled. She threw a full-fledged tantrum the moment she received the news. This was what she usually did on the extremely rare occasions she didn't get what she wanted, but this time, it was to no avail.

What could her agent do? *Make* the station conduct the interview? This was not her pliable father she was dealing with, the agent wanted desperately to remind her (though, of course, in the interest of his professional career, he didn't). These were people who cared little about her wealth and even less about her tactless temperament. Besides, this rumor of a potential global contagion was possibly a breaking story not to be rivaled, not even by the Delilah's boundless ego. Filled with her own childish fury, Delilah paced the nearly eleven hundred square feet of her penthouse loft hotel room, incensed that anything, even a potential outbreak of Biblical proportions, would deprive her of something she wanted. She picked up the phone to call her father—she'd give him an earful and he'd do something about all this—but before she could finish dialing the numbers, a chilling realization presented itself. If the people around her were somehow infected with a terrible disease, then she was vulnerable as well.

What if the hotel receptionists who had handed her the card key to her room were infected? What if the guys who had brought up her luggage were infected? What if the hotel's entire staff was infected? Suddenly, the rumored crisis became very real to the spoiled socialite. In the process, she had forgotten that she was still holding the phone receiver. She let it fall from her hands, now. How could she know that it, too, wasn't infected? Panic welled up in her breast, and it didn't matter that she didn't know what this possible infection was. It also didn't matter that she as yet hadn't heard any real news at all about its existence, or lack thereof. All that mattered was that she could potentially be affected by it. Her blind panic mounting by the second, she stripped off her clothes and rushed to the bathroom for a hot, purging shower. She scrubbed the shower head, the water dials, and most of the shower's walls, with one of the new loofah sponges that had been stocked in the bathroom. To watch her scour things to a glistening shine as she was doing, one might not have guessed that this young woman had never scrubbed a single thing in her life.

Then, she snatched up another brand new loofah and commenced to showering. Once that was finished, she threw on some fresh designer clothes and undergarments, rushed out of the room and to one of the hotel's elevators. Her intention was to head straight for the reception desk and demand that someone report to her room post haste to sanitize the entire place immediately. The phone in her room had a specially dedicated line to the reception's desk for such things, but Delilah was loath to touch anything in her room just now. In fact, she had rigged up a series of gloves made from the new towels left in her room, which she fastened to her wrists by strips of bath rags that she had torn to pieces for the purpose. She left one bath cloth whole to hold to her mouth as protection from possible airborne infection. She truly looked a mess, all rigged up as she was, but right now, it didn't matter to her how she looked, which was another first.

She hit the necessary buttons on the elevator with her unsightly towel-gloved hands and soon descended to the ground floor. She had nearly reached the desk, all but hysterical by this time, when a new and terrifying thought gripped her. If the hotel staff was indeed infected with this nameless pandemic, wasn't she putting herself at further risk by being in such close proximity to them? And if that was the case, how could she possibly expect them to sanitize her room, as they would certainly bring the infection with them in the first place? Everything was so confusing and Delilah began to fancy that it was becoming more difficult to breath, what with all the pathogens entering her lungs. She struggled to hold her breath, even beneath the cloth, and of course, that didn't work. She looked down at her exposed arms. Certainly, the horrid disease was attacking her unprotected flesh at that very moment!

She screamed aloud from the crushing frustration and everyone in the lobby, including the receptionist, stared on, bewildered. She screamed again at the people to stop staring at her and pounded on a nearby chair for obedience.

"Please calm down, Ma'am." Advised the receptionist. "What seems to be the problem?" Delilah looked at the women in simultaneous fear and disgust. Part of her was looking for signs of decay that she was sure would be the result of the spreading disease. Much to her alarm she noticed that the whites of the woman's eyes were, indeed, noticeably yellowed. She looked quickly over the rest of the receptionist and also noticed that the woman was feverishly scratching her arm, and what looked like dead skin was falling from the spot in the process. Immediately, Delilah wished that she had not seen the proof she was looking for, but it was right there before her eyes. It would've been better had it been all in her head (even though that alone had already scared her to hysteria), but it wasn't. It was real...and she was next.

Not caring anymore about the shocked and staring faces, Delilah sprinted to the elevator and back to her room. She nearly broke down her room door rushing into it, and locked every lock once she was in. She wanted to yell for her father. She snatched up the phone with her awkward gloves and pressed the numbers to her father's cell phone furiously. The bulky towels wrapped around her hands pressed three and four numbers at a time and made it impossible to make a call this way. She grunted in anger. She wanted her father desperately. Somehow, his money would make things better. It always did. But in order to make the call, she'd have to unwrap her hands and risk contamination. She threw herself onto the bed and squealed in the ear shattering tone of a frustrated newborn, unable to think of anything else to do. All of her fancy clothes, her thousand dollar hairdo, not even this $2,800 a night luxury hotel room—none of it was effecting its usual magic whereby everything in life, no matter how unpleasant for everyone else, was cool and comfortable for her, and thus, she was left lost and afraid.

Just like a small, abandoned child who screams in tantrum until she's sore from exertion, only to find that her tirade has failed to produce what was sought after, Delilah found that her outburst meant absolutely nothing here.

If she wanted to talk with her father, she'd have to pick up the phone like any other human being and dial the numbers…and, yes, risk infection in the process. Filling incredibly sorry for herself for how cruel reality was treating her, she did just that. Lenard answered on the first ring. One of the things his wife had taught him before her passing was to answer promptly whenever the women in his life beckoned.

"Oh, Daddy!" Delilah shouted, before again bursting into panic-stricken sobs. For the next forty-five minutes, she unloaded all of her angst upon his shoulders (or rather, into his ear). She had no idea that at the very moment she had called, her father was in a meeting with some of his colleagues discussing the very thing that had her upset. She hadn't been watching the news. In fact, she hadn't been doing anything except engaging in raging fits—but if she had been, she would've known that the possible infection was no longer a rumor, but a substantiated reality. Seemingly within the last few hours, women of every age, color, and nationality all across the planet, began displaying the jaundiced yellow eyes and itchy, flaking skin just like the receptionist Delilah had seen earlier. In reality, though, the phenomenon had been taking place and spreading slowly amongst the collective female population since the meteor incident. It was just recently that these unusual symptoms had spread to enough people to make things truly alarming.

Lenard's business partners had called the meeting with him because, as they spent most of their time at luxury hotel locations owned by the company, they mistakenly thought that perhaps whatever was happening to their wives and daughters had something to do with their hotel buildings. It was during the meeting, an hour or so before Delilah's frantic call, that Lenard's secretary informed him that he may want to turn on the news in the conference room where he and the associates sat. All of them were blaring the same headlines.

"Well, at least we know it has nothing to do with our hotels," one of Lenard's professional partners joked dryly, as every news station available informed the public that something, nobody yet knew what, was affecting the female population of the world.

Lenard stepped out of the meeting and did his best to calm his shaken daughter. He assured her that he would be on one of his private jets to New York as soon as possible to personally pick her up. True to his word, he adjourned the meeting and was in New York City within hours. He picked up his daughter and they returned to their mansion straightaway. As soon as they made it home, Delilah demanded that all the help, the butler, the driver, the maids, etc., be instructed to return to the modest apartments on the mansion's property where they lived when they weren't working. As much as she wanted to be waited on, she didn't want anyone in the house to spread the infection, especially since the female hired help were all showing the same yellow eyes and scaling skin.

After the place had been vacated, Delilah again rushed to her room and locked her door. Her room was typical of wealth; fully equipped with plenty of square feet, a huge adjoining bathroom, large, flat screen T.V., a king sized heart-shaped bed, even a fridge. She basically had everything she would need to survive comfortably for many days, so Lenard understood that he may not see her for some time. Meanwhile, he phoned a few of his friends in high places—many of them on the payroll— to get whatever information he could about what the hell was going on.

Among these friends were some prominent doctors and scientists, many of whom Lenard had made handsome contributions to their causes and establishments (like financing the trip of the son of a globally renowned plastic surgeon to intern under a notable, albeit pompous, scientist somewhere in the middle of Antarctica, in exchange for that surgeon performing some controversial plastic surgery for Lenard's wife in the comfort of their home). Lenard learned that the affected women were showing signs of what looked like a completely new form of cancer, as well a specific kind of anemia. Lenard wasn't familiar with many of the terms some of his contacts were using, so he asked them to explain what they were trying to say in laymen's terms. The information that he was eventually left with was that basically, the woman had somehow recently undergone a complicated change in their systems that was causing their skin to reproduce unnaturally fast—hence the scratching and subsequent shedding, and that one of the only things medical professionals knew of that caused cells to display uncontrolled growth like this, was cancer.

As far as anyone knew right now, this ubiquitous cancer, if it was, in fact, cancer, was accompanied and possibly even caused by a marked change in the way the women's blood was using and transporting oxygen. Every woman studied showed a marked decrease in red blood cells. This was what was probably responsible for the yellowed eyes. All this wasn't exactly laymen's terms, Lenard noted, but it all boiled down to the fact that, for some reason, women's bodies were suddenly handling oxygen very differently than normal (or perhaps, struggling to handle a different kind of oxygen) and their bodies were not transitioning well. The other consensus was that it had all started with the first sighting of that mysterious 'meteor'.

Chapter 6

Mr. Reynolds was now lying safely back in the emergency room of the research station. The room was about the size of an extra-large living room and was equipped with an operating table, a few pieces of medical equipment, and two stainless-steel chests of medical supplies. Large halogen lights loomed high in the ceiling alongside moderately-sized vents attached to powerful vacuums that were responsible for the emergency room's ventilation. The powerful system sucked air from the room through these vents while other vents closer to the floor resupplied the room with fresh air from the outside. The glacial Antarctic air was highly inhospitable to germs and airborne pathogens, so this special ventilation system ensured that the air in the emergency room was as clean, probably more so, than any other hospital in the world. Unfortunately, it also meant that the air in the room was ridiculously cold.

Sure, there was a small separate system that heated the incoming air, but it was working in semi-permanent nighttime in a land where 0°F is considered unseasonably hot during the daytime. There was only so much it could do to warm the air. Naturally, everyone kept on thick layers of clothing as they stood around Scientist Reynolds now. They had checked him for any obvious wounds, but having found none, they left him thickly clothed as well. Geoffrey had already relayed what had taken place to everyone at least three or four times, but these were scientists he was talking to. By definition they didn't believe in miracles, and if nothing else, this was a miracle of horror. What *really* happened was what every one of the other scientists wanted to know. Geoffrey was surrounded by professionals whose minds were steeped in logic via years and years of practice, and his claim of why Mr. Reynolds was lying here totally unconscious was anything but logical.

Though no one spoke the idea out loud, the possibility that Geoffrey had actually assaulted Mr. Reynolds crossed everyone's mind. Other than a dark and raised patch on the scientist's shoulder, there was no bruising or other sign of struggle on either Geoffrey or Mr. Reynolds. All of Mr. Reynolds's vital signs were normal, and, except for him periodically moving his lips and rapidly moving his eyes that would suggest the scientist was not unconscious, but merely sleeping, he seemed fine. Someone suggested that perhaps he should be moved out of the station and back to the States to a better equipped facility in case something more was wrong with him that they couldn't see. After all, the emergency room of the station was, as its name implied, only designed and stocked for absolute emergencies. It was far from an extensive operating theater and if any extra medical attention was needed, it would certainly not be given in this hocked-up first aid center.

The problem with having Mr. Reynolds escorted out, however, was that the only quick transportation off the station was by helicopter, and the station was as far from anything resembling a commercial airport as the emergency room was from a full hospital, so calling for a helicopter to be dispatched was, by no means, a trivial thing. Anyone calling for one of the special, and extremely expensive, helicopters that were on standby for such a trip, would have to answer with their career should the situation turn out to be anything other than an absolutely dire one. There was no way to tell if the current situation *was* dire. Mr. Reynolds was breathing normally, and there was no sign of life-threatening trauma. For all appearances, he was simply unconscious. On the other hand, every person in the room would readily agree that the meteorite fragment was something new, something the likes of which none of them had ever experienced before, and if the account Geoffrey had given was true, then the proper authorities would have someone's head if it wasn't reported right away.

No one was sure what call to make, so they decided that Mr. Reynolds would remain under observation for the equivalent of a normal night, eight hours, upon the completion of which, if he was not awake to answer for his own well-being, then the difficult phone calls would have to be made. Shifts were allocated so the comatose scientist could be watched round the clock while the others slept and everyone returned to their bunk-filled sleeping quarters. For all their efforts, no one seemed to be able to sleep. These were minds of people whose profession required that they delve deeply into the unknown, and there was much that was unknown here. Something big, something *huge*, was amiss, this much was certain, and no one could resist summoning his deductive reasoning to try to unravel the one question that plagued them all: What was the rock and what happened?

When the eight hours were up and Mr. Reynolds was still not among the lucid, the scientists were exhausted and not completely coherent, themselves. It was difficult enough to sustain a healthy circadian rhythm with no daylight, but to also be forced awake by overreaching imaginations...well, the stumbling feet and drooping faces of Mr. Reynolds's peers would strongly suggest that such a mixture was in direct opposition to alertness.

Once everyone had shuffled to the coffee maker for that sweet, brown gold of caffeine, they each took a chair and began discussing a plan. Everyone knew what must be done. They had, in fact, already agreed upon it, but still no one wanted to assume the potentially unlucky responsibility. The fact that everyone's constitution was half-mast at best wasn't helping things. Geoffrey decided he had had enough and that he would make the dreaded phone call. His career had yet to really begin, but more importantly, he had seen with his own eyes what happened to Mr. Reynolds. If the others were undecided on whether or not to believe his account, *he* wasn't. Just like everyone else at the station, Geoffrey had been briefed rigorously on the protocols of how to call for help in just such an event.

He stepped briskly toward the glass case that housed one of the special satellite phones used to contact help in situations like this, but before he could reach it, one of the other scientists spoke up in the first harsh tone Geoffrey had heard (outside of Mr. Reynolds's, of course) since he first got to the station.

"And just what do you think you're doing, Son?" the scientist asked, coldly.

"I'm calling for help," answered Geoffrey, as professionally as he could. He was already seething at the fact that either these people had mistaken him for a liar, or didn't have enough balls between them to consider anything other than their own precious careers. He didn't want to add to the mess that was already on everyone's hands.

"Yeah, I can see that, but if you know how to call for help, then you know damn well that an *intern*," the scientist laid great emphasis upon the word, "shouldn't be calling for help unless none of the scientists are able to do so themselves."

Of course Geoffrey knew as much. He also knew that the scientist speaking to him so roughly knew what Geoffrey was doing before he asked, mainly because he (Geoffrey) had just told everyone what he was going to do before he stood from his seat. Geoffrey stood with his back to the group and his face to the phone in the glass case. He hadn't moved an inch from where he stopped when Benjamin, the other scientist, spoke to him. He wanted badly to turn upon his superiors, to yell at them that he was forced to make the call precisely because *they* were unable to do so themselves, because they were all spineless cowards. He wanted to scream at them that a man—an incredibly pretentious man, albeit, but a man nonetheless— was unconscious on a stainless steel table in the middle of the room and they, a bunch of supposedly professional, grown-ass men and women, were too concerned with their reputations to even let someone know, but Geoffrey knew that, as right and just as it may feel to lash out, it would do absolutely no good at all.

Instead, he took a deep breath. "Well, would one of you call please?" he asked between painfully clenched teeth, still not bothering to turn to face the others. "*I'll* take the heat." He knew that the gesture would be insulting, but he couldn't resist at least a little defiance.

"Yeah, *intern*," same emphasis, "we'll do that, but in the meantime, you can just have yourself a seat."

Geoffrey took another deep breath and returned to his chair. Benjamin glared at him for a few long moments and then rose to his feet to retrieve the phone. He got to the glass case, lighted a hand upon the knob, and stopped. "And you're right, you *will* take the heat for it." he snarled, before making the call.

Everyone was tense as they waited for the helicopter to arrive. Benjamin reassigned shiftsso that someone would always be present with Mr. Reynolds. Geoffrey was not included. Nearly as offensive to the scientists as the fact that they may be jeopardizing themselves by phoning home base for a potential false alarm, was the fact that it may get out that a lousy intern was the only one with enough guts to do the right thing should this turn out *not* to be a false alarm. To avoid that happening, they were fully prepared to discredit Geoffrey in any way they could when the time came. They would draw attention to the fact that he was alone with Mr. Reynolds when he became unconscious— highly suspicious—and that the crazy story he gave them upon their arrival only heightened that suspicion.

But how would they explain the fragment, and that it was Geoffrey—the lousy intern—who had initially noticed it in the first place? No one wanted to think about that. They would just have to cross that bridge when they came to it. Meanwhile, the normal observations of the sky continued as everyone waited for the helicopter, and, as he had expected, Geoffrey was assigned to only the most tedious tasks; jotting down the most meticulous and redundant findings, fetching coffee, etc. Meanwhile, no one discussed or otherwise drew attention to the fragment that was still glowing in the distance. The scientists all agreed that they would tend to *that* once Geoffrey and Mr. Reynolds were long gone. Perhaps, they'd even figure out a way to guide this latest turn of events to work in their favor.

Things went on like this until a couple of hours before the helicopter was scheduled to touch down. There were no brightly-lit helipads around, and the all but completely snow and ice covered research station didn't stand out from the rest of the white Antarctic desert enough for a high flying air craft to see it clearly, especially in the current six month darkness, so protocol was for diesel fuel filled barrels to be lit in rows as a makeshift runway. Geoffrey was assigned most of work (as he had also anticipated) and within hours, he and Mr. Reynolds were airlifted away from the station and to a more clinically suitable facility, where he was extensively questioned and studied. Initially, Mr. Reynolds was going to be taken to a hospital facility in what looked like a heavily-guarded military base, and Geoffrey was to be taken elsewhere, but he insisted that he be taken wherever Mr. Reynolds was so that he could be there when his superior awoke or he assured his rescuers that he wouldn't answer a single question.

It wasn't that he had suddenly grown a heartfelt affection for the scientist, or even that he was trying to be obstinate. Rather, he knew what story the other astronomers were likely spreading about him, that he had possibly done something untoward to Mr. Reynolds that had resulted in him ending up unconscious. Geoffrey wanted to be there when Mr. Reynolds awoke (assuming that he *would* eventually awake) so he could hear his name cleared of foul play with his own ears. Otherwise, his fledgling career may not be all he would stand to lose. The official-looking men in the helicopter were in no mood to have demands leveraged upon them by the likes of a simple intern, but they acquiesced. The gravity of this action was not lost upon Geoffrey.

Even though he had raised the protest convincingly enough, a large part of him didn't expect to be taken seriously. He was almost certain that he would have to throw his father's name around a little (and even then, he didn't know if he expected much) and honestly, he was struck nearly dumb that his demands were met so quickly and with such little opposition. He understood that if the other scientists had implicated him in an assault on one of the most prominent astronomers of modern times, he could be held legally, even against his will, and possibly indefinitely, pending questioning of a very different kind.

And he was right. However, as the helicopter landed and he and Mr. Reynolds were both handed over to a small group of men that were even more officially dressed than the others, it became apparent that he was not going to be treated like a criminal, but rather, like royalty. Sort of. As the chopper approached the ground, he could see that a large rolling bed was waiting for Mr. Reynolds. The scientist was carefully carted off and Geoffrey was asked to have a seat in a plush, ultra-modern looking wheelchair that was waiting for him. Behind the wheelchair stood a formidable looking who was at least a foot taller than the rest of the men surrounding him, and was dressed head to foot in army fatigues. Geoffrey rightly assumed that this was the leader of the group. "I can walk on my own. I don't need any help." Geoffrey assured this towering battlefield brawler. His mouth was suddenly very dry. "Thank you."

The guy, apparently not hearing anything Geoffrey just said, took the opportunity to introduce himself. "My name is Lieutenant General Daniel Brimmers." The man extended a powerfully large right hand.

Geoffrey extended his own hand for the greeting shake and found that it was completely swallowed up, and nearly crushed in the other's awesome grip. Looking up into the lieutenant general's benevolently smiling face, it was clear that the man was not even applying a fraction of his full strength. Once the handshake was over and Geoffrey's hand had been released, he let it drop to his side but brought his other hand to it, trying to rub the soreness out of it (and perhaps make sure all the bones were still intact), as inconspicuously as possible. The faint smiles lighting the faces of the lieutenant general's men suggested he wasn't doing a good job with the inconspicuous part.

"Now, Mr. Summons," the skyscraping lieutenant general resumed, "if you will have a seat, I will see to it personally that your stay here is as comfortable as possible."

Lieutenant General Brimmer's voice was deep like the guttural bellow of an earthquake, and Geoffrey wouldn't have been surprised if the helicopter behind him would have folded up its wings and fallen over out of sheer terror, had he commanded. If that wasn't enough, the man's natural appearance demanded at least as much respect as the sound of his voice. It was obvious that he was well over 6 feet tall and, even beneath thick layers of green and black fatigue gear, it was also obvious that he was all muscle. The lieutenant general's muscle structure wasn't the refined muscle that Geoffrey imagined he would find on a gymnast or a runner. No, the lieutenant general was all bulk. He imagined a lean Hulk in army fatigues...then the monster of a man that would eat that Hulk and steal his clothes and that was Lieutenant General Daniel Brimmers.

The lieutenant general's jaw muscles were set squarely, pushing out against the taut skin of his face like they were made of solid stone. His neck was the stump of an oak tree covered in human flesh and his hands, well, Geoffrey already had more experience with those than he would've liked to. But for all his brutishly terrifying attributes, the lieutenant general was as kind to Geoffrey as an old friend. Geoffrey didn't know if the guy had heard him say that he could very well walk, but after that handshake, and a better look at his physique, he sat in the wheelchair without further protest.

"Thank you, Mr. Summons," said the lieutenant general, as he wheeled the chair around as easily as if it was still empty. The men from the chopper returned to the aircraft without a word. Lieutenant General Brimmer's men regrouped around him and Geoffrey seamlessly as they marched down a narrow, paved walkway toward a large brick building with heavily-shaded windows. It would appear Mr. Reynolds had already been wheeled away, in the same direction. Geoffrey strained to see *anything* of the place around him, but the platoon of men surrounding him, though not nearly as formidable as the ole' lieutenant general there, were doing a damn good job of blocking his view. The thought that they were purposely blocking him, that he wasn't *supposed* to see a lot, didn't escape him either.

From what he could see around or over the heads of the men, there were tall buildings everywhere and all of them looked exactly like the one into which he was being wheeled. When his convoy was nearly to the entrance of the closest building, he ventured to ask a question. He had to clear his throat twice before he could gather the nerve to post an inquiry to the beast of a man behind him. "Lieutenant General?" asked Geoffrey, suddenly sorry that he was here.

Just as before, the lieutenant general's voice was teeth clatteringly sonorous, but his tone was nonthreatening, perhaps even compassionate, as he answered, "My men call me Lieutenant Dan, you may refer to me as such if it would make you more comfortable." Oddly enough, Geoffrey thought that it would. It just felt safer to think of the lieutenant general as the legless war veteran who had softened a little as Forrest Gump's first mate, as opposed to the brute mammoth who could easily snap his body in half at the slightest inclination.

"All right… Lieutenant Dan, c-can I ask a question?"

Geoffrey couldn't see Lieutenant Dan, but his voice, still as unnerving as an oncoming train, sounded shocked, as he answered, "Of *course* you can, Mr. Summons."

"Am I going to wherever they've taken Mr. Reynolds?"

"Yes, you are, Mr. Summons." Answered Lieutenant Dan, matter-of–factly, "My men on the chopper alerted me to some of the…suggestions you offered, and arrangements have been made for you to be in close proximity to Mr. Reynolds. Is there anything else you would like to know, Mr. Summons?" The question, at least to Geoffrey's ears anyway, sounded more like a warning than a genuine inquiry.

"No, thank you. Thank you, very much." Geoffrey lied.

Lieutenant Dan brought the wheelchair and the surrounding convoy to a halt about thirty-five feet from the door of the building as he talked with Geoffrey. Now, he made a nearly imperceptible gesture with his head and one of his men pulled what looked like a small radio transistor from his pocket and hit a series of buttons. All this was done behind Geoffrey's wheelchair so he didn't see it. What he did see, however, was a marvel of engineering. There came a soft hissing from somewhere on the ground, then the entire concrete walkway leading up to the front door of the building before him, as well as a couple feet of turf on either side, began to move. Geoffrey was sure that he was seeing things, but it was difficult for his brain to decide what he was seeing. His frame of reference was off. At first it looked like the ground, except for the sliver of walkway and earth directly before him, was rising. It wasn't until widening slivers of light from beneath the turf began illuminating the walkway that he realized that about an 8-by-30 foot section of concrete and earth before him was sinking.

The soft hiss of hydraulic motors became more distinct as the unseen platform continued its descent. Soon, the platform was at a forty-five degree angle. They were on the same grass-lined concrete path, but it now led to a new and previously hidden entrance. Geoffrey saw the yawning opening to a well-lit corridor some feet below the door that he had originally assumed he was to enter. Lieutenant Dan wheeled him into the corridor and the other men followed closely behind. Once everyone was inside, the hydraulic motors lurched to life again as the platform rose back to ground level. In his mind's eye, Geoffrey imagined himself outside watching the earth realign itself like magic. He knew the seamless platform would raise the walkway and a foot or so of surrounding grass on each side back to its original position in such a way that the most observant eye would never know the difference. He also realized that he was being shown all this meant that he was involved in something much deeper than an assault case. What it could possibly be that he had gotten himself into occupied his every thought as he was wheeled down the long and excessively-bright corridor to God only knew where.

Fortunately for him, though (at least depending on how he looked at it), he wouldn't have to worry about being in suspense much longer, because before long, he was wheeled into a large room that was more comfortably lit than the blinding hallway, and placed in front of a large, one way mirror. On the other side of the mirror lay Mr. Reynolds; or rather, what had become of Mr. Reynolds. Geoffrey could see him, but the scientist could not see his intern. Just as before, the only thing that showed between Mr. Reynolds's open eyelids was the glossy white of missing irises. What's more, the scientist had obviously lost weight: A lot of it. The human frame that lay on the other side of the mirror from Geoffrey was little more than a lightly-padded skeleton. Obviously, something horrible had happened to Mr. Reynolds in the short time since the now-terrified intern had seen him last and the only thing Geoffrey kept thinking now was, *Damn, if I had only just gone to medical school like my father told me!*

Chapter 7

At that moment, Delilah was still locked in her room, safe behind her walls from the chaos that was enveloping the world outside. But that safety, like all safeties, was not to last forever. In fact, a virtual squadron of uniformed men and black government SUVs were darkening the grass of her sprawling front yard, and a few of them were in the process of marching to her front door even now.

Lenard was in his living room sipping a piping-hot cup of coffee heavily laden with whiskey, when a firm knock sounded at his front door. He had been deep in thought, trying to force into some kind of discernible order the vast amount of alarming information he had earlier received from his professional contacts. He was so deep in thought, in fact, that he didn't hear the increasingly loud knocking coming from the front door. He also failed to notice the shadows of men passing by his living room windows, as unannounced government guests took up key positions all around his house and the surrounding property. He did notice things, however, when the knocks stopped…and the front door opened. Had he not been already facing the door, he likely would have missed that as well, but since he was, he immediately jumped to his feet, intending to give the hired help a grand earful for entering the house without his permission, especially since the door was locked and they had been ordered to return to their apartments. The mug in his hand was the third cup of spiked caffeine, and the disorientation that nearly snatched his equilibrium away.

He very slowly set the cup down on the small table beside the chair from which he had just risen, and shielded his eyes with his hands until he felt sufficiently steady. Even before he was ready move his hand, he began his verbal assault.

"What the *hell* do you think you're..." he began, but as he took his hand his away, he was welcomed with an even more unexpected surprise. "...doing?" he finished, all the anger in his voice instantly and completely drained. Before him stood not his maids and his head butler, but about five or ten suited men, all of them wearing latex gloves, and large caliber pistols in holsters at their sides. More were trickling through the front door every moment.

"We are federal agents, Mr. Hanson, and we need to know where your daughter is." informed the suited man nearest to Lenard. Even as he spoke, other men were searching the house. Two or three climbed up the flight of stairs that led to Delilah's room. Lenard turned toward those men as they rapidly ascended the steps.

"Hey, this is private property!" Lenard yelled "You get the hell out of here right…" An excessively painful hold upon the soft of Lenard's shoulder halted his heated demand before he could finish. He winced in pain as the grip forced him to return to the chair. The agent who had spoken with him loomed over him with his hand still on his shoulder, though he had let up on the pressure.

"Mr. Hanson, we are federal agents. We need to speak with your daughter, *immediately*…it is a matter of national security." The agent drew his face close to Lenard's as he spoke (as if that were necessary, considering Lenard's shoulder felt as if it had been all but broken). Lenard, still grimacing from the smarting in his shoulder, opened his mouth, but only he and God knew if he was going to cooperate or if still had enough fire in him to merit another painful hold, because before he could get any words out, his daughter's ear-shattering scream filled the room. Obviously, the men had found their target. The agent holding Lenard's shoulder stood upright just in time to watch two specially-trained men restraining a very animated Delilah with a good measure of difficulty.

They brought her down the stairs with perhaps more difficulty (and certainly more expletives) than would've been rendered by a hardened terrorist. She was taken outside to one of the black trucks waiting there. The agent placed his hand again upon Lenard's shoulder (the very same spot as before, no less) and kindly advised him to remain calm.

"Your daughter will not be harmed," was the only consolation he offered Lenard as they both listened to her panicked screams die out behind the thick armoring of specially-plated SUV doors. She yelled for her daddy to help her, but to no avail. All Lenard could do was look on and impudently demand answers that he may never be given from men he had never seen before. Meanwhile, the truck into which Delilah had been loaded, drove off of the Hanson property, accompanied by five or six identical black trucks. Delilah, now in the back seat of the truck, behind a thick iron grating that separated her from the cockpit, was still kicking and screaming—quite literally—for immediate release.

One of the agents was sitting in the back with her, so naturally, he found himself the recipient of most of her verbal and physical duress. She spat, she clawed, she yelled, she thrashed, and basically did anything that would make this whole fiasco as uncomfortable for the strange suited men around her as it was for her. After sustaining more than one or two bloody scratches from his fiery patron, the agent in the back gave Delilah a single warning that she should calm down or else. Of course, she didn't calm down, so the 'or else' came in the form of device that looked like a very miniature flashlight. The first opening the agent got in between Delilah's hazardously hysterical thrashing, he pressed the device hard against her neck. Five tiny syringe heads pierced her skin, and almost instantaneously, her limbs went slack. She slumped down with little more than a weak whimper onto the truck door nearest her. Her head bumped helplessly against the window with the truck's movement for a few moments, until the agent sat her limp body up straight where her head could lay back on the seat, and so, with her head back and mouth agape, she gave no further problem.

When she returned to consciousness, she was lying on a bed in a dimly-lit white room. Immediately, she tried to return to her screaming and thrashing fit, but somehow, her body wouldn't cooperate. She calmed down enough to lift her head and see that she was restrained. A thick leather strap bound each of her ankles, another, her midsection, another, her chest and shoulders, and yet two more, both her wrists. The wrist straps secured her arms to what looked and felt like thick, plush armrests one would expect to find on an expensive recliner. Once Delilah got over the initial shock of finding out she had been harnessed like a maniac—which she *had* been acting like, ironically—she noticed that someone had changed her clothes. When the agents had initially abducted her from her room, she was in a nightgown (designer, of course) as she didn't want to take any chances that the mysterious infection was clinging to the clothes she'd been wearing, and, more importantly, her.

Now, however, she was in a white linen dress. The stark realization that someone had disrobed her while she was unconscious, and had seen her without her clothes without her permission, brought with it a fresh fury. She kicked and beat, though ineffectively, against the leather restraints until the bed beneath her sang as if it would soon fall apart. And she sang with it…sort of. The ear shattering screams of frustration that she released would've likely caused any glass objects near her, had there been any, to instantly and violently explode into a glistening mushroom cloud. The set of lungs on this young lady was simply amazing. Her angry screech was deafening. It was much louder and of a much higher pitch than any she had ever produced before (she had never had cause to protest like this), and it strained her vocal chords to their very limit. It also gave her a splitting pain just behind her temples in the process. But none of this mattered to her at the moment. The only thing that mattered was that not only did someone have the audacity to come into her home and abduct her, but they also drugged her and stripped her bare.

Her single-toned, mountain-moving screech continued until a door opened and a man, a doctor of some sort by the looks of him, in a completely white uniform with matching white, bootie-covered medical shoes, entered the room. He had two thick earplugs stuffed snugly into his ears. Delilah was so busy squealing that she didn't notice his presence for some time. Meanwhile, he took up his position near the head of her bed and waited...and waited. As a medical professional, he could properly appreciate the awesome stamina it must take to sustain such a strenuous note. Every vein in Delilah's face and neck bulged against her skin. By the looks of things, she could've easily given herself an aneurism, but that didn't seem to matter to her.

Soon, the doctor became genuinely alarmed that Delilah would do serious damage to herself if she didn't stop. He was just about to call for more sedative when exhaustion beat him to the punch. Delilah's bawling dropped one to two decibels at first, then nearly all at once, she was reduced to a very hoarse cough. As everything continued to catch up with her, she found herself so tired that she could hardly move. Finally, she let her head collapse back onto the pillow, and showed no other signs of life beside an exaggerated rising and falling of her chest, her mouth open to inhale as much precious breath as possible. The doctor gazed at her and stroked her forehead gently. She didn't protest. She had no more energy left for that.

"Well, while you are a *captive audience,*" the doctor began. He thought the pun distasteful even before he said it, but simply couldn't resist, "let me take this opportunity to try and help you understand what's happening…" The doctor told Delilah that his name was Ian Crangler, and that he was the nation's top rated specialist in his field of medicine (he was surprisingly mum as to exactly *what* field of medicine he was talking about). Dr. Crangler told Delilah that she was an extremely important person now, but again, he was mum as to exactly why. In fact, the most specific information that he gave her was that mankind had been infected by an alien virus that made childbirth from this point on, fatal for both child and mother. She was the only female on the entire planet who had not been infected with this horrible virus and in her bloodstream was the only source of a viable vaccine. The fate of all mankind rested literally in her hands.

Chapter 8

Geoffrey was still watching Mr. Reynolds from the other side of the large pane of one way glass. He was just about sure that he couldn't stomach any more of the gruesome sight, when the door to Mr. Reynolds's room opened and a man in a white overcoat with matching white pants and bootie-covered medical shoes, entered. With his pale white skin, beneath a spotless outfit, in a completely white room, the man looked like an apparition as he strolled almost casually beneath bright white lights, to where Mr. Reynolds lay. Geoffrey had seen his father in medical garb plenty of times, but never like this. If it was possible to add to the strangeness of Mr. Reynolds's current condition, the man in the lab coat did, and only added to Geoffrey's struggle to adjust to all this.

Meanwhile, the doctor hit a button on the underside of the bed. The astronomer's ankles were bound with white leather straps, and his wrists were strapped with white leather straps to two armrests supporting his arms. He wore loose white plastic gloves on his hands. Slowly, the bed began to lift Mr. Reynolds's head and torso, while lowering his legs and feet.

After a few moments the bed had transformed into something like a recliner. The armrests tilted as Mr. Reynolds was forced upright, his mouth still forming soundless words and his eyes still missing irises.

The doctor grabbed the stethoscope hanging around his neck—also white—and placed it over the Mr. Reynolds's heart. After a few seconds of listening, he nodded solemnly as doctors usually do, and raised his hand and gestured. Apparently, he was calling for assistance. Meanwhile, he hit the bed button again and the recliner now raised Mr. Reynolds's torso and midsection upright. The armrests rotated smoothly into a semi-vertical position along with the transforming divan, until Mr. Reynolds was positioned nearly erect. A few moments later, two men entered the room wearing equally-spotless white uniforms and pushing medical equipment. Even the stainless steel equipment was draped with what looked like thick, white curtains. The two men brought the doctor a small rolling cabinet and quickly left. Lieutenant Dan stood on the other side of the one way glass with Geoffrey, but he didn't look nearly as confused as the intern. In fact, his chiseled face looked as calm as if all this was standard procedure. Back on the other side of the glass, the doctor worked his hands in a pair of latex gloves and produced a butterfly needle, and a small plastic vial from the rolling cabinet. He drew blood from Mr. Reynolds's arm into the vial. He then drew another larger vial full of blood, one that already had some other liquid in it, and returned them both to the cabinet.

After that, he used the machines that were brought in to run some simple tests. He hooked up leads to the scientist's body from the machines, and situated goggles over Mr. Reynolds's eyes. Then, he exited the room. The scientist seemed oblivious of anything taking place around him. Geoffrey, on the other hand, was hypnotized by the scene. Moments ago, he hadn't even been sure that he could continue to look on but now, he found himself enthralled with expectation of what could possibly happen next. Geoffrey was so enthralled, in fact, that the sound of an opening door in the otherwise deathly silent room startled him out of the corner Lieutenant Dan had sat him in when he had taken the wheelchair away sometime earlier.

The doctor he had just seen with Mr. Reynolds, entered the room. He spoke with Lieutenant Dan briefly, then turned to Geoffrey. His gaze was intent upon the intern's hands as he spoke. "Hello, young man." He said "How are you feeling?"

Geoffrey didn't answer at first. "I'm doing fine." he lied, after what felt like a long while.

"Good." The doctor answered, drawing closer, but not *too* close, to him. His gaze never strayed from Geoffrey's hands (both of which were trembling by this time). "Now, I'm going to ask you a few questions. It is very important, *extremely* important, that you answer me completely and honestly. Do you understand?"

Geoffrey's lips trembled as he answered, "I do understand and I promise I'll tell you whatever you want to know." Lieutenant Dan's formidable presence was a powerful motivation to speak the truth.

The doctor continued in slow, measured words, as if he could afford to take no chance of his terrified subject mishearing him. "Did you touch the meteorite fragment?" he asked.

"No, no I did not." Geoffrey answered quickly.

"Did you touch that man," he pointed to Mr. Reynolds, "*at all*, after *he* touched the fragment?"

"I didn't...I hit him with the shovel, really hard I think, but only because I didn't know what else to do, but I didn't touch him at all after that." Geoffrey answered.

The doctor exhaled slowly. He seemed to speak with considerably less anxiety after this. He carefully took Geoffrey's still trembling hands in his own and examined them, turning them over, moving them this way and that, until he was satisfied. He then pulled up a chair and asked Geoffrey to tell him everything that happened from the moment he spotted the fragment to the moment that he and the astronomer were carted off in the chopper.

The doctor leaned close and looked intently into Geoffrey's face. "You need to tell me everything that happened. I warn you to not omit the smallest detail. I need to know everything."

Geoffrey obliged, telling the doctor absolutely everything there was to know, even about the plot the other astronomers had forged against him. No one in the room seemed too concerned with the affairs or the hypocrisy of the other scientists, but as Geoffrey recounted things pertaining to the fragment and Mr. Reynolds's subsequent reaction to it all eyes were intent upon him.

At last, Geoffrey finished his account. The doctor sat up in the chair and rubbed his lower lip, absorbed in deep thought. Lieutenant Dan, looming behind him, frowned as if considering something important. After a while, it seemed like the both men had completely forgotten that Geoffrey was in the room. He looked around. It was painfully obvious that he wasn't going anywhere anytime soon. Perhaps, he would never see the light of the day in the free world again. If he was ever going to get any answers, it was probably now or never.

"Excuse me," he said, or, more accurately, whispered, his voice was so low. He cleared his throat and tried again, this time a little louder. "Excuse me." Lieutenant Dan was the first to break out of his daze.

"Yes, Mr. Summons? What is it?" asked the lieutenant general.

"Well, actually," began Geoffrey, with more than a small measure of cautious reserve "I was wondering…what's going on? Obviously, that fragment is more important than I know, but why?" he wanted to ask more, but as everything thing else seemed to be tied to this one inquiry, he waited to see what, if anything, would be answered. Amazingly, the doctor was yet in his daze. Lieutenant Dan tapped his shoulder and he started back to reality.

"What is it, Lieutenant?" the doctor asked.

"Mr. Summons wants to know what's going on. What do you think?" Lieutenant Dan didn't sound like he was making a genuine inquiry as much as simply jesting. The doctor, however, must've not known that, because the tone in which he answered was, indeed, sincere.

"My vote is we tell him." He answered. Suddenly, Geoffrey wasn't so sure that he wanted to know anymore. That didn't matter of course, because the doctor continued, "First chance I get, I'm going to call my ex-wife and estranged daughter. What can it possibly hurt now? Besides, what information we can get out of him and the comatose astronomer over there may be of some assistance to us. If so, they may be responsible for saving billions of lives, not to mention the future of mankind. Either way, I say let 'em in on our dirty little secret."

Lieutenant Dan looked back at Geoffrey as if thinking this over. Even lost in thought, his face was like his jaw: Hard and firmly set. It didn't look as if the doctor's logic was winning out. A terrifying thought entered Geoffrey's head. By the looks of things, he was already on the wrong end of the whole, 'I could tell you but then I'd have to kill you' thing. The doctor had already shared that there was a 'dirty little secret' (one *hell* of a dirty little secret, as far as Geoffrey could tell), that was carefully guarded by the government, so Geoffrey had been effectively stripped of all hopes of maintaining plausible deniability, but he still hadn't been given enough information to make such a risky position even remotely worthwhile. In short, he had been given too much information for his own good, but not enough for his own welfare.

The doctor must've read the concern on Geoffrey's face because he continued to persuade the lieutenant general, "Listen, Lieutenant Dan—that's what everyone around here calls you, right? Well, look, I'm certainly not trying to tell you how to do your job, as I certainly wouldn't appreciate you advising me on how to perform mine, but don't you think this kid has a right to at least know? Even in what you do, even in war, there are rules, aren't there? I don't claim to know all the idiosyncrasies of your chosen profession, but if I'm not mistaken, I think one of your men told me something like it's unlawful to shoot an enemy combatant while they're parachuting down and can't defend themselves." Lieutenant Dan gave a reluctant grunt acknowledging that fact.

"Well, if the *enemy* deserves at least some kind of consideration, doesn't this young man?" the doctor asked rhetorically. "Neither he nor the astronomer in there knew what the hell they were getting into when they started messing with that fragment. That fragment may be the very reason he never sees his family and friends, everyone he's ever known, alive, again…" Geoffrey's eyes widened considerably and he stopped breathing involuntarily at the sound of this assertion. *Damn, I really should've been a doctor like my dad told me!* he thought to himself.

The doctor continued, "The least we can do is tell the poor bastard what's going on here."

Lieutenant Dan looked at Geoffrey, and for the first time, Geoffrey saw his frighteningly-cool demeanor give way to something even more disconcerting; genuine displeasure. Uncomfortable beads of perspiration presented themselves all across Geoffrey's forehead almost instantly. The lieutenant general looked displeased. He stepped around the doctor toward Geoffrey's chair, and his (Geoffrey's) life flashed before his eyes. One of the lieutenant's deathly huge hands lighted upon Geoffrey's shoulder. With the slightest clamp of his fingers, he sent a hot jolt of pain through Geoffrey's arm, elbow to neck. Geoffrey winced but didn't budge: Not from resilience so much as the fact that the lieutenant general was so strong that he was virtually holding the intern's entire torso upright with his single vise-like hold.

Lieutenant Dan narrowed his eyes and leaned in toward Geoffrey. Geoffrey's heart beat as if it would burst from his chest any moment. Lieutenant Dan had a look on his face as if his body was building up too much pressure and he planned to release it into Geoffrey's face. Instead, with a deep sigh, he abruptly released his painful grip on Geoffrey's shoulder and straightened up.

"The doc's right, Mr. Summons. That meteorite fragment you found marks the change of the entire world as you know it. And it *is* very likely that you'll never see your family and friends alive again."

Lieutenant Dan heaved another deep sigh and slowly returned to his original position behind the doctor. Once he got there, he continued his oration. "This location," the lieutenant general waved his hand in a wide arc toward the entire grounds. "is a highly classified and heavily-guarded fortress. And as with all fortresses, this one was meant to protect something. Something more important than money, more important than any high tech computer, and more important that any one weapon." He turned and again leveled his guarded gaze upon Geoffrey, "Knowledge. We have known about alien life in our part of the universe for decades. We've been bringing back primitive alien life forms from the moon and mars since we got there. What looks like alien bacteria or fungus, nothing complex but *life*. But nothing ever lasts long once they get it back home. Everything always dies once it's been subjected to our atmosphere. Everything. It always just turns to dust."

The lieutenant general's voice heightened a note or two as he continued, "Even received some kind of transmission from the 'higher functions', as the science personnel like to call 'em. That crowd figures that if alien intelligence can send a readable signal, then they have to be at least as smart as humans, and since they're aliens, it's probably best to assume they're smarter than we are. So, anyway, they finally receive a transmission from these 'higher functions' and it's in numbers. It's been fifteen years, and the guys in the offices still can't figure it out. Whole messages written in numbers."

"Well," interposed the doctor "it does stand to reason that if there is a universal language, it would be some kind of math, or something like it. Numbers are the only things that are likely to be the same on other planets."

"That's right. You did say that you took up some kind of math before you got into medicine in college." Lieutenant Dan observed.

"Infinitesimal calculus," the doctor clarified "and I only *got into medicine* as you say, when I got here fifteen years ago." He turned his attention back to Geoffrey, and continued Lieutenant Dan's narrative, "But even stranger than that was *how* the message was sent. It came on a burst of pure energy. Light, Son!" the doctor nearly yelled, "Nothing can travel faster than light, not even information, so these foreign intelligences have found a way to actually use light itself to carry information. Light is of prime importance in one way or another in many fields, including, and especially, medicine. With the improvements we could make to lasers for instance, if we could learn to manipulate them better, we could possibly perform more complex surgeries with them and completely disinfect open flesh even while it's being removed or repaired. The Cleaning Lights we all passed in the corridor are just a start of what could be done with the knowledge we've already garnered from these alien intelligences. And that's just the tip…"

"Cleaning Lights?" Geoffrey asked.

"The lights you passed in the hallway leading here. You couldn't have missed them. Didn't you notice that they were much brighter than any lights you've ever seen before?" Geoffrey had noticed that the corridor's lights were incredibly bright, but after the whole hidden entryway thing, he didn't take as much note of the phenomenon as he likely would have otherwise.

"What about them?" Geoffrey asked.

"Well, what they are," answered the doctor, with the same faint rise in enthusiasm as had been witnessed in the lieutenant general a few moments ago, "is the best sterilization agent the world has ever seen. When you came in here and passed under and through those lights, your body was nearly instantaneously purged of most of the potentially dangerous microbes, spores, bacteria, etc., that live on your skin…as well as in your body."

"Potentially dangerous?" asked Geoffrey with a noticeable tone of alarm.

The doctor quickly answered, "No, nothing that we did: Nature, Son. You see, you already have literally hundreds of millions— maybe more—living microorganisms that call your body home. Your mouth, your skin, your eyebrows, even that full head of hair you young people are usually unworthily blessed with, is all saturated with hordes of bacteria, and yeast. Now, most of these microorganisms are good for you, but some aren't. As far as we can tell, the vast majority of them are fatal to alien life forms that haven't had millions of years' experience in the hostile environment of our planet to build up an immunity."

"Are you saying that you have…real life *aliens…here*?" Geoffrey asked, astounded. He hadn't used the phrase 'real life' for anything since he was a kid, but now he felt sort of like a kid: A confused, helpless kid.

The doctor looked at the lieutenant general before he went on. Lieutenant Dan just answered his look with a gruff grunt. "Hey, Doc, you're the one thinks he has a right to know." Was all he said.

The doctor turned back toward Geoffrey, "Yes, Son, we do, but not alien*s*. We have only a single foreign entity housed at this particular facility at the moment, and we're not sure yet that it's from the life forms that sent the fragment." With that, Geoffrey's assumptions were confirmed. He knew, he just knew, that that meteorite fragment was much more than it appeared. Up until this point, there was no way for him to know for certain that all of this wasn't because of his alleged assault of Mr. Reynolds. If that were so, he'd be in big trouble, but with this new information, there arose a new, more vibrant fear. Was Earth under attack by alien life forms that could hurl incapacitating glowing rocks into our atmosphere whenever they wanted? If they were—which seemed to be where things stood at the moment—then he was, in fact, still in huge trouble…and so was the rest of the world.

The doctor's voice, as he continued his harrowing narrative, was the only thing that helped usher Geoffrey back to reality. "We've had others at less technologically advanced facilities, but it would seem that their housings, their bodies if you will, cannot bear to be in close, unguarded proximity with the microorganisms that I spoke of earlier, that are associated with virtually all human beings. A few days in any human's presence, no matter what we did to prevent it, and they all eventually ceased to function."

"They died?" asked Geoffrey.

"Yes, and turned to dust like nothing we've ever seen…radioactive dust. Those lights in the entranceway corridor that you and Lieutenant Dan traveled through to get here, effectively killed or vaporized at least 85% of the harmful microorganisms residing on or beneath your skin, and especially a flora of microorganisms residing within your respiratory system." The doctor's tone took on an introspective air, as he continued, "My team and I were already making great strides in the practice of bloodless, laser-aided surgeries, but it wasn't until we were fortunate enough to have some of this alien technology fall into our hands that we discovered how to unlock more of light's, how shall I say, greater potentials. We still have some ways to go, but with time, I'm sure we can do even more unimaginable things with what we're discovering."

"So, those lights can kill germs and things…*inside* my body, from the *outside*?"

"Precisely." The doctor nearly shouted, jabbing a finger into the air.

"And you developed them?"

"Yes." The doctor answered, then as something of a side note, "Well, I had some help, but yes, I developed them."

It would seem that the purpose of most of this oration was to draw attention to the fact that it was the doctor who had authored this great stride in the field of medicine. Geoffrey thought about Mr. Reynolds wanting his name attached to some new discovery so desperately that he was willing to put himself in the kind of danger that got him where he was right now. It would seem that even aged and seasoned professionals were still just children at heart, trying to secure the shiniest toy and claim it for their own. At the very least though, Geoffrey was getting some valuable information, so the rest mattered little.

The doctor continued to laud his latest achievement and its vast implications until he said something else that piqued Geoffrey's interest. He explained how the lights made the entire underground facility essentially a huge, high order clean room, when he noted that all this was done in addition to the fact that the lights never needed to be changed or repaired. When Geoffrey asked how that was possible, the doctor was more than happy to explain, "…and that's the fascinating thing!" The doctor was almost giddy. "There are no lamps in these lights, as you can see if you look at them closely enough. They have only what we call containment units. And, also, they have no cords, because they don't use electricity. Why would you think that is?"

Geoffrey shrugged his shoulders. He opened his mouth as if to answer but then closed it without a word. He had no idea how the lights could operate without electricity.

"Because these fixtures," the doctor gestured to the ceiling, toward a set of lights that were identical to the ones in the corridor, except that they weren't as bright, "don't produce light, they *store* it." The creases in Geoffrey's forehead as well as the way he simultaneously raised an eyebrow and squinted said that all this made no sense to him. The doctor went on with the explanation, growing more excited like a kid showing off his shiny new toy. "It is accepted among scientists that light exhibits both wave *and* particle properties. Now, I'm sure you understand the wave properties of light, as it's the part of light that you can see," The doctor's energy was reaching a peak. "but you're probably not familiar with the *particle* properties of light. That's the part of light that, under the right circumstances, you should be able to *feel*." Geoffrey's eyes lit up in understanding.

"We've," Here, the doctor's tone suggested that he actually meant *I*, "found a way to synthesize light into a physical presence!" The doctor sat back in his chair silently, satisfied to let Geoffrey awe at his fully-revealed, shiny new plaything.

And marvel, the intern did. This latest revelation cast light—quite literally—on a lot of other things, and Geoffrey was trying desperately to take it all in as fast as it was coming. After a few moments of enjoying the stark amazement plastered on the intern's face, the doctor continued, "Now that we've found out how to make light a material presence, there's no limit to the things we can do with it, including sending information by it. That's what we think happened with your astronomer friend in there," the doc gestured toward the one way glass, "That fragment he touched was covered in light, you said, right?" Geoffrey nodded. "Well, we believe that information about whoever sent that fragment may be contained in that light."

"So, what's happened to him, then?" Goeffrey asked.

"I believe his body is absorbing that information. One of those machines in there will wake him out of his daze, at least that's what we're shooting for. If it works and he comes to without severe brain damage, he may be able to give us all the information we need about this alien life force and its home planet, or perhaps even galaxy." The doctor lowered his voice conspiratorially, "Your friend in there may hold information that is the key to understanding the entire universe…but more importantly, to help us avoid the complete and total annihilation of all life on our planet."

Chapter 9

"I need a heart monitor in here right now!" the doctor yelled.

"And get me an oxygen machine!" another demanded.

The scene was chaotic, nurses and assistants rushing in every direction, struggling to gather machines and medical materials that were being screamed for much more quickly than they could be produced. Meanwhile, Delilah gazed on at the entire scene with an unusual mixture of pleasure and panic. She was well-used to being fussed over. Her father always made sure that she had a virtual army of chefs, beauticians, maids, and even surrogate shoppers to do just that, but the chaos that was ensuing over her now—the only thing she had done was alerted the doctor that she was feeling a little out of breath—was quite alarming. Just outside her monotonously white room, she saw white suited professionals stumbling over each other to retrieve the things that were being yelled for.

In her room, three male doctors were doing the yelling. One stood beside her bed checking her pulse, another stood at two large windows that faced the hall in the front of the room, from which she watched an intermittent haze of white uniforms rush to and fro. A third stood at a large mirror recessed into a side wall of the room. He was mouthing something to the mirror, but in the blur of bodies and voices surrounding her, Delilah didn't think too much of it. One of the scrambling white suited people rushed in with a machine that had been yelled for.

"Get the hell out of here!" the doctor near the window yelled savagely. "*No one* is to enter this room except us!"

The bewildered orderly, looked as if he was about to ask where the doctor wanted the machine then, but he didn't get a chance, because the doctor interrupted by roaring, "I said, get the hell out of here, *now*! And tell the others to leave whatever we call for out in the hallway! *No one* is to enter this room except us!" Once the unfortunate, and confused, intruder backed out of the room, the doctor turned to Delilah. The smile on his face looked forced. "I'm sincerely sorry about that, Ms. Hanson." The doctor said. He spread his hands in exasperation. "Help. I'm sure you can relate."

Delilah didn't open her mouth to answer. The only thing that was going through her head was, *What the hell is going on?* Meanwhile, the first doctor continued to check her pulse. The second, the one who was talking to the mirror, walked over as well. He looked at the first doctor questioningly. "Pulse is slightly higher than normal." The other answered the silent inquiry.

"I thought so," said the mirror whispering doctor. "I think we should step outside for a moment."

"But..." the other began to reply.

"*I think we should step outside for a moment.*" Interrupted the first, through bared teeth. The pulse checking doctor finally got the hint and all three headed to the door. Neither of them bothered to answer a single question plaguing Delilah's mind, as they did so. The door didn't shut all the way after they exited and Delilah heard them talking just outside. "We *cannot* upset this patient in any way, form, or fashion. We all know that, so what the hell is going on here?" Delilah listened on, excited at the prospect of getting some questions answered. "We need machines and supplies, but I've already told these damned orderlies a hundred times to never enter..."

"Well, first of all," returned the first voice. Delilah felt dreamy and slightly tired and couldn't tell who was talking to whom, "they're not orderlies, they're government certified security clearance worthy nurses." Delilah couldn't tell which of the doctors was talking, but she could tell by the thick, insubordinate tone, that this latest bit of information was fodder that the doctors had been reminded of countless times. Delilah could all but see eyes rolling in disgust even as the words were

Steven A. Spellman

spoken. She knew the look well. It was often her own.

"Well, I have to record that her pulse has risen and the big wigs will want to know why." Came the reply.

"I know, and we can't sedate her any more while we get these machines set up. If we can synthesize a vaccine, it's going to have to come from her blood, so we can't afford to keep drugging her." Before she could stop herself, Delilah let out a brief, but reverberating squeal of horror at hearing that she had been drugged…again.

Obviously, one of the doctors heard her because the only conversation that followed was a quick proclamation of "Oh!" before the door was pulled closed all the way and three highly-concerned doctors quickly passed the front windows to her room. Fresh repulsion flooded Delilah's breast. She knew *something* was wrong with her, otherwise she surely would've been screaming at the top of her lungs hours ago for her father to be contacted and for her to be taken out of this place that very instant.

Even now, it was much more difficult than usual for her to get upset—*Delilah upset*, that is—and she knew that it must be the effects of the sedatives flowing freely inside her. Anyone who knew Delilah would've assumed that those sedatives were the extra strength variety to quell the Hanson fury as they had, and they would've been right. As Delilah lay beneath leather straps and dim lights, revulsion began to subside and in its place rose up a fiercely strong feeling that she was being watched. By the feel of things, it was the room's odd *mirror* that was doing the watching. She wanted to yell, but it was just too difficult to summon the energy for her usual tantrums, so she just lay there pouting, wanting to cry, but unable even to summon the comforting tears of self-pity.

After a while, another doctor entered the room. "Hello, Ms. Hanson." The doctor said.

Delilah had been staring at a far wall, still pouting over just how unfair her situation was, but turned her head sharply at the voice. It was not the voice of someone she would consider a friend, but it was familiar and right now, that counted for more than she'd have ever thought possible.

"Help me get out of here, Ian." Delilah pleaded. "Get me out of here. Get my dad. Get me out of here please!"

"Whoa, slow down, Miss Hanson. Just calm down," answered the doctor.

"I want my daddy!" Delilah was so frustrated and confused that she didn't care if she sounded like a lost four-year-old. It was also possible that she didn't care because a lost four-year-old is exactly what she felt like, yet again.

Either way, the doctor didn't seem too disconcerted as he said coolly (or at least it sounded cold to Delilah), "Listen, Miss Hanson,

I'm going to do my best to explain to you what's going on, but I need you to promise that you'll calm down. If I can't get you to make that promise, then frankly, Miss Hanson, I can't help you."

Delilah glared at the doctor. It wasn't that she was still under the delusion that she could get her way with loud, harsh words or, as in this case, long, harsh stares, as much as it was simply force of habit. As many overly privileged people just like Delilah already knew, getting what they wanted all the time with just the flick of a credit card or the punch of a button (usually on the phone, to call good 'ole daddy, so *he* can flick a credit card) can grow on a person. Just like a well-baited hook in the mouth of a fish, once a person gets a good taste, it's hard to let go. Once the fruitless staring match had run its course, Delilah reluctantly relented and agreed to 'play nice.'

"Great. That's absolutely fabulous, Ms. Hanson. But one other thing before we get started: I'd prefer that you refer to me as Dr. Crangler. I'm a professional and I'd appreciate being addressed as such." Delilah gritted her teeth so hard that it was a miracle her gums didn't touch, but eventually she nodded. It would seem that she had fallen greatly from the high and mighty command giver she had been just a few days ago. Without a doubt, she much preferred her former state, but she was beginning to realize that if she was ever going to get a shot in hell at returning to the way things were, she'd have to cooperate, because her money and looks obviously didn't give her the upper hand in this strange place.

"Now, Ms. Hanson," *Dr.* Crangler continued "I need to get some machinery set up in here. I need to run some very important tests on you and I need to get it done as quickly as possible. I apologize for my comrades who were here just now. But I promise you that you will not be seeing them again. Only I will attend to you from this point forward."

"I want to know what's going on first." Delilah said, in a noticeably stressed tone, and through strained lips. She had agreed to cooperate. She hadn't agreed to like it. The doctor sighed audibly.

"All right, Miss Hanson," said he "I think that's fair. You've been snatched from your home, sedated," thankfully he had enough tact to not add, *repeatedly,* "and brought to a place that I'm sure is unfamiliar and scary to you. But I must warn you, Miss Hanson, what has happened and the unwitting part you now play in all of it is not easy to explain...or believe." As the doctor noted, Delilah had been through a hell of a lot already. This past year had awarded her with experiences that were literally out of this world and Dr. Crangler may've been surprised at exactly what she would believe at this point.

Instead of going through all that, Delilah just nodded her head faintly and said, "Okay."

"Good, that's good," answered the doctor. He pulled a chair out of the hallway and took a seat near the head of Delilah's bed where he could talk to her face to face. He explained to her that an alien life form had saturated Earth's atmosphere with a brand new and unique kind of deadly virus that was specifically designed to attack only the female population. The effects of this virus were that, besides the ubiquitous yellow eyes and unnaturally flaking skin, neither mother nor child of any infected person would survive childbirth. From what they had seen already, the virus was permanent and was the first disorder ever to affect every member of the female population on Earth, regardless of age, ethnicity, nationality, way of life, or any other notable difference.

The virus was designed to spread by something every woman needed to live—oxygen—which turned out to be its greatest and most ingenious strength and simultaneously, its most exploitable and only known weakness. Dr. Crangler explained that this was because of oxygen's highly-adaptive and corrosive nature. The virus attached itself to oxygen molecules and saturated the world's entire supply of fresh air within hours, but because oxygen has the ability to change so rapidly, the virus survived only long enough to infect anyone breathing the planet's air, but not long enough to sustain itself for any extended length of time otherwise. Also, due to the volatile and changing nature of oxygen and the complex way the human body uses it, the virus ceased to be contagious once it had found a female host.

"This is where you come in, Delilah." Dr. Crangler said. "You were the only female occupant on your space flight and since there were no women aboard the International Space Station, you were the only female outside of Earth's atmosphere when the meteor appeared." Dr. Crangler licked his lips and leaned in. "You were the only female in the entire world who had not contracted the virus." The doctor's eyes narrowed, "As far as perpetuation of mankind is concerned, you are now most important person on the face of the planet." Delilah lay slowly in her bed and was silent and still, her features as blank as if she was in another world. Her mind couldn't encompass the awesome information that she was just given. Had it not been for all she had experienced, including her current surroundings, as well as the thick leather straps that held her down and constantly reminded her that this was reality and not a horrid nightmare, it was likely she wouldn't have believed any of the nonsense the doctor just fed her.

Unfortunately, denial or naiveté were no longer viable options. She believed that all Dr. Crangler was saying, but understanding it...well, that was a completely different animal altogether.

After a long silence, the doctor spoke up. "I understand this a lot to handle…" he mused to himself for a moment "yeah, a *hell* of a lot. But as I told you before, the only thing I can offer you is the truth, and right now, the truth is not easy. Not easy at all." A few more silent moments passed, when the sound of a light tapping from the mirror filled the room. "I really need to get these tests underway. I have a couple of other important gentlemen that I need to attend to soon." He stood and looked down at Delilah. Her mind was still wandering off in the recesses of space. "Do you have any questions, Miss Hanson?" he asked.

Surprisingly, she did have a question. Her eyes cleared with an almost alarming quickness, as she turned her face to the doctor's. "What happens to the women…you know, if they try to have kids?" The question was so sincere and innocent, and the look on Delilah's confused face so childlike, that, for the first time, the doctor felt a pang of sympathy for the young women. He hadn't exactly hated her (perhaps he would have if he knew her better) but he certainly wasn't fond of her. He knew her story, not only from the publicity that had always been lavished upon her, but from classified surveillance documents that were compiled upon her. He knew that disappointment and lack were not words that she was familiar with, that, like most people who didn't have to earn their own money, she assumed the world revolved around her (how ironic that now it was closer to the truth than it had ever been, and it was nothing like she had expected), and deep down, he resented her for it.

From the moment she had been brought to the secret underground facility, he vowed that if nothing else, he would show her that she was not the boss here. Now, she could've been his own daughter for how plaintively she was reaching out to him for answers. "I don't think now is the time, Miss Hanson," he said with sincere angst. Suddenly, he didn't want to further crush her world by explaining to her the gruesome effects this virus had upon the beauty of childbirth. "Maybe, a little later, when you've had time for all this to sink in."

"Now." She answered, simply. This was not one of her usual *if you don't do what I say, I will have you fired!* demand. Rather, it was the firm resolution of a woman who felt like she had earned the right to some answers. The doctor looked at her intently. He looked back down at his chair and slowly lowered himself into it again. As delicately as he could, he tried to paint an understandable picture of something that was anything but. In a low voice loaded with gravity, he explained what was already happening to women around the world. Thanks to the ingenuity of properly-functioning hormones, a pregnant woman's body normally alerted her when it was time for the carried child to be introduced to the world. Then, once that

91

precious newborn had been expelled into the harsh world of overly bright lights and overly loud sounds, its own hormones (and maybe a firm tap from a doctor or other) would alert it to begin breathing.

That was all before The Virus. Now, the bodies of yellowed eyed, scaly skinned, pregnant women did not alert them to the proper time of childbirth. In fact, it was as if their swollen, pregnant bodies didn't know that there *was* a time to give birth. The first women to experience the phenomenon after The Virus suffered the worst, since no one yet knew what to expect from this strange and sudden ailment. Perhaps, there was a teenage girl who didn't want her parents to find out that she was pregnant, or perhaps, she didn't know herself. The child inside her would grow and move and function normally. The problem was that this continued on indefinitely. Said teenager, anxious to keep her condition a secret, and in addition, unfamiliar with the natural progression of pregnancy, didn't register alarm as she should have, when ten months, eleven months, perhaps an entire year passed and the overgrown child remained yet in the young womb.

The alarm would register, though, when the unbearable pain came. It was not the pain of childbirth. This agony was the pain of her delicate insides being pushed and stretched heinously beyond their limits. There were those who were so desperate to hide the shame of being labeled "loose" that they literally burst from a continually growing baby that their bodies would not birth as nature had dictated. Of course, the mother and child both met a severely slow demise. Pregnancy was always a difficult, and many times, uncomfortable experience for many women, but even the harshest pregnancy paled in comparison to a frightened and pain plagued teenage girl being tortured to death by 44 weeks and twelve to fifteen, or possibly more, pounds of compressed baby crushing her lungs and internal organs like an angry, expanding water balloon.

Just like a water balloon that is continually being filled beyond its ability, so the unfortunate mother would eventually (but only after an awesomely agonizing and drawn out decline) fall over dead, her internal cavities having torn to bursting. Even those who were not so unfortunate, were no better off. Grown women, married women even, would draw closer to their appointed time of delivery and anxiously await the tell-tale signs of impending labor only to find that days, weeks sometimes, passed, and nature had not taken its course. Many of these women were eventually taken to the hospital only to have their questions of what was wrong answered with the blank faces of trusted medical professionals who were genuinely as confused as they. All the lab tests showed that everything was right on paper and computer screens, so why had women suddenly stopped going into labor…at all?

Labor could not even be induced due to The Virus, but at least there were still C-Sections to thank God for, right? Wrong. This is where, if anyone doubted that something of biblical proportions had taken place in modern day society, they were converted. When a seemingly healthy woman was cut open to release the child, as soon as her insides were exposed to open air, she began to convulse violently and scream hysterically in pain from her exposed regions. Before the doctor's eyes, whatever internal flesh of hers that was exposed to the open air, if only for a few brief moments, would instantly undergo a graphic deterioration whereby living flesh would dry to something like a grey paste then into a thick, grey powder and finally, into fine dust. It was something like morticians were used to seeing in fully decayed corpses, only much more quickly.

If that wasn't enough, as soon as the freed child would take its first independent breath, it would gag violently. Nothing any doctor tried to do seemed to make a difference as newborns—every single one of them—choked to death off of fresh air. Every procedure or variation thereof in the book, as well as more than a few highly-controversial ones that were not in the book, were performed, but they all ended with the identically ghastly and fatal result. Somehow The Virus had further changed how female bodies reacted to the oxygen in the air. Their virus-saturated lungs and blood streams processed incoming air and changed it so it could be continually propagated within them, but if any unfiltered oxygen was introduced into the body (i.e., through an open wound) the disastrous effects already described would follow. Harsh, considering that a skinned knee or a deep cut could mean an agonizing demise. No one understood why men weren't affected.

The same was true for the baby. It, too, was infected with The Virus and so, was fine as long as it was being supplied with oxygen filtered through its mother's now diseased lungs, but as soon as it took a single breath of its own...There were many questions that had yet to be answered, like, if Doom's Day had finally come at last, and why did the Grim Reaper only have a thing for women, and especially, pregnant women? No one (at least not the in the general public) had the answers. If there was one thing that there was no lack of, it was sheer, head balding, nerve wracking, panic.

After Dr. Crangler finished this narrative, he gazed at Delilah, trying to gauge her response to all she had just heard, but she just stared at the ceiling, neither here nor there, vacancy obvious in her eyes. "Miss..." the doctor began.

"Thank you." Delilah answered before he could finish. Her voice was as distant as her gaze, as if she was yet far away on her space flight and was talking from the International Space Station orbiting the planet. Dr. Crangler couldn't tell if she knew what she was saying, but it didn't matter. The information he had just given her would've been overload for anyone's circuitry. All things considered, he figured she was handling things as well as could be expected. She continued to stare blankly at the ceiling directly above her and the doctor decided to take the opportunity to run those tests he had mentioned. While he did, Delilah showed no further notice of him or his lightly-whirring machines, or the cold attaching leads and needles that came from them, but just continued to stare silently at the ceiling, her gaze as uniformly empty as the white walls surrounding her.

Chapter 10

After about five hours of deep, unbroken sleep Geoffrey sat up, yawned, and stretched his limbs until the bones in his jaw, shoulders, and fingers cracked and popped like a symphony of ill-used elderly joints. Geoffrey felt anything but old. In fact, this little rest of his had infused him with new life. This entire roller coaster ride of unexpected events had drained his physical and mental aptitude to the point of bare boned exhaustion. He had slept harder than he could ever remember sleeping before. Now, however, his returned energy infused him like a tall frosty glass of cold water to a man who had been stranded in the desert for days. The irony of all this was that he had, in fact, recently come from a desert—a desert of ice. But for all his replenishment, the all-encompassing white of the sheets, blanket, and even the mattress on which he was now sitting—as well as everything else in the room—reminded him of the unfathomable reality at hand that he briefly escaped in slumber. That alone seemed to tire him again, though in a very different way.

Welcomed with this strange dichotomy, he rubbed his temples, yawned again (this time with no popping), and stood. He was still fully clothed, which meant that he went to sleep like that (something he never did) and as he thought about it, he didn't remember going to sleep in the first place. A thought crossed his mind and he took a look at the creases of his arms. Just as he vaguely expected, there were small, nearly unnoticeable imprints in his flesh that signified needles had recently broken through his skin. He had obviously been drugged. He lifted his shirt so he could see his chest, and when he did, he noticed the second thing he already expected; small round areas of fine, sticky grains left behind by the adhesion portion of chest leads.

Things were so crazy already that he wasn't as alarmed by the fact that he was drugged and tested as he would've been on any other occasion. He was still not comfortable knowing that he was completely at the mercy of people who were, for all intents and purposes, complete strangers. The next thought that entered his head was, where was Mr. Reynolds, and if anything had changed with him since he'd seen him last. He turned his head this way, then that, searching for the large, recessed wall mirror. He remembered how he, Lieutenant Dan, and the doctor had observed the astronomer through the one way glass, but now there was no mirror in this room. There were, however, two large windows that looked out onto a hallway, but Geoffrey could easily see through those so he was sure they were not for surveillance. It wouldn't have mattered anyway if anyone *had* been keeping tabs on him while he slept. Judgment Day had apparently come for mankind and somehow the loss of privacy didn't matter much anymore.

He stretched his limbs a third time, not from a need to work out the sleep, as much as a lame attempt to postpone dealing with the inevitable. As he already knew, the inevitable, by its very definition *must* be dealt with, so he stood and headed toward the windows, looking out onto an equally white hallway. He had never seen everything so universally white in his life. *There must be a special reason for it*, he thought. As much as he could, considering his limited vantage point, he looked this way and that, but there seemed to be no one in sight.

"Hey…someone?" he yelled. Somehow, he was certain that, though he saw no obvious surveillance equipment, he had not just been placed in this room and forgotten about. "Hey…someone?" he yelled again. No answer.

He turned and took a more thorough look around the room, searching the walls and ceiling until he found what he was looking for. At the very top of the room's far western corner, where the ceiling and the wall meet was a small, off-white spot on the wall, a large dot about the size of a camera lens, in an otherwise snow colored room. The only way Geoffrey could even tell it from its surroundings was that it was raised away from the corner. He walked casually to it, raising his hands and waving.

Before he even walked all the way to the corner, the doctor from earlier opened the door and stepped in.

"I see you've located our hidden camera, young man." The doctor said, kindly.

"It would seem so, but, um…"

"You want to know how things are going with your astronomer friend, correct?" asked the doctor.

"Yes, and a few other things…if that's possible."

"Well, I'll answer what I can, Mr. Summons, but only what I can. Lieutenant Dan is responsible for guarding you while you're here, and he's much more of a *government* man than I am. I'm sure you already know, the government doesn't relinquish *all* of its secrets that easily. As far as Mr. Reynolds is concerned, you'll be seeing him in just a little while. But first," The doctor looked over Geoffrey like a mortician in some movie or cartoon trying to assess measurements for a custom coffin "we'll need to get you cleaned up."

The doctor reached into one of the deep pockets of his white lab coat and produced a white note pad and a small, white pencil. He handed the articles to Geoffrey. "I'm going to show you to the sterilization shower, but first, I need you to write down the size of your clothes. Shirt, pants, shoes, underwear, everything. And be very precise."

Geoffrey gazed down at the colorless writing material. "Why is everything white here?" he asked, turning the pad and pencil over in his hand.

The doctor sighed lightly. "I just got finished dealing with another Nosey Nancy not too long ago, Mr. Summons. Can't we get you cleaned up and changed before we begin with the twenty questions routine?"

"What's the rush? It doesn't look like I'll be leaving this place any time soon…if ever. And who was the other guy that had questions?"

"Other young lady." The doctor corrected. "And a very popular young lady out in the free world, or so I hear. But you need not worry about her, you won't be making her acquaintance any time soon."

"Why is that?"

"Well, let's just say that your astronomer friend is a very important person now, but if he's important, than this young lady is *extremely* important."

Geoffrey could not decipher the doctor's mysteriously dark assessment and didn't try. Instead, he said, "*Okay*, well…why is everything here white?"

"Right," sighed the doctor, "You're a persistence one, aren't you, Mr. Summons? Well, let me try to explain it to you in as much of laymen's terms as I can." Geoffrey could easily sense something of the same brand of egotism that he had grown used to in his dealings with Mr. Reynolds, but it didn't chafe him nearly as much. There were more important things to be concerned with.

"All the lights in this entire facility," began the doctor, gesturing toward the ceiling, "are virtually identical to the Cleaning Lights in the entranceway, except they are not nearly as powerful. They don't need to be. As I told you before, the Cleaning Lights that you passed through when you first entered all but completely sterilized your body inside and out, but your body needs a large array of bacteria and other microorganisms to function properly. It is one of the many necessary symbiotic relationships that man has been forced to acquire in order for us to survive our atmosphere." The doctor paused to give Geoffrey a moment to digest the information. "So, besides acquiring many of these microorganisms from our surroundings, the body itself also produces a number of them. The lights in this room as well as in rest of the facility are to keep these newly-forged microorganisms in check..." The doc glanced down at his watch (also white), "...as is the sterilization shower that I'm supposed to be escorting you to."

"Right, but you still haven't told me why everything's white. Is it to help control these...microorganisms?"

"Yes and no," answered the doctor cryptically, "The Cleaning Lights are just one variation of this particular technology that we were able to garner from the foreign intelligences we've been studying. What you experienced with the fragment, we think, is that technology at full blast. Now, I'm sure you can see why it wouldn't be very beneficial for us to have much contact with *that*, don't you?" Geoffrey nodded solemnly. "Now, what we've found," continued the doctor, "is that if we introduce certain variables into the equation, we can get different applications from that technology. Safer applications." He glanced down at his watch again. "Well, anyway, we've found that certain colors...excite this particular application and increase its power. The only problem with that is that if the Cleaning Lights are too strong, they'll kill off more of us than just microorganisms. They would start actually soldering organ cells, which means goodbye lungs, heart, brain...you get the point."

Geoffrey certainly did.

"We've found a few colors that cause this reaction, but until we know how every color will affect the lights, we think it's best just to keep things neutral. We believe that's why the fragment fell near the research station where you were in the first place. That light was intended to carry the fragment, but the miles and miles of unbroken white landscape in Antarctica most likely altered its application."

"These lights can kill us?" Geoffrey asked, with some alarm.

"Mr. Summons, if we don't figure out what's going on here and how to stop it, the human race is a goner anyway. And besides, like I already told you, we can't study living alien specimens without them. You take a risk with every breath you draw, Son, that's just the nature of existence. This is no different." Geoffrey didn't ask any further questions, and it likely wouldn't have mattered if he had, because after the doctor finished talking, he made it clear that Geoffrey was to head to the shower, without further delay. The doctor led Geoffrey through a virtual maze of hallways that were as large as the entranceway corridor but, as the doctor had said, not as brightly lit, until the two of them at last came to the sterilization shower.

The shower was unlike any normal shower Geoffrey had ever seen. He expected as much: This whole fiasco was like a crazy dream and a normal shower would've been too close to reality to be properly at home in this dream. The room the doctor led him into was, for all appearances, just like the others, except that the light was of a much different and lesser quality than the rest of the facility. The lights were regular lights and it was amazing how dull and dirty they looked now that Geoffrey's eyes had grown accustomed to the Cleaning Lights. The difference was so profound that it was almost like stepping out of the noon day sun into relative darkness. When Geoffrey's eyes adjusted to the gloom, he saw the other obvious difference in the room. The walls and the ceiling, even the floor were all permeated with small, shallow grooves. Geoffrey looked at them closely. He didn't think they were cameras, but he couldn't tell what they were.

"All right, Son," said the doctor, "You will only be in here for about fifteen minutes. Shortly after I leave, you will hear instructions on what you're supposed to do. I will meet you afterward. I have another patient to attend to." Geoffrey had the distinct feeling the doctor wasn't talking about Mr. Reynolds. Before he could ask any further questions, the doctor had closed the door behind him and was gone.

"Right." Geoffrey whispered to himself. "And so, the fun continues."

"Geoffrey Summons?" a voice that sounded amazingly close, asked, just then. Geoffrey nearly leapt out of his skin.

"Yes?" he answered tentatively, once he could steady his breathing.

"Disrobe, please." the voice said blandly. Geoffrey couldn't tell if it was a woman's voice, a man's, or computer generated for that matter. Either way, it sounded devoid of any particular interest. Geoffrey mused to himself that this was probably for his benefit. With the unexpected voice reminding him that he was being watched, he was glad that the person using it wasn't giving the impression that he, she, or it was enjoying this little moment of voyeurism (especially since he couldn't tell with any certainty whether or not it was a *woman's* voice). Even as he disrobed, he was still uncomfortable. This seemed to be just another link in the chain of unusual things that he had been involved in lately. Geoffrey took off his shoes, then his shirt, with the unassailable hesitation of man undressing in front of an audience of strangers for the very first time.

Then, he thought about the aliens the doctor had mentioned studying. How must they feel, being monitored and probed, as Geoffrey was sure they were? Did they feel as humiliated as he did now? Were they able to *feel* humiliated at all? What *did* they feel, being in the hands of absurdly foreign entities as human beings (certainly *humans* were the aliens to them) and that, being endlessly tested upon and perhaps even vivisected, for the sake of furthering knowledge?

"Would you *completely* disrobe, please?" the voice said, startling Geoffrey a second time. He had been so lost in his own train of thought that he stopped undressing. He looked down. His fingers hovered, frozen, over the buttons of his pants. He finished unbuttoning his pants, slowly lowered them to the floor, then stepped out of them. It was truly unnerving to undress before an audience for the first time, even if that audience was well hidden behind camera lenses somewhere.

He wedged his thumbs into the waistband of his briefs as he had done countless times before and again, he hesitated. He was painfully aware that this was his final article of clothing.

"I assure you, Mr. Summons, that the staff here has no interest in making a peepshow of you. This is nothing more than a necessary procedure and the sooner we begin, the sooner we can finish." Geoffrey recognized the wisdom of the androgynous voice. It was right, the sooner he got on with this, the sooner it would be over with. The fact that it was confirmed that multiple people were watching didn't help much, but he couldn't just stand here forever.

He dropped his briefs and stepped out of them. Slowly. The worst part was over. From behind him, Geoffrey heard a faint whirring of a machine gearing up somewhere behind the walls. He turned toward the sound and saw a small drawer moving away from the wall. The box section extended in increments until it came out about a foot and a half.

"Place your clothing in the receptacle please." The voice beckoned. Geoffrey dutifully obeyed. Completely naked, he gathered his things up and placed them in the drawer. "Step back please." Geoffrey did so.

Once he was about twelve feet from the white box, the entire thing slid back into the wall. It was amazing. The movement of the compartment was smoother than anything Geoffrey had ever seen, and once it was flush to the wall, it was virtually impossible to tell that it had ever been there. As Geoffrey gazed on at the spot where the phantom box had been, two things suggested that it had not been a figment of his imagination: The absence of his clothes (which was *certainly* not just in his head), and the strange transformation that began to take place right before his eyes. The full outer face of the box, now level with the wall, became clear.

The entire side of the compartment facing Geoffrey gradually became transparent, like a white mist dissipating into the open air. Soon, Geoffrey saw his jumbled clothes again in the walled cubicle. Once the area was completely clear—so much so in fact, that it looked like Geoffrey could reach right in and pull his clothes back out if he wanted to—he saw a faint movement at the base of the drawer. His clothes began to move as if they were being agitated from below. A bright white-purple flame, also unlike anything Geoffrey had ever seen before, gathered steadily at the base of the box and then, in a startling instance, rose up and instantaneously reduced his clothes to nothingness. In a flash, the odd flame engulfed the pile of clothes and left nothing, not even ashes, in its wake. Then the wall quickly turned to opaque, and to completely white, just it had been before.

To Geoffrey's stunned eyes it all happened so fast. *Had it even ever been there in the first place?* Geoffrey asked himself. Was his mind finally cracking? As he contemplated this possibility, there arose a faint hiss that seemed to come from everywhere in the room and at the same time, mists of water shot out toward Geoffrey from every angle. The mists were so fine and warm that Geoffrey didn't immediately register he was even getting wet. He was rubbing contemplative circles in his chin when he noticed that his hands felt moist. He pulled his hand away from his face and found small beads of water building steadily on his skin like he was sweating. He felt his face and looked at the rest of his naked body. He found that indeed his entire body was 'sweating' as well.

"Okay, maybe I *am* cracking up." He whispered absently.

"No, Mr. Summons, you are perfectly sane." The voice from before asserted. The involuntary jump that Geoffrey gave, jolted more than a few beads of 'sweat' from his body. This was the third time whoever was on the other end of this intercom system had startled him nearly senseless.

"Would you stop doing that, please!" he yelled in the heat of his suddenly-risen blood pressure.

"Terribly sorry," answered the voice "...Is that better?" asked the voice, much slower, and at a considerably lowered volume.

"Yeah, I guess so," returned Geoffrey, after breathing deep in an effort to re-steady his heart rate.

"Good. We want nothing more but for this transition to be as comfortable as possible." Geoffrey thought that if someone were, in fact, trying to make this transition comfortable, they were doing a terrible job, but he kept it to himself. "The moisture you feel," the voice continued, "is purified water. It's quite harmless, I assure you. It will open the pores of your skin and prepare it for the sterilization shower."

What kind of shower am I taking, that I need water to prepare me for it? Geoffrey wanted to ask, but again, kept it to himself.

"If you will look behind you and to your far left, you will see a pair of pumice stones. In about five minutes, the water will stop and the room will fill with a chemical mist that may feel a little...disconcerting at first. Please don't panic. It is a completely safe agent and will not harm you. Once this agent fills the room, you are to use one of the pumice stones to lightly scrub your head, scalp included, and torso. Then you are to use the second stone to scrub your bottom half. I will tell you when to stop and give you further instructions afterward. Before you begin, remember to scrub gently. It is imperative that you do not scrub too harshly. Do you understand what you are to do, Mr. Summons?" the voice concluded.

"I do." Geoffrey answered. He turned to where the voice indicated and found the two pumice stones. They seemed to be floating in mid-air at the opposite side of the room. He stepped toward them, gliding unclothed through the airborne mist of purified water, and saw that they weren't floating, as they appeared, but were sitting on a thin, white tray that was jutting away from the wall. With all this white everywhere, Geoffrey felt like he was experiencing snow blindness. He grabbed one of the stones and waited for the mist to subside. It did after a few minutes, and just as the voice had stipulated a colorless and tasteless mist soon rose in its place. This mist was actually vaguely white, but in a white room, he didn't notice it. The mist was certainly not painless, however. In fact, a few moments had passed since the water dissipation and Geoffrey was just about to ask the faceless voice if something was wrong, when his skin began to tingle as if a thousand small spiders were crawling all over it.

An alarming warmth pervaded him as well. He rightly assumed that this was the sterilization agent that had been spoken of, except that it was a little more than simply *disconcerting*. It was downright scary. The tingling grew more profound, but the scary part was the heat. If it felt like a thousand spiders were trekking his skin, then the increasing heat was like each spider had a microscopic incinerator attached to each of their legs. It was not like heat from the sun on a hot day or mechanical heater that had been turned up too high. It felt more like completely separate heaters had been implanted in every exposed inch of his flesh, and were being gradually turned higher with each passing moment.

He grabbed a stone and went to work. The sooner he got this over with the better. In his haste, however, he did exactly what the voice had ardently advised against and scrubbed too hard, and it only took a single swipe to remind him, because with that single swipe, which happened to be on his upper left arm, the flesh involved screamed—no, *roared*—its disapproval. It took every ounce of his strength not to buckle to his knees in agony. The harrowing sensation had now found raw flesh, and it was exciting times, to say the least.

"Please, Mr. Summons, gently." The voice admonished, but Geoffrey needed no reminder now. After this little mishap, he rubbed the stones across his body with much greater care. In the process, he saw something, dirt perhaps, rise from is skin like steam as he lightly rubbed it, and dissipate into the invisible mist. Once he was finished, a large section of the wall slid into itself, and provided an entranceway to an adjoining room. The voice instructed him to enter, and in the room, he found a fresh pair of clothes—everything white, of course.

"Please, just wait where you are, Mr. Summons." said the voice after he had dressed "Dr. Crangler will be with you shortly."

"Crangler...so that's the doctor's name. With a name like that, guess I wouldn't tell anyone either." Geoffrey whispered to himself. After about twenty minutes had passed, Geoffrey began to think that he had been forgotten. "Hello...Hello?" he asked into the air. The voice didn't answer. "Hello...Hello?" he repeated. Again, no answer. After another twenty minutes passed, Geoffrey decided that he had, indeed, been forgotten. The room he was in was the same as the others except that there were no windows.

"Well, at least there's a door." He mused aloud. He walked to it and turned the white knob, certain that it wouldn't open. Much to his surprise, it opened into a white hallway—big surprise. Geoffrey traveled the hallway, passing the windows of one or two empty rooms, until he came to an inhabited room. In this room, about ten people were sitting in a semicircle, watching a large monitor recessed into the wall.

On the large monitor, in bright vibrant colors, a disturbing scene was taking place. There was a woman on an operating table, and by the looks of things, she was suffering greatly, because she was screaming and thrashing violently. That wasn't the most troubling thing on the screen: The woman's belly was swollen to epic proportions. Though Geoffrey father was a doctor, he didn't need that to know that something was horribly wrong with this woman. The woman's abdomen was stretched to the size

113

of an exercise ball, and if that wasn't enough, it looked like the ball was *moving*. The skin covering the irregularly shaped thing, whatever it was, was shiny and large, superficial tears, like hideous stretch marks clearly showed the broken dermis underneath. Blood droplets surfaced into the gashes like a gorged sponge forced to rid itself of too much fluid. The blood droplets flew this way and that with the sheer violence of the woman's agitation.

The woman's belly was so impossibly tight and stretched that it was amazing that whatever was in her hadn't burst out long ago. As Geoffrey looked on, horrified, and mouth agape, he noticed that every now and then, he could see hands, feet, knees—a very large baby—pushing out against its fleshy confines. It was disgustingly similar to alien movies Geoffrey had seen. Three doctors stood over the woman. One of them produced a scalpel while the others struggled to hold the woman still. The woman's belly was so taut that no sooner had the scalpel touched it, it burst into a jagged series of lines roughly toward her genital area. Geoffrey felt he was about to throw up or pass out—perhaps both—except that all his attention was completely enthralled in the bloody drama before him.

From the large, ragged wound that extended from where the doctor's knife had grazed the woman's flesh, just beneath her breast bone, all the way to her vagina, a child much too large to still be in its mother's womb, was moving in the gory opening. The doctor reached into the bloody wound and pulled the child out. The woman had stopped moving and Geoffrey found that he hadn't even noticed when her thrashing had stopped. Obviously, the trauma was enough to finally send her over the edge into eternity. Meanwhile, the much larger than normal child moved and writhed, but didn't scream as Geoffrey knew normal newborns did. The doctor called for a nasal aspirator and sucked thick mucous through the newborn's nostrils. Immediately, it coughed violently, but as it tried desperately to breathe afterward, it began to choke just as violently. Geoffrey could not hear any sounds from the monitor but it was still heart wrenching, watching the child as it opened its mouth wide to cry, only to gag and jerk when it could draw no air.

The doctor holding the child reached out and one of the other doctors passed him a small face mask. He covered the child's face with it, but it didn't take an expert to see that it was having no effect. Watching the child jerk and convulse so pitifully made Geoffrey desperately want to turn his head, but he simply could not. He was frozen in place. Eventually, the child's jerking lost strength until there was no movement at all. Geoffrey hadn't noticed, but he had been balling his fist so tightly while watching that his fingernails had drawn blood from his palm. Back on the monitor, the doctor took off the mask covering the lower half of his face and spoke into the camera. It was Doctor Crangler. He almost didn't see the doctor unhinge the mask at all because just then, the bland whiteness of the walls, the spectators' suits, even the edges of the monitor, were swallowed up into abysmal blackness, as Geoffrey at last fainted and his body dropped heavily to the white floor.

Chapter 11

"All right, Delilah, you made it through months of ridiculous training for that space flight and you've been dealing with obstinate and mostly ignorant help most of your life. You can do this. Besides, you were trained by the best." With her fingers, Delilah made an invisible cross just above her chest as she whispered, "God bless the dead," for her late mother. She was trying to encourage herself but it wasn't as convincing as she would've liked. Still, she had to start somewhere. She sat up in her bed now, peering down at the white leather restraints that no longer bound her hands and feet. One of Dr. Crangler's subordinates had released her from them earlier while the doctor was away. In fact, now that she was less hysterical she realized that most anyone in this facility—besides Dr. Crangler, that was—seemed frightened of her, as if she was a delicate piece of china.

The harrowing explanation of things that Dr. Crangler had given her earlier was quite sobering, but it was not something that her mind could fully grasp just yet, perhaps not ever. After all, it's not every day that a girl is told in gruesome detail how women and children all over the world were dying slow, agonizing deaths and that she was possibly the only hope for their survival. So now that she was awake, had a brief reprieve from the endless testing, and was unbound for the first time in what felt like an eternity, Delilah tried to regather her wits. To do that, she did the only thing she knew how to do. She put the things that were not pleasant as far back in her mind as she could and resolved to not deal with them until she was left no other choice. She then tried her best to make order out of whatever was left. Unfortunately for her, though, most everything now fell under the category of not pleasant to think about. In addition, she was in a place where it was obvious that her father's money and influence didn't matter, which was something she had never experienced before.

The more she pondered on it, the more she was reminded that she was out of her element and that things were out of her control. The same old frustration welled up in her breast and was amplified by the fact that she knew her tantrums wouldn't restore her to the world she knew and was comfortable with. She felt her temperature rising in stride with her angst, when her mother's firm voice resounded in her head. "The world is meant to be ruled by women, My Darling." From what Dr. Crangler had told Delilah, she wielded considerable power (though it definitely didn't feel that way) now, by virtue of her being the only woman left not infected with The Virus.

"The strongest man who ever lived," continued the voice of her mother, "was conquered by a woman, and I named you Delilah because I want you to remember that there is no man so strong that you cannot conquer."

Delilah was not interested in conquering a man just now. She was only interested to returning to something that vaguely resembled normalcy. "Is that so?" her mother's voice asked inside her head "Well, who here seems to be the person most likely to be able to make that happen? As far as you can see, who here seems to really wield the most power?" Delilah's mind instantly answered for her; *Dr. Crangler*. He was obviously the one in charge around here. In addition, it seemed like he just might be warming up to her. She felt disgusted that the only course of action left for her was to humble herself to trying to win the affections (or at any the rate, the influences) of a *man*, but it was better than the alternative. She also found some consolation in something else her mother had taught her.

"If money can't get it for you (and God knows you probably don't need it if you can't buy it) then use your feminine charms, My Darling." her mother would say, "They ain't just for looks. Besides, the only thing worse than not having it, is not using it."

"That's right," Delilah admonished herself, "the only thing worse than not having it is not using it to your advantage." Much to her relief, she found that she felt a little better. Had she forgotten that God (but more importantly, her mother) had blessed her with to-die-for hips and breasts, flawless skin, and a face that could bend the strongest of male wills? Well, if she had, it was high time to remind herself...as well as a certain white-suited doctor. It had been so long since Delilah had used her beauty for anything other than to evoke envy (until now, money usually did the trick) that she felt quite lost as to the specifics of going about things. Everything had always come so easily to her, and if she did desire the attention of a certain male, it took little more than a briefly-flashed smile or a careful flourish of her shapely hips to secure that attention. She knew that that just wouldn't do for Dr. Crangler. What's more, he was old: Dinosaur ancient actually, possibly even in his late *forties*, and it was probable that it would take a considerable campaign to get the job done, especially with his expressly advanced age.

It shouldn't be that much of problem though, Delilah mused. He was still a man, after all, and what red blooded male—Big Bang old though he may be—could resist a gorgeous woman, especially when that woman was Delilah Hanson? And so, though she had never had to use her considerable...*assets* in such a manner before, she figured she'd just have to learn along the way. She had flown into outer space after all. She could do this.

"Thanks, Mom," she whispered, and ran her tongue across her full lips so that they'd be nice and moist should Dr. Crangler show up any time soon. A few seconds later, as if the preparation alone had summoned him, the good doctor walked through the door.

"Hello, Miss Hanson." The doctor greeted. "Please Excuse the delay…oh, I see that one of my helpful assistants undid your…well, I see that you are up and about." He didn't seem happy that Delilah's restraints had been removed, most likely because it was not at his command. "I had to help another patient to the sterilization shower, and it would seem that he, like you, had some pressing questions that he needed answering…so, how are we feeling?" Delilah had been to the doctor's before and it always struck her as highly unusual that they would ask how 'we' are doing, as if they, too, were a patient.

I'm sure you're doing just fine, but I on the other hand… Delilah wanted to tell the doctor. Instead, she flashed the brightest smile she could muster and asked, pleasantly, "What's a sterilization shower?"

Dr. Crangler heaved a barely audible huff. "How about we commence with the questions a little later, what do you say?"

"Of course, of course, whatever you want." Delilah answered, still maintaining her most winning smile. Dr. Crangler looked puzzled, but other than that, showed no sign that he was in the slightest affected by Delilah's considerable charms. It was here that the thought crossed Delilah's mind of how she must look. She hadn't bathed or seen a hairdresser in God knows how long, and she was sure her plan would work better if she could benefit from a good, long shower and some necessary feminine additives. "But, may I ask, Dr. Crangler," the smile increased in intensity a few watts, "when will *I* be able to get a shower?"

"Actually, very soon, Miss Hanson. That's precisely why I came, to prepare you."

"Oh, Dr. Crangler," Delilah said, pursing her lips and flourishing her hand (she felt quite silly engaging in all this flirtatious nonsense, but one glance at her surroundings reminded her that silly was better than imprisonment) "I'm a big girl. I don't need to be *prepared* for a shower. I know how to bathe myself," then, with a flutter of her eyelids, "I promise."

The puzzled expression returned to the doctor's face, and remained a little longer this time before he replied, "That may be the case, Miss Hanson, but I assure you, you will need preparation for *this* shower."

"What kind of shower is this?" asked Delilah, the coyness in her voice beginning to break. Dr. Crangler explained the process of the sterilization shower and by the time he finished, Delilah had lost all of her unusually demure mannerisms.

"What?" she asked, quite alarmed. To be abducted—even for the survival of all mankind—was one thing, to be drugged, another, but to subject her delicate skin to the torture that the doctor just described, and then to be monitored in the process by an unseen audience, well, that was over the line. *Entirely* over the line. Absolutely not! To hell with her plan (at least for now), Delilah would not and could not, go through with this.

The doctor's lips were pulled tight. "Calm down, young lady!"

"*You* calm down!" she advised back. "I need a shower, and not that nonsense you're trying to sell me! There's no way in hell I'm doing that!" It was obvious that she was deadly serious.

"Miss Hanson, if you don't calm down, then I will have to sedate you…again," said the doctor. For a split second Delilah's agitation waned as she took this into consideration, but it quickly returned. Certainly, she didn't like the idea of being drugged against her will…again, but even that was more acceptable to her mind than what Dr. Crangler had described of the sterilization shower.

"Then that's what you're gonna have to do, *Dr. Crangler*, cause I'm damn sure not going to cooperate! I need a shower—a normal shower—as well as more than a few other things. Body wash, facial cleansers, just to begin with…" Delilah was irate by this time, and though the doctor would've gladly put her back in her place, he found it impossible to get a word in edgewise over her high-pitched squeal. He just stood silently, glaring hatefully at his suddenly untoward patient, as she made her ardent demands.

He was still standing there when a voice reverberated from somewhere in the walls. "Dr. Crangler, report to Operations immediately, please." It sounded as if it was being broadcast in high definition and the abruptness and closeness of it halted Delilah midsentence, somewhere between demanding a hair stylist and reminding Dr. Crangler that he was a damn fool if he thought she was getting into the sterilization shower. Meanwhile, he rewarded his patient with one last hateful glare, heaved his shoulders in dismay, and exited the room to obey the edict given him.

Once he closed the door behind him, Delilah took the opportunity to catch her breath. With all the energy she just expended, it took her more than a few minutes to accomplish the feat, but she eventually did. Once her chest had stopped its violent heaving, she chided herself for letting her plan be obliterated so easily. The more she thought about it, the more she was convinced that she had had no other choice. The sterilization shower sounded like a torture chamber: A torture chamber from which her flawless skin would never recover. She was just about to cry over the fact that she had most likely destroyed any hope she may've had of getting what she wanted, when her door opened again and a painfully resolute Dr. Crangler reentered. In his hand was a large, white notepad and matching white pencil.

"It has been arranged for you to take a regular shower, Miss Hanson," he hissed her name, "and if you would be so kind as to write down the products you require, they will be provided as well." It was apparent by the doctor's strained features, that, since his departure, he had been somehow coerced into cooperation.

Although Delilah couldn't quite fit the pieces of this sudden change together, that didn't matter just now. What mattered was that she was finally getting what she wanted. The doctor reluctantly handed her the writing utensils and exited the room in a huff. She lost no time making an extensive list of name brand facial treatments, hair moisturizers, lotions, and the like, until she was satisfied. When she finished, she waited to see if anyone would come to retrieve her list.

When no one did, she began to yell for assistance. "Hello? Is anyone there?" she beckoned into the open air. She wasn't a gadget geek, but she knew there must be some kind of surveillance equipment in the room, even if she couldn't see it. Sure enough, it wasn't long before someone came to her aid. A white-suited man she had not met before, came through her room door. "Where's Dr. Crangler?" she asked.

"Dr. Crangler is, uh, busy at the moment. I will take your list and if you'll follow me, I'll take you to your shower. Dr. Crangler will be with you afterward."

Delilah thought this over. "I need the things on that list first. I can't wash with regular soap. Just doesn't work for me. And the shower you taking me to, it's a *regular* shower, right? With running water and a new loofah and everything, right?" the assistant nodded, even though he had no idea what a 'loofah' was. "Good. Good. Well, first, I need these things, and I'll follow you wherever I need to go." The assistant looked flustered as he took the list and backed out of the room. After about two and a half hours passed and Delilah hadn't heard or seen any sign of another living person, she began to fear that perhaps she pushed her luck too far. Perhaps, she was mistaken in assuming that she had the upper hand. Perhaps, she had dug herself into an even deeper hole than that which she was already in. These and other similar apprehensive musings quickly dissipated, however, when she heard the heavy locking mechanism of her door giving way, and in walked two of the doctors from earlier, each pushing a rolling cart filled with the things Delilah had listed.

Everything was there and the exact name brand that Delilah's lengthy list stipulated. She looked at the arrangement and smiled. This was the closest she had felt to home since all this craziness began. The doctors left her to her things but one returned a few moments later with a gown, underwear, shoes, and a few other things—everything white—for Delilah to change into after she had taken her shower. Most everything fit, and she felt pampered (or at least close to it) again. With her vigor—not to mention her assessment that perhaps she could work an angle on this situation after all—renewed, she asked for Dr. Crangler.

"He will be with you later on, Miss. Hanson. After you've had your shower." One of the doctors answered.

"Please tell him I'd like for him to keep his promise, please." Delilah returned. "He said that *he'd* show me to the shower and I'd appreciate it if he did." The doctor addressed looked puzzled, almost the same look that Dr. Crangler displayed earlier, but eventually acquiesced. Delilah knew what he must be thinking, but didn't bother to correct him. She would've much rather been in her own home where the only people she summoned in the first place were those on the payroll, but since this was obviously not the case, she preferred to deal with one white-suited stranger at a time, and right now, that stranger happened to be Dr. Crangler. The two doctors in attendance left her, but not before assuring her that Dr. Crangler would be with her shortly. It didn't escape her notice that they, too, spoke and dealt with her as one might deal with expensive china too valuable to be broken.

It was ironic that now Delilah truly began to understand, at least in a manner relevant to her, the truth of what Dr. Crangler had told her about The Virus that was wreaking havoc on womankind and how important she now was since she seemed to be the last woman on the planet who had not been infected with it. The absolute gravity of the situation was still not something she was able to digest, but if there was any part of the story she *could* grasp onto for perspective, it was the fact that she was extremely important. Even though Dr. Crangler had set out to make this haughty young lady understand that here she would not have her way so effortlessly as she was used to, it would seem that he may not be as much in the advantage as he would've liked. Now, as is often the case, the weightier struggles of mankind would be predicated upon the incredibly less important contentions of a select few—in this case, a select *two*.

Chapter 12

When Geoffrey came to, he immediately noticed two things. One was an eerie crawling sensation on his skin, as if a thousand more spiders had been added to the ones from earlier, and though they seemed to no longer be armed with the microscopic incinerators, they were still performing what felt like terrain practice on his flesh. The heightened sensation sent a deep shudder through him but did nothing to quell the feeling. The other thing he noticed was that his room now had a small array of furniture in it. Beside the bed he found himself on, he was also now privileged with a small recliner, a settee, a simple rolling table (on it were a few magazines with covers that suggested the information inside was as bland and sterile as this secret facility), and a small desk equipped with two drawers. All of was—of course—white.

Geoffrey was glad to see that there were some additions to his room, but disappointed to find that two of the most important additions, a television or a radio, were still missing. "Well, at least they gave me something to look at besides four blank walls." He mused aloud. He got up and scratched his arm to see if it would help stop the invisible roving spiders. It didn't.

He checked the new furniture more closely and found that everything had been sturdily built and that the recliner was fine, white leather. No standard issue stuff here. He checked the drawers of his new desk. Both were filled with containers he wasn't familiar with, but they looked to be hygiene products he had never seen populating the aisles of any Wal-Mart. He picked up a few of the containers and studied them more closely. The labels had detailed user instructions, but were nondescript otherwise. Geoffrey expected as much. What he didn't expect was the hand that lighted on his left arm and the voice in his ear.

"Geoffrey," said Dr. Crangler. Geoffrey's heart skipped a beat—a couple of beats actually—and the spot on his upper arm where the suddenly materialized doctor had touched, the same place that he had rubbed too hard earlier in the sterilization shower, protested instantaneously. He nearly knocked Dr. Crangler to the floor in an attempt to shake his hand loose before he could catch himself.

"Sorry, Son, I was actually trying *not* to startle you," said the doctor once he narrowly avoided being assaulted.

"Well, you failed. Miserably." Geoffrey observed heatedly, gently stroking his upper arm. "Have you been in here the whole time?" The doctor nodded. "Why didn't I see you, then?"

"I've already explained to you," the doctor began, "why everything in this facility has to be white, but one of the adverse effects of that is that when your eyes see little to no difference in their surroundings, they can start to play tricks on you. You're familiar with what happens when you drive for any distance through heavily-forested routes?"

"Yeah, you get really tired, really fast."

"It's something like that. Everything starts looking the same and, well, you can miss things."

There was one thing Geoffrey definitely hadn't missed and though it was nauseating to remember, he needed answers. "What was that I saw on the monitors, Dr. Crangler? What happened to that woman?"

The doctor sighed. "What you saw is what every woman who intends to have a child can expect to happen to her, unless we find a way to defeat this virus." The doctor sighed again, more heavily this time. He began stroking his chin and though his eyes were meeting Geoffrey's, his gaze seemed to be focused inward. "We've tried test tube babies, in vitro fertilization, everything we can think of. Nothing works. As soon as the eggs are implanted their infected by the mother's blood and we don't yet have the technology to grow children completely without a womb…"

"Is there any way I could be taken out of here for a while?" Geoffrey interrupted. The doctor started at Geoffrey's voice. He had almost forgotten his presence completely.

"What was that?" he asked now that Geoffrey had his attention again.

"I wouldn't mind seeing some of those heavily-forested areas now." Geoffrey answered quickly. He had wanted answers but the answers seemed more than they were worth at the moment.

"We'll have to see about that," was the doctor's only reply.

"Well, to what do I owe the pleasure of this visit, then?" Geoffrey asked, seeing that he could expect to receive no further answers on the subject just now.

"You're going to talk to your friend, Mr. Reynolds, today." Dr. Crangler answered matter-of-fact.

Geoffrey's face lit up. "Really?" he asked.

He was surprised at his own vigor. It wasn't that he was excited to see Mr. Reynolds, rather, he was excited to see *any* familiar face besides those of the doctors'. "So, he's out of his coma, or whatever was going on with him? Is he all right? Does he remember anything?" Geoffrey was almost giddy.

"No offense, Son, but if I never have to deal with another slew of pressing questions from a patient again in my life, I won't be too upset." observed the doctor. "Hopefully, most of your questions will be answered when you speak with him. But, before we go, I need to show you how to use some of the things that have been brought for you." Dr Crangler reached into the top drawer of the desk and pulled out a rectangular container with a small perforation on the upper side. He pulled out a cloth that resembled a thick paper towel. "I assume you've been experiencing the after effects of the sterilization shower?"

"You mean the feeling that ants have taken over my skin?" asked Geoffrey, sardonically "Yeah, I've been experiencing it all right. What the hell is that anyway?"

"Well, like I said, the human body has long since formed a symbiotic relationship with the microorganisms that the shower rids you of. The sensations you feel are your body's way of trying to adjust without them. But your body has become so dependent on some of these organisms, that it cannot function properly without them. That's what this is for." he gestured toward the cloth that was now sitting atop the container. "These are special. They're saturated with a unique compound of chemicals that aid your skin in adjusting to the lack of certain bacteria. I developed it myself." Dr. Crangler beamed just as he did back when he was explaining the Cleaning Lights to Geoffrey. "You are only to use them once a day. Be very careful that you remember that—only once a day."

"Oh, don't worry." advised Geoffrey, seriously, "After that little shower incident, you can believe I understand the importance of following directions to a tee now."

"Good. Good. All right, I'm going to leave you alone for about an hour. As soon as I leave the room, you are to rub this chemical over your entire body. When I return, I will escort you to Mr. Reynolds's room and I will instruct you on what you are to do. Do you understand?"

"Sure, cover myself in whatever's on those towelettes and wait for you to return with further instructions."

"Good. Good. I will see you in an hour, Mr. Summons." Dr. Crangler exited the room.

Geoffrey watched him as he left and realized it was easy to see the truth of the effects all this white could have on the human eye. With his lab coat, pants, and shoes, the only visible part of the doctor was his hair, and that, too, was not far from white. In reality, it looked like Dr. Crangler had exited as soon as he turned his back to Geoffrey because he blended in so well with the surroundings.

"What if *we're* the aliens?" Geoffrey spoke to himself, as Dr. Crangler closed the door behind him. "What if we're really the ones mounting the invasion?" It was certainly a plausible question, but not one that Geoffrey's already taxed mind was prepared to delve into. Instead, he headed toward the desk. He grabbed the thick cloth that the doctor had left out and undressed so he could cover himself in its thick chemical mucous as he was instructed. He had no clock by which to gauge time, but when the doctor returned, he thought that it had been a full hour.

"Are we ready, Mr. Summons?" Dr. Crangler asked from the door way. "I thought I'd announce myself before I entered your room. It would seem that you can be quite violent when you're startled." Geoffrey figured the doctor was trying to lighten the mood, so he answered in a brief, dry chuckle. The doctor glanced at the desk. The towelette container was back in the drawer, but the one Geoffrey had used was crumpled up on top of it. "Good. Good." Answered the doctor "I see you've used the cleansing cloth."

"So, that's what those nasty things are called, huh?" Geoffrey said, looking at the discarded cloth with more than a little distaste. Whatever mixture of chemicals the cloth was saturated in felt like moist snot on the skin. It was discombobulating in other ways as well. As soon as Geoffrey applied it, it spread on clear and seemed to evaporate into thin air, leaving behind only a sensation similar to being covered in syrup. Moments after application, Geoffrey touched his skin and found that it was perfectly dry as before, even though he still *felt* the chemical solution quite profoundly. Even now, it was like his skin was gasping for breath beneath the layer of chemical syrup, but as he lifted his arm to his face, there was no smell, no moisture, no sign that he had anything on his flesh besides the clothes he was wearing. "Yeah, this may be good for me, but I'll tell you what, it certainly doesn't feel good."

"The itching sensation from the shower is gone though, isn't it?" asked the doctor. Geoffrey thought for a moment. It was, in fact, as well as the raw area on his arm. Both uncomfortable sensations had disappeared.

"Six in one hand, half a dozen in the other, I guess, huh?"

"If *you* say so." Answered the doctor. He grimaced at having a discovery of his treated so lightly. "If everything is in order, Mr. Summons, then follow me, please." The doctor, held the door open. As the door shut behind Geoffrey, he heard the electronic locking mechanism kicking into place.

"You know, you say that we're here so you can maybe learn how to beat this virus, but it's really looking like we're just prisoners here. I mean, can't I call my dad just to let him know that I'm all right?"

"Listen, Son, I don't handle all that. I have enough on my hands as it is...now, pay attention." They neared another hallway and the doctor stopped. "Now, listen very carefully. The person you are about to talk to is not the Mr. Reynolds that you remember. I'm sure it will be quite a shock when you see him, but whatever you do—*whatever* you do—do not startle him. He is in an extremely fragile position and it is imperative that we get whatever information we can out of him before we lose him. Do you understand?" Dr. Crangler drew his face close to Geoffrey's, and Geoffrey was a little frightened by the sudden gravity that filled his features. In the short time he had known the doctor, Geoffrey had never seen him so serious.

"I understand." Geoffrey answered, though he really didn't.

"Now, I'm going to be communicating with you while you're in there." Doctor Crangler handed Geoffrey a small electronic ear bud. "I'll be walking you through this, step by step. Now, like I said, it is imperative that you not startle him, so I need you to be calm. Take a deep breath." Geoffrey dutifully obeyed, though it did nothing to calm his increasing tension. "When you enter the room, if he talks to you, talk back, but keep the conversation light. Don't mention anything that may upset him."

"What's wrong with him? You sound like he's possessed…am I gonna be in danger going in there?" Geoffrey interrupted.

"Not at all, Son. Not at all." The doctor answered hastily. Geoffrey knew he was lying. "Now, all you have to do is stay calm. If he talks to you, talk about whatever he wants to talk about. Tell him whatever he wants to hear. But if he does talk to you, I want you to ask him what has he seen, what has he heard."

"What has he *seen*?" Geoffrey asked, his concern growing by the second.

"Just do it, Son." The doctor said, shortly, "This is very important. Billions of lives hang in the balance on what your friend may know. Now, just be calm and I'll walk you through it every step of the way. Now, put the earpiece in your ear." Geoffrey did. "Good. Good. Take another deep breath." Geoffrey did that as well. He was thoroughly frightened by now, but what alarmed him more, was Dr. Crangler's behavior. He had never heard him repeat himself so many times, had never seen him so wound up. He almost sounded as if *he* was the one going into the danger blindly. Geoffrey did his best to steady his nerves (he did a miserably poor job), and followed the doctor down another corridor. At the end of this corridor were two doors. One was the room were Mr. Reynolds was being held, and the other was the observation room on the opposite side of the one-way mirror from which Geoffrey had gazed into the astronomer's iris-less eyes when they first arrived. Suddenly, it seemed like he had been here for months, years, maybe. As he neared the door to where Mr. Reynolds was, he remembered how he had thought, that the observation room must be the worst room in the world. Now, he felt there was a room worse than that—the one he was about to enter. "Is everything ready?" the doctor asked into the open air.

"Everything is in place." A genderless voice answered.

"Good. Good. Now remember," he spoke to Geoffrey again, "remain calm. You are in no danger. I will walk you through it, just stay calm."

"I will." Geoffrey lied, as the locking mechanism on the door filled the air with the tell-tale *hiss click* that it was opening. Dr. Crangler nudged him a little, and he stepped into the room in the dreamlike state of reserved terror. He didn't know what to expect, but even his wildest fears paled in comparison to what he eventually saw. When Geoffrey entered, he could see Mr. Reynolds's special seat. It was still facing the one way mirror, was in a seated position, and looked empty. Almost. It looked like it had been lined with flesh colored cloth. The cloth lined the seat and back portion, and a thick strip of cloth lay on each armrest. Geoffrey looked cautiously around the room.

"Mr. Reynolds?" His mouth was dry. He wet his lips and whispered again, a little more loudly this time. "Mr. Reynolds?" There was a nearly imperceptible grunt from the upper back area of the bed. Geoffrey was about to call for Dr. Crangler and ask him if this was some kind of joke. He had been brought here to speak with Mr. Reynolds, but there was no one in this room, just a strangely-colored cloth-lined seat.

Instead, he took a closer look at the seat. Now that his nerves had calmed a bit, he could appreciate the unusualness of this bed/seat—or anything else in this facility—being draped with any material that wasn't white. He took slow, calculated steps toward the chair. As he neared it, it seemed to him that he felt warmer, but not enough for him to be certain. Once he had reached the seat, he noticed that the cloth held a certain vibrancy. He drew closer still and lowered his head to inspect the cloth more carefully. It was glowing, a faint kind of glow that Geoffrey had never seen before, as if a light was stuffed inside the deepest folds of the cloth. The quality of the glow was such that Geoffrey knew the light must be the same as he had seen encasing the fragment. Thinking this over, Geoffrey looked over the rest of the seat. He looked down at the seat and noticed that the cloth was cleaved into two identically-shaped pieces, hanging loosely down to the floor, eerily resembling what flattened human legs may've looked like. At that moment, there was another, more profound grunt coming from the upper back area of the chair where Mr. Reynolds's head would've been (if he'd been in the chair, of course). As he followed the thick padding of cloth up to where the grunt was coming, he noticed that this portion as well assumed a strange shape, strongly resembling a flattened human torso.

A highly unpleasant thought finally coalesced in his mind. He looked into the flattened face of this human effigy and his horror was confirmed. The head of this flattened cloth effigy bore two glowing eyes, the eyes of what was left of Mr. Reynolds and they were looking directly at Geoffrey. Geoffrey started backward, putting about ten feet between himself and the living remains of Mr. Reynolds. One thing, and one thing only, went through Geoffrey's mind as he stared at the impossibility before him: *What the Fuck!?*

It went through his mind so much that when he thought he could finally open his mouth to say Mr. Reynolds's name—to see if it was really him, if he'd respond—the only thing that came out was, "*What* the Fuck?" He balled up his fists and rubbed his eye sockets with them. He did it a second time. Sure enough, the impossible reality before him was…well, still before him. "Mr. Reynolds?" he finally gasped. The glowing eyes were intent upon Geoffrey, but the only audible response was the same faint grunt. Geoffrey took a single step closer. Now that he was sure that this patch of flesh cloth, this…this thing, was a living person, a living person he had once known, he felt incredibly sorry for Mr. Reynolds. He took another cautious step forward. His entire body was trembling badly, but he paid it no attention. From the other side of the one way mirror behind him, multiple sets of eye watched (chief among them, Dr. Crangler) as he took yet another calculated step forward. The spectators on the other side of the mirror heard every sound made in Mr. Reynolds's room. They heard Geoffrey whisper Mr. Reynolds's name a third time.

They clearly saw everything as well. They saw after this third whisper from Geoffrey, he straightened up stiff as a board. Geoffrey looked around frantically in every direction as if he was hearing something, though the men on the other side of the mirror only heard Geoffrey's frantic shuffling. Then, he clapped his hands over his hears. "Stop!" he yelled, "Stop!" One of the spectators on the other side of the mirror jumped from his seat and was about to go remove him from the room, but Dr. Crangler lifted an authoritative finger.

"Sit down." He commanded.

"But if he agitates the subject,"—referring to Mr. Reynolds—"with the state he's in…" the concerned spectator tried to point out.

"If my assumption is correct," interrupted Dr. Crangler, with menacing calm, "this is the *subject's* doing. Just give it a few moments, let me see what happens." Dr. Crangler tapped a small ear bud in his ear. "Mr. Summons. Mr. Summons." Geoffrey showed no sign of response. In fact, he had not responded to anything the doctor spoke into his ear bud since he entered the room.

A few long, tense moments passed and Geoffrey slowly calmed down. He stared at the living remains of Mr. Reynolds more acutely as he took less cautious steps toward the flattened body. Dr. Crangler couldn't see Geoffrey's face directly, but the cameras hidden in the walls showed every aspect of both men on separate monitors he had set up for the purpose. From these monitors he could see that as Geoffrey approached Mr. Reynolds, he had an expression on his face as if he was, indeed, listening to something.

Dr. Crangler gasped. "I was correct. The subject *is* communicating with Mr. Summons."

"But, he isn't saying anything." the spectator from earlier observed.

"He's communicating with Mr. Summons...*telepathically*." The doctor was now standing inches away from one of the monitors, as if he could somehow delve into the phenomena better, the nearer he drew to the image on the screen.

"Are you sure?" one of the others in the room asked, with more than some excitement in his voice, "If he is, then this changes everything."

"Silence!" Dr. Crangler demanded. Geoffrey was calling for something.

"Notebook and paper!" he yelled.

"Notebook and paper!" echoed Dr. Crangler from the other side of the mirror. The doctor sent one of his assistances to carry them to Geoffrey, while he continued his observation of the situation. The assistant stood at the door until the locking mechanism unlatched, opened the door to as small a crack as possible, and threw the pad and pen into the narrow opening. Geoffrey retrieved the pen and pad and returned to his telepathic friend. Standing in front of him, he began to write furiously. He wrote like this until he filled the entire notebook. He called for another, and then another. This went on for almost three hours, until he had filled every page of every notebook, front and back. Other than occasionally halting to retrieve another hastily tossed notebook, he didn't stop for a break or a breath, in between. He didn't stop to look up at Mr. Reynolds. In fact, barely anything of him moved aside from the hand that held the notebooks and the hand that filled each of them to the brim with cryptic writing. When he finally finished the third notebook, he backed into the mirror behind him and slid slowly to the floor like a man exhausted. The last of the notebooks was still clutched tightly in his grasp.

For a few long moments, he didn't move a muscle, but remained transfixed on the severely deflated Mr. Reynolds. The wasted astronomer's glowing eyes returned the gaze. The two sat in this posture, completely still—it didn't even look as if Geoffrey was breathing—until at last, a startling and sudden change took place in Mr. Reynolds. He opened his eyes wide as if he was suddenly alarmed. He leaned the deflated oval of his head back, pressing hard into his chair. He held this taut position for a few long seconds and gradually the glow that characterized his shrunken flesh faded from his extremities, moving into his eyes. As this was happening, the light in his eyes intensified. Geoffrey gazed on motionlessly, and so did every person watching from the other side of the mirror. Once the last of the glow had gathered into his eyes, it loomed there for a moment and from there, faded as well. It dissipated from his open sockets like thick steam and disappeared into the open air of the room. In a flash, the lights went dark and the every monitor on the other side of the mirror filled with static. The listening devices wired into the walls of the room also went dead.

About fifteen minutes passed, but it felt like a verifiable eternity since no one could see what, if anything, was taking place in Mr. Reynolds's room. Dr. Crangler was not about to step foot in the room's suddenly dark recesses and he knew that none of his assistants would either, no matter how stern the directive. Everyone just remained where they were, too astonished to speak, too astonished to stir, too astonished to draw much breath. Eventually, the lights in the room re-illumined, which was noteworthy of itself. The lights in the facility were not like normal lights: Complex physical and chemical reactions fueled by electrical currents that could be stopped and reinstituted at will. As the doctor already mentioned, these lights were actually physical presences simply housed in containment units, so for them to go out and come back on wasn't like a normal light responding to a simple power outage. It was more like water leaking from a container and suddenly reappearing back in its place a few moments later. This did not escape Dr. Crangler's notice, but it was not something worthy of his full attention at the present.

What was worth Dr. Crangler's notice, however, was the fact that when the lights returned, they showed a room with only one person in it. Geoffrey was sprawled full length on the floor, eyes closed and unmoving, with the notebook clutched tightly to his chest. His newly-telepathic associate, however, was no more. The only thing left of him was a thin coating of dust, lining the wheelchair in the same orientation as his cloth-like flesh was mere moments earlier. The monitors kicked back into life, and after a few moments, Dr. Crangler turned his attention to Geoffrey. He stared intently at Mr. Summons on the monitor nearest him.

"Thank goodness, he's breathing!" he exclaimed, watching the young man's chest rise and fall with some regularity. Dr. Crangler was an extremely professional man. It wasn't often that he got so excited over the welfare of a patient. He wasn't necessarily excited that Geoffrey survived whatever had just taken place, for his own sake, he was glad that the young man had survived because that meant that there was yet a chance for him to pick his brain and possibly immerse himself in extra-terrestrial knowledge the likes of which he never would've garnered from his physical experiments on the aliens. Dr. Crangler was also excited that possibly Geoffrey's mind now contained information that may show him how The Virus could be successfully combated.

The doctor didn't need to worry over potential information, for, in the three notebooks that Geoffrey had filled in his writing frenzy, were many more answers than could possibly be understood in a single lifetime by any one man. The books held apocryphal answers, answers that were never intended to be discovered by the likes of human kind.

Chapter 13

Once the initially paralyzing awe of what Dr. Crangler later dubbed the 'Arnold Reynolds incident' had subsided, the doctor entered the room Mr. Reynolds's room and retrieved Geoffrey. It was only after the doctor had entered the room and remained alive for a long while that any of his assistants would venture in to help him. They placed Geoffrey in one of the special wheelchairs and carted him back to his room where he was monitored closely. He was unconscious for nearly four days. During this time, Dr. Crangler spent almost every waking moment poring over what Geoffrey had written in the notebooks, but for all his concerted efforts, he could make no sense of any of it. It didn't look like any kind of language native to Earth—once the doctor had time to think it over, he supposed that he should've expected as much—but rather a strange dialect of symbols and seemingly random lines.

When Geoffrey finally returned to consciousness, Dr. Crangler's was the first face he saw. Before that, the doctor had been waiting anxiously by one of his observatory monitors, alternately watching Geoffrey sleep, and combing through alien symbols struggling to make some sense of them all. As soon as the monitor showed his patient stirring for the first time in four days, he wanted to rush in and inundate him with all types of questions. The irony was not lost upon him that now *he* was the one with all the 'pressing inquires', and had it not been that he knew the eyes of his colleagues were upon him, he likely would have. In fact, he found it nerve wracking just maintaining a professionally slow stride on his way to Geoffrey's room. Even though in the presence of his staff, he made an official decision to ascertain Geoffrey's state before asking him to remember what had happened, he made his way down the hall with all three notebooks neatly tucked under his arm. In truth, he didn't remember taking them along. He had spent so much time with them over the last few days that they were like a part of him now. When he entered the room, Geoffrey was looking around blankly as if he had just arrived at the facility for the first time. He didn't seem to notice the doctor's presence, so Dr. Crangler took the opportunity to place the notebooks out of sight in the bottom drawer of Geoffrey's desk.

"How are you feeling, Mr. Summons?" Dr. Crangler asked, careful not to raise his voice or make any sudden movements. Geoffrey opened his mouth but nothing came out. He cleared his throat harshly.

"Thirsty…and hungry, I think," he finally answered.

Dr. Crangler was so excited to see that Mr. Summons had not only survived the ordeal, but appeared to be fully functional, that he could hardly contain himself. Almost instinctively, he began to reach for the notebooks in the desk drawer, but caught himself. "Do you remember anything, Mr. Summons?" he asked with equal caution.

"Thirsty…and hungry." was the repeated response.

Dr. Crangler rose and stepped out of the room briefly. "All right, Mr. Summons, food is on the way. Now, do you remember anything?" He asked upon his return. His ill contained pleas were met with the same response. It became clear to the anxious doctor that no information would be gained from Mr. Summons until he had been given some sustenance. Quite agitated now, the doctor left the room again and returned some time later with a large container of food and another of drink. Geoffrey finished it in record time and demanded more. A second helping was produced and, after Geoffrey likewise demolished this round, he was satisfied. He pushed the empty container away and the doctor couldn't help but notice that he indeed looked better than when he first awakened.

"Thank you. Thank you very much." Geoffrey answered. "I felt like I was gonna die of thirst *and* starvation." Dr. Crangler opened his mouth, but Geoffrey interrupted, "Look, I know what you want, and I'll tell you everything, but not right now. I don't know what Mr. Reynolds did to me, but I feel like my head may explode if I try to think any more. I need to lie down and get some rest. After that, I'm sure I'll feel better and I'll tell you whatever you want to know." If Dr. Crangler intended to respond now, Geoffrey didn't notice because he was already lying back down on his bed. The doctor reluctantly gathered the notebooks from the desk drawer and tucked them back under his arm, then he cleaned up the empty food and drink containers. Under normal circumstances, he would've had someone else do such menial work, but he wanted no one in this room interacting Mr. Summons until he could get every bit of information possible out of him. Afterward, he returned to the notebooks, but with the same futile results. After a few hours, he decided to get some rest himself. The only thing that helped him quell his internal anxiousness was that he knew that he needed to be fully alert if his subsequent interview with Mr. Summons was going to be a success, and he certainly needed for it to be a success. This was a once in a millennia—more than that, once in human *history*—opportunity. Until now, he could only study the physical properties of alien life forms, but before him loomed the possibility of studying the *mind* of far advanced intelligences. He felt as if he could burst.

Apparently, he was more tired than he realized, because when one of his assistants woke him to inform him that Geoffrey was awake and was calling for him, nearly six hours had passed. He rushed to Mr. Summons's room, notebooks in tow. When he entered, he found Geoffrey sitting up on his bed. He looked refreshed but somehow aged, though just barely. Otherwise, he looked like his old self.

"Hello, Mr. Summons." greeted Dr. Crangler amiably.

"Hello, Dr. Crangler." answered Geoffrey, "I see you haven't let those notebooks get far from you."

The doctor peered down at the notebooks, "No, I haven't it would seem…how are you feeling?"

"Much better, much better indeed. That food and rest really did wonders. Say, how long was I out before I woke up the first time? I vaguely remember blacking out back there with Mr. Reynolds, but after that, everything's fuzzy."

"Are you saying that you remember something after you fainted?" asked Dr. Crangler.

"Yeah. Must've been some kind of dream or something. Mr. Reynolds was there and I think he was trying to teach me something or something like that. I don't remember much else. After then, I woke up and all I can remember was being very thirsty and very hungry."

"Interesting." The doctor mused aloud. He took a seat and placed the notebooks in his lap.

"So, how long had I been out? A few hours?" Geoffrey persisted.

"A few hours!" exclaimed the doctor. "You were unconscious for four days."

"Four days?" apparently, it was Geoffrey's turn to make an exclamation, "Are you *sure*? It didn't seem like that long at all."

"Of course I'm sure. I monitored you personally every day…" the doctor would've continued, but he refrained. Not only did he not want Geoffrey to know how frantic he had become concerning these latest developments, but protocol required that he not draw any attention to the fact that his patients were being monitored every second of the day, at least not in their presence anyway. It wasn't like anyone expected that they didn't know, the powers that be just thought it best that they not dwell on that fact too often, and with difficult, temper tantrum throwing patients like Delilah, no one questioned the logic. "Yes, Son, you were unconscious for four days." The doctor finished simply.

"Wow!" was the only response Geoffrey could muster.

The doctor gave Geoffrey a moment to calibrate himself before resuming, "Do you remember anything of what Mr. Reynolds was saying in this dream you mentioned?"

"Not really. That's how my dreams always are. When I wake up, I usually can't remember much about them."

The doctor opened one of the notebooks in his lap and presented it to Geoffrey, "These are the symbols you wrote when you were in the room with Mr. Reynolds, just before you lost consciousness. Do you have any idea what they represent?" The doctor's voice was tense. Geoffrey looked down into the open leaves of the notebook. At first there wasn't a sign of recognition on his face as if he was reading something somebody else had written. Then, the next moment, his eyes lit up with recollection.

"I'm sorry Dr." he began. The doctor began to pull the notebook back, when Geoffrey snatched it from his hands. He looked at it more closely. "Yes! Yes, I do know what these symbols mean!" The violence of Geoffrey's sudden movement caused the doctor to leap on his bed, startled. "This is what Mr. Reynolds was teaching me. I remember it now. He was teaching me how to read these symbols. When I was with him in the room, he told me to write something down, then he showed me all these symbols, and when I was asleep, he taught me how to read them."

"He *told* you to write?" asked Dr. Crangler, "In your *head*?"

"Yeah, don't ask me what that was about, 'cuz I couldn't describe it to you if I tried, but he spoke to me in my mind. He made me hear and see things that were more clear than what I'm hearing and seeing right now."

"So you can translate this?" Dr. Crangler was nearly overwhelmed himself.

"Sure, if you get me some more notebooks, I can write it all down right now."

Dr. Crangler snapped his fingers impatiently toward a corner of the room. As soon as the notebooks and pens were produced, the doctor shoved as many into Geoffrey's hands as he could hold. Geoffrey began scribbling in them as furiously as he had done back in the late Mr. Reynolds's room, but now that he was not being infused by whatever physic energy Mr. Reynolds had been emitting, he found that he needed to rest after filling the first two notebooks to capacity. Dr. Crangler wanted desperately to press him on, to have him finish the entire translation as soon as humanely possible, but common sense warned him that if he pressed too hard, he may foul up this whole endeavor, and that was a risk he simply could not afford. He advised Geoffrey (albeit unwillingly), to take as many rest breaks as he deemed necessary, but to finish recording what he knew as quickly as possible.

"You can't imagine just how important this information may be." Dr. Crangler asserted solemnly as he disappeared out of the room.

"You may be surprised." Geoffrey whispered after the doctor was gone. He lay down to rest, but did not sleep. Instead, he just lay there with his eyes shut tightly. Behind his closed lids, he saw a panorama of alien symbols as well as the ideas they signified, in human language. After about thirty minutes, he would get up, grab a notebook, and complete the next round of translations. This went on for hours and hours—with Dr. Crangler carefully watching the entire time—until all the notebooks were filled. After Geoffrey finished the last page of the last notebook, he lay back down again, but this time, he did sleep. He slept long and hard, as he had before, and no wonder; he had just written untold thousands of words freehand, of things no human mind would've been able to conceive otherwise. Meanwhile, Dr. Crangler quickly retrieved the notebooks as soon as it was clear that Geoffrey had finished with them. After replacing them with fresh ones (just in case Mr. Summons had more to write), he made a swift beeline for his office, but not before informing every member of his staff that under *no* circumstances was he to be bothered until he stipulated otherwise.

Afterward, he sat down in front of a broad table and a bank of monitors by which he could see both Mr. Summons and Miss Hanson, and dove headfirst (almost literarily) into the notebooks Geoffrey had recently filled. He expected to find great things, and not only would he not be disappointed, but even his loftiest expectations were exceeded by what he eventually found.

Chapter 14

When Dr. Crangler finally lifted his head from his all-consuming studies, he too, looked somehow slightly aged. He didn't realize it, but he had been completely and totally engrossed in the material for hours. He would've gladly remained in his ardent studies if his body hadn't demanded reprieve. He stood up and stretched. In the process, every inch of his frame groaned with agitation. He decided to take a short walk through the halls of facility, if for nothing else, to allow him to return to studying the notebooks without oversurfeiting his middle-aged body. He hit the button to unlock his door and was startled to find a few of his assistants waiting just outside.

"Dr. Crangler," one of them spoke hastily, "the Hanson patient wants to see you. She won't…"

"I don't have time for Miss Hanson right now." the doctor interrupted.

"But she…" the assistant tried to resume.

"Give her whatever she wants." the doctor barked. The assistants turned flabbergasted faces toward each other. Delilah was making some pretty unusual demands—at least by the standards of men who knew little of pampered feminine preferences—and the assistants frowned at one another. To supply her with what she was asking went greatly beyond the bounds of protocol. Besides, it was Dr. Crangler who demanded that she be given only what he authorized. Well, he had just authorized *everything*, and at the moment, it didn't look like it would bode well for the person who tried to talk some sense into him. Every one of the assistants had, like the doctor, worked extensively in this facility and had been grilled on the proper chain of command, and in this particular chain, the doctor was the preeminent link. If he said that Delilah Hanson was to have whatever she wanted, then Delilah Hanson was to have whatever she wanted. The unnerved assistants went to fulfill their orders while their withdrawn superior roamed the white halls nearest his office with nothing other than alien symbols and their translated meanings dominating his every thought.

Once he felt that he had walked enough, he returned to his office (and more importantly, to the notebooks) and again, soon lost himself in study. Much of the information in the notebooks dealt with vivid, albeit utterly confusing, truths about the alien intelligence from whose planet the fragment originated. It described the nature of their foreign community as well as space-time in general. It spoke of the composition of stars and the peculiar science of galaxies and though, thanks to Geoffrey, it was in English, Dr. Crangler couldn't make heads or tails of much of it. There were, however, more than a few observations that the doctor understood. Among these revelations was the fact the fragment was actually an infinitesimally small piece of the alien's home planet. As it turned out, the aliens that the doctor had been studying were the same species that sent the fragment. Dr. Crangler had speculated that the alien bodies were simply 'housings', and he was more correct than he probably knew. According the information in the notebooks, this alien community was comprised of a single super consciousness inhabiting many such 'housings'. Common knowledge and ability was spread amongst the aliens using light as a vehicle. This, of course, explained how Mr. Reynolds could suddenly be privy to alien secrets just by touching the fragment. The manipulation of light as a way to spread information was simply ingenious. Unfortunately, though, this alien intelligence was trying to use that ingenuity to end all human life on Earth.

If an intelligence wanted to share (or in this case, *spread*) something to someone that was hundreds, or perhaps millions, of light years away, then the only practical way to do that would be to use light. Since what was being spread was a virus, the best way to spread it efficiently would be to use something native and abundant on the receiving planet by which The

Virus could easily propagate: Earth's oxygen supply. Earth had hosted alien encounters before, not many, but enough to give some merit to the fabulous claims with which the public at large was familiar. Though much about these alien encounters was heavily fabricated, one thing the movies got right was that every attempted invasion by aliens somehow ended in defeat. The fact of the matter, as the aliens apparently learned, was that Earth was a planet abundant in resources, many of which could not be found on any other planet in the universe, but it was also a planet abundant in organisms that subsisted off of those resources. As a result alien entities had no defense against these hostile and unsympathetic organisms. As had been observed by one of the great writers on the subject, man had paid in his own blood, to the tune of billions of lives, for the right to reside among the kaleidoscope spectrum of bacteria and flora, viruses and diseases, plagues and natural disasters, that also called Earth home.

The very thing that man, in all his consorted wisdom, could not overcome, himself—microorganisms and the diseases they inspire—always proved to be the undoing of alien entities, so the aliens regrouped and devised another plan. Earth was simply too valuable to be allowed to languish in the hands of ignorant humans with their trivial pursuits and overinflated senses of self. If the aliens could not invade the blue jewel of the universe directly, then they would annihilate its hordes of mankind with a virus, purge its unforgiving atmosphere, and claim it as their own. According to the notebooks, the virus that was plaguing the planet at present was, by no means, the first. The Black Death was the most well-known (though it was not known that it had been instituted by aliens), and to a lesser extent, the Great Plague, but the mostly-overlooked fact of the matter was that since The Black Death that had eventually claimed over half the population of an entire continent, a catastrophic plague of some kind had been ravaging the planet every ten years or so, right up until relatively modern times. The only reason for this brief cessation of viral hostilities was that those unseen aliens had recognized that man could not be eradicated so easily. Man's numbers had dwindled dramatically, but still, he somehow survived every invasion, every systematic spread of disease, basically everything that could be thrown at him aside from destroying the entire planet with him on it. It was as if *he* was the plague and intelligences far exceeding his own could not formulate a cure.

So came the next phase in the war that only an elite few had recently recognized that the planet was even engaged in. Man had apparently earned immunity from eradication by disease, but he was still not invincible. Sure, his body had become expert at killing off diseased cells, even if it meant the sacrifice of his own cells, which he would simply regenerate what he could and adapt to life without the ones he couldn't. As natural selection clearly showed, where he failed, his offspring would only grow stronger. It was astonishing at first for the extraterrestrials when they discovered that deadly viruses were actually administered by man himself—flu shots, for example—with the result that he only forged a greater immunity, but his profound ability to recoup and regenerate was also his weakness. Just as the most efficient diseases don't stop at simply killing off cells, but, like cancer, actually manipulated the body into producing more of *itself*, so the aliens devised a virus that would distort the way man produced his very offspring. This virus didn't need to kill every man, woman, and child to be effective, it only had to effectively stop them from reproducing.

Once Dr. Crangler took another break from mulling over this and other information, his eyes were red, his face was sullen, and his mind was exhausted. He was a man well used to professional fatigue, but even he had not given so much energy to such unfettered study as this since his med school years fifteen years ago. Much of the information about The Virus he already knew, but with this new, supplemental information, a picture of the reality at hand began to coalesce in his imagination that was even more viscous and appalling than he was prepared for. Even though he had experimented on alien bodies extensively, he had never really viewed them as beings capable of feelings and emotions. To him, they were potential foreign invaders, advanced beings with remarkable intelligence, but no other relatable qualities. They were things to be studied and defended against, but certainly not things to be *related* to. Now, realizing that aliens had been experimenting on humans eons before the reverse was true, he felt suddenly violated. He had never attributed human emotion to these beings, but now he saw them as cruel and evil, affecting the demise of millions, even billions of precious human lives in their relentless pursuit of acquisition.

Then the doctor's mind began to wander to many of his own studies of other organisms on the planet. Hadn't he, just like the other doctors and scientists of the world, performed countless experiments upon animals, other organisms, and at times, even people, in order to manipulate their resources for mankind's own endeavors? Hadn't man routinely wiped out entire populations of fellow organisms for the sake of its own betterment? If this line of logic was to be followed, then who was to say that the organisms on the planet that were not to man's liking didn't deserve to exist more than man himself? After all, many of them had been here long before man. What if what this alien life form was attempting to do was actually poetic justice? Musings like these didn't sit well with the doctor, so he cast them aside. It was not comfortable imagining that *he* was the culture in the Petri dish and *aliens* were, in fact, the dominant species, peering over him, deciding his ultimate fate. Man was the rightful heir to Earth, Dr. Crangler reminded himself, and he resolved to double his efforts to thwart this, the aliens' latest attempts to forever remove man from his blue marble throne. Mankind would not be subdued on his watch, the doctor told himself. It all sounded really good, but just now, Dr. Crangler felt that he had only enough resolve to do one thing, and that was to lay his head on his desk and rest. He didn't realize that he hadn't slept in the last thirty hours, so totally was he enthralled in Geoffrey's notebooks, but his body did, and it assured him that it would not cooperate any further without a break.

Chapter 15

Geoffrey sat up in his bed and looked around. He had just awakened a few moments earlier and felt more refreshed than he had since he got here. The hypnotic effect of having little to no visual stimuli was both draining and oddly confusing, so the significance was not lost upon Geoffrey that he felt much better in spite of his unchanging surroundings. He wiped his eyes, stretched his limbs, and thought for a moment. He had it! The fact that he had finished with the notebooks was the reason he felt so sublime. Finally getting all of that information out of his head and onto paper was like clearing an insanely crowded fish tank of most of its occupants. He fancied that he thought more clearly, saw more clearly (which wasn't saying much, since there was only white to see), and even his body was replenished. His appetite had returned as well.

He turned toward the upper corner of the room where he knew the surveillance camera was hidden and motioned that he was hungry. While he waited, he thought over a few things until his mind inevitably found its way to the subject of the late Mr. Reynolds. It struck Geoffrey as odd that he hadn't thought more of what happened to the astronomer before now, but with the doctor constantly pressuring him to finish the notebooks, it was no wonder he didn't have much time to think on anything else. Now that he finally had time to think, he wondered what became of the scientist. Oddly enough, though, he wasn't as alarmed for Mr. Reynolds as he would've thought. Somehow, he knew that the scientist was all right, wherever he was, just like he knew that there were three men watching him via the hidden camera, and that Dr. Crangler was sound asleep somewhere in the building. Among the things he didn't know, however, was just *how* he knew these things. He thought about how Mr. Reynolds had communicated with him telepathically before being reduced to dust. It was an experience that he couldn't put into words. Geoffrey imagined that it would be like trying to explain colors to one born blind, or perhaps trying to explain the phenomenon of thought to a vegetable or a rock. When Mr. Reynolds spoke into his mind, he heard the words more clearly than if they were spoken audibly, but he couldn't *hear* them, exactly. The images Mr. Reynolds introduced into his mind were more distinctive than if they had been plotted by a great artist, but he didn't *see* them, exactly. This was the only discernible explanation he could give, even to himself, of what had taken place in that room.

That was the connection he was looking for. He knew three men were watching him on monitors in the facility, but he *didn't* know. Whatever Mr. Reynolds had done to him caused this new ability. Still, he had yet to decide if the change was good or bad. Nearly thirty minutes passed with Geoffrey trying to make some kind of order of everything he'd experienced when he realized via his new extra sensory perception that one of Dr. Crangler's assistances was coming down the hall with the food he asked for. Sure enough, not a full minute later, the locking mechanism on the door sounded and the door opened, revealing a very nervous assistant with a white Styrofoam tray of food and a matching drink. The assistant stepped halfway across the threshold of the room and, only looking at Geoffrey briefly, set the food items on the floor near the door. Meanwhile, Geoffrey thought he heard someone's voice. It seemed to be coming from far off in the distance and was too faint for him to distinguish what it was saying, but he was almost certain that it was the voice of a man. When the assistant quickly closed the door behind him, the voice ceased and Geoffrey thought nothing else of it.

He made quick work of the food. There was no trashcan in his room so he put the tray and cup back where the assistant had left them and motioned to the camera for someone to pick them up. Afterward, he sat idly on his bed for a few long moments, before deciding he could use the tray as a diversion until someone came to pick it up. After all, he didn't yet have a television, a radio, or even a window to look out of, and he had already gotten all the rest he was going to need for some time. First, he poked holes in the tray, then he pinched it at its corners, then, remembering that the doctor had taken the notebooks he had written in, but not the pencil, he retrieved it from the desk drawer and began drawing on the tray. The doctor had left other notebooks but for whatever reason the image in Geoffrey's head seemed to be searing itself upon Geoffrey's brain, as if it were too potent to be held in for even a second. There was no time for looking for notebooks. Geoffrey scribbled fiercely on the tray. He felt as if his head would burst if he stopped. After a few moments, he looked at the image he had drawn. It was a hideous thing, an image with a frame and a head but nothing like any animal or human he had ever seen before. He glared at the monstrosity he had drawn for a few seconds and the holes in this side of the tray as well and let the tray fall from his hands with a sigh.

"I *really* need a television." He whispered to himself.

Chapter 16

While Geoffrey sat, bored and alone, on the edge of his bed, Delilah reclined on a leather sofa, watching television and nibbling on premium quality chocolate (white chocolate, no less) truffles. A small radio sat on a rolling stand beside the partially eaten box of truffles, as well as a small cup of cold milk. Aside from these additions, the room also now had a three drawer desk that was considerably larger than the desk in Geoffrey's room, and filled with all manner of designer products. Delilah had certainly not returned to the lap of luxury to which she was accustomed, but, considering the circumstances, she was on her way. She continued nibbling on expensive chocolate confections and watching television until she decided she was bored with whatever program was on. She changed the channel, then changed it again, but was equally disappointed. She changed it a few more times, but with the same result. Frustrated, she stood and yelled at the camera in the upper corner of the room that she needed to use the restroom. A short time later, the locking mechanism in her door unlatched and a light tapping immediately followed the *hiss-click*.

"Come in." said Delilah to two of Dr. Crangler's assistants.

"You need to use the restroom, Ma'am?" one of them asked.

"I do not. But if I did I wouldn't want *men* escorting me there." She scowled at the thought. "I'd appreciate a room with an adjoining bathroom." It sounded more like a demand than a suggestion. The assistant looked at his fellow assistant with more than a measure of consternation. "Uh…" he faltered, turning back to Delilah.

"Never mind." She broke in. "I'll talk to Dr. Crangler. When is he coming?"

"He…will be with you shortly." The assistant shuffled and seemed to not want to maintain eye contact with Delilah. In the volatile condition in which he had last seen the doctor there was no telling *what* he would do or *when* he would be anywhere.

"All right, well just show me to the bathroom," returned Delilah. The assistants led Delilah to the nearest lavatory. "Could you please not stand right at the door?" Delilah asked not so politely, once she was at the bathroom's entrance. "Could you possibly stand down there somewhere?" she pointed about twenty feet down the hall. "I am a woman after all, and it's just not comfortable having a bunch of guys hanging out while I use the bathroom." She smiled assiduously at the assistants until they slowly backed down the hall to the spot she indicated. While she went into the bathroom, the two conversed amongst themselves in barely audible whispers. "You know we'll probably be fired for giving in to these crazy demands of hers, don't you?" one assistant asked the other.

"It's what Dr. Crangler ordered." The second assistant answered. "If any trouble comes of all this, it's not *our* fault. You know how many times we were told to follow the doctor's orders to the letter—foremost by him—and that's what we're doing. When the shit hits the fan, they can't blame us for following orders. Besides, from what everyone's saying, if they can't find a cure in the girl's blood to The Virus, then nobody's gonna be able to have kids anymore, so it's probably for the best that we keep her comfortable." The other assistant nodded in solemn agreement. Regardless of what was suddenly ailing Dr. Crangler, it was his shoulders that would bear the brunt of this whole thing and it was he who was responsible for coming up with answers, certainly not his lowly assistants.

About twenty minutes passed by the time Delilah finally exited the lavatory. The assistants were standing silently in the same spot, but now they rushed to her to escort her back to her room. "So, is there any chance I can get that room with a bathroom attached to it." asked Delilah, as she followed the assistants back to her quarters. "Isn't it bad enough that I haven't been outside since I got here? I mean, I understand that I'm important and all, but can't I make a single phone call? My father could send some of the help from my house to wherever this place is. They know what I need, and then you guys wouldn't have to walk me to the bathroom like a three-year-old." Delilah didn't really think that the servants at her home would be brought here, but if she could get in touch with her father, he may be able to free her of this horrible confinement, so she figured that any argument that supported that objective deserved at least the chance to be aired. Unfortunately, the reality soon surfaced of how she was abducted and subsequently drugged right there in her father's presence. If these people could trespass on private property and take her while her wealthy and affluent father was right there in the room, there was probably nothing he could do now that she was held prisoner in this god-awful colorless facility. It was definitely not an encouraging realization to dwell upon, but Delilah partially consoled herself by the fact that she was making headway in getting her demands met at the moment. If nothing else, it was a start.

"Where is Dr. Crangler anyhow?" she asked as she approached her room. One of the assistants stopped at one of the large double windows that lined nearly every room like this in the facility. He peered into the window and sighed deeply in relief. "He's right there, thank God." Said he "So, Miss Hanson, if you have any further request, they should be directed to him." Delilah saw the doctor, or rather the back of him when she walked to the window where the assistant was standing, as he surveyed her room. The door was already opened so the leading assistant led Delilah in quickly, and just as quickly stood to the side just inside the room. The remaining assistant did likewise after Delilah entered. Meanwhile, Dr. Crangler, hearing the steps of his awaited guest, turned on his heels with a swiftness and anger that belied his age and professional reserve.

"What…!?" the doctor barked, unable to articulate a spirited assault for the tide of anger that currently engulfed him. "What…!?" he tried again. He gestured in every direction and it was clear that he could hardly control himself. "Report to Operations, *immediately*!" he demanded to his two silent staff members, once he calmed down enough to speak a complete sentence. "*Immediately*!" he yelled again, even though his assistants were already making their hasty exit. He watched with a grimace as they passed the double windows of the room toward the operations department. Then, he turned around to Delilah, who was sitting quite comfortably on her new white leather couch. "Miss Hanson…" he began.

"Listen, Dr. Crangler," Delilah kindly interrupted, "I don't know how long I've been here, but it feels likes months. I mean, guys in black suites trespass on my property, take me from my house, *drug* me," she sounded especially displeased with this last bit, "and then bring me to whatever this place is, where guys in white suits stick me in a room—one without a connected bathroom I might add—and just leave me to rot. I mean, really. Everything's white all the time, I'm just now getting some of the products I need, and no one will tell me when, or *if,* I'll ever leave this place. Now, you said that I was important, that you needed me to find a cure for this virus thing that's out there. Well, if I'm so important, why shouldn't I be treated like it?" Delilah paused to give the doctor a chance to answer, but he just stood there, seething, glaring at her as if she was truly insane. "You know," she continued, completely undaunted, "it wouldn't be a bad idea to let me call my dad and have him send some of the help here. I mean, it would…"

"Absolutely *not!*" demanded the doctor. "As a matter of fact, all of this…this…*stuff,"* the doctor gestured toward Delilah's latest room additions, "will have to go back immediately, including you. I'm going to have you moved back to the room you were in as soon as I have all this nonsense removed."

One of things that Delilah had demanded from Dr. Crangler's nervous assistants in his absence was that she be moved to be a different room, the room she was in now. She had already figured the doctor wouldn't be so receptive to the other things she had gotten changed, but she didn't think he would cause such a fuss about her being relocated to a different room. After all, she reasoned, what was the difference? As far as she knew, the entire facility was nothing more than a hodgepodge of equally blank rooms, but, even so, there was a reason she had herself moved to a different location, and she had no intention of returning, as she firmly asserted to the doctor.

Delilah stood her ground. "Absolutely *not!*" she returned, "I *am not* going back to that room or any other room."

The doctor was about to assure her in no uncertain terms that indeed she was, but didn't. Getting the information from Geoffrey's notebooks was still his main objective, and he didn't want to be further distracted. Even though he was furious with his assistants as well as the absurdly arrogant young lady standing before him just now, he didn't want to waste precious focus he needed elsewhere, engaging in combat with Miss Hanson. Any other time—*any* other time—he would've been more than happy to show this spoiled little *celebutant* who was boss here, but not this time. Instead, the doctor asked, "And exactly why not, Miss Hanson?"

"Because, I'm not a peep show, Dr. Crangler." answered Delilah with heightened fervor. Unfortunately for the doctor, his reluctance to engage in territorial mortal combat with Delilah was only encouraging her to be more bold in her campaign to get her way. "It's not like I approve of it, because I certainly do not, but it's one thing for you people to have cameras everywhere," she continued, "but it's a whole other thing for me to have to see this huge window all the time where I know people are watching my every move. And since I haven't seen another woman around here yet, I know that there are most likely nasty, maybe old, men on the other side of that window-thing you have set up. Oh, yeah, that's right. I know there's somebody on the other side of that window in my old room. I saw your guys talking to it when they thought I wasn't looking." Delilah gave the doctor a knowing look that was meant to inspire guilt. Meanwhile, he just stood there, dumbfounded at this woman's arrogance, but again, this was not the time for the battle he would've enjoyed engaging with her.

The doctor sighed in exasperation. "I need to run some tests on you and I don't have time for this at the moment, *Miss Hanson*." he hissed her name, "If you will just cooperate with me, then we can get this over with as soon as possible."

It was more than apparent to Delilah that she was wearing the doctor down, which was exactly her intention, and she couldn't have been happier (except, of course, if she was immediately released from this place). She smiled innocently and nodded slightly in intimation that she would cooperate. The doctor, for his part, exited the room in great strides (Delilah fancied to herself that his very steps were those of defeat), and returned some time later, trailed by three of his assistants—none of whom were the ones from earlier, not surprisingly—each was carrying or pushing some kind of medical apparatus. Once these pieces of equipment had been properly set up in Delilah's new room, the assistants left a second round of medical equipment, then a third. By the time they were finished, Delilah thought that she may have to undergo medical tests until the Second Coming; and oddly enough, this was not far from the doctor's intention. The myriad of blood tests, stress tests, disease screenings, more blood tests, etc., was indeed of paramount importance, but by no means did all of them have to be performed in a single day. Delilah had not grown an immunity to The Virus, she just hadn't contracted it, so synthesizing a cure from her blood would be much more difficult than it would otherwise, but the cure—if it could even be found—would certainly not be produced in a day, a week, or even a single month, so performing all the these arduous, painstaking tests at once was essentially meaningless.

Unfortunately for Delilah, the only purpose for doing things this way was to cause her as much discomfort as possible. Of the many things she didn't know about this secret facility was that Dr. Crangler was not, as she had assumed, the top ranking official here. He had superiors that he had to answer to that Delilah would never lay eyes upon—some of the same officials that had authorized her abduction, in fact. Now, these officials knew (mainly because Dr. Crangler had explained it to them), that the work to be done concerning Delilah was a delicate endeavor. Delilah's body had to be functioning completely up to par for the doctor to be able to extract the kind of biological samples he needed to possibly find a cure for The Virus. That meant that Delilah had to be free of diseases, contaminants, and other things, but it also meant that she could not be excessively stressed, as the effects would be just as hazardous. Unfortunately for Dr. Crangler, this meant that he could not vex this terribly spoiled young woman like he desperately wanted to, but it wasn't to say that he couldn't pursue other routes to annoy her, and right now, one *other route* was to run tests on her until she was past exhaustion, and then run more tests. Of course, if Delilah had known what was going on, she would've used this information to her advantage, but she didn't, so the doctor used it to his.

He ran Delilah on a small treadmill for a myriad of stress tests, drew blood until her arms nearly looked like a heroin addict's, and then ran her again. He was as falsely polite to her as she had been to him as he connected all manner of uncomfortably-cold leads to her torso and

179

legs and recorded the findings. He pricked her fingers, cut unnecessarily long samples of her hair, forced her to pee in countless cups, and all while, his attending assistants looked on with considerable confusion. When he finally finished, five and a half grueling hours later, Delilah was asleep nearly as soon as he informed her that they were done for the day. After everyone had left, he looked at Delilah, a little surprised at just how unprofessional he had been, before leaving the room himself. He didn't have much time to dwell on the ugly facets of human nature because he still had to sort through the results of the many tests he'd performed, and try to make sense of them. After all, even though he and Delilah would likely resume cold war combat as soon as she awoke, there was still a virus to cure, and the destruction that was being wreaked above ground would not wait.

Chapter 17

Days passed before Delilah saw Dr. Crangler again and though there was a new set of assistants assigned to her now, she soon managed to work them to her own benefit as deftly as the last bunch. Not only did she get a few more pieces of furniture in her room, but she also pressured the new guys into getting her some new clothes and hair accessories—*colorful* cloths and hair accessories. This was Delilah's boldest move yet and it wasn't a great surprise to her that shortly after her newly-acquired things showed up, so did Dr. Crangler. The assistants were still in Delilah's room setting up her new things when he arrived. She was trying to convince one of them to give her an amateur foot massage when the locking mechanism of her door unlatched and the doctor roared in.

"I want Miss Hanson moved to another room and everything cleared out of this one right now!" the doctor bellowed. "I specified at the briefing that there was to be nothing of color placed into her room unless I approved it personally!" The doctor's fists were clenched and trembling, his face was flushed, and his words came in angry gasps.

"But you said not to disturb you for any reason, you said…" one of the assistants began.

"Damn it all!" shouted the doctor, "I don't care what I told you. I said no color in this room!" The assistants traded confused glances. Looking at how similar the bewilderment was on each of their faces, Delilah had a nearly overpowering urge to burst out in hysterical laughter. It was always a great joy for her to be reminded that she had the ability to put men into such great disarray. Meanwhile, the doctor continued, "Now move Miss Hanson to another room and clear this one out immediately!" The two disorientated subordinates struggled nearly in vain not to stumble over one another as one headed for a piece of Delilah's furniture to drag it out, and the other for Delilah. Delilah had been enjoying the chaotic scene, but now, she sprang into action. Rising to her feet in one swift movement, she held her arms out in front of her in intimation that she wasn't going anywhere.

"Hey, Hey! Stop right there!" she yelled so loudly that everyone in the room, the doctor included, was startled motionless. "I already told you, Dr. Crangler, I'm not going back to that room or any other one. Now, I've been trapped here long enough without anything but white walls to look at. I'm not a barbarian, I'm a woman. And if you expect me to cooperate with you so you can get whatever it is you're trying to get from me, then I'm going to have some things." With this heated declaration, the battle between the doctor and Delilah was brought to an undeniable head. She had waited long and worked hard to secure the things that now populated the room, and the thought of having to be taken backward so easily was more than she could take. A year ago, these clothes (they weren't even designer for goodness sake!), these pieces of furniture, the girlie hair things, all of it would've been little more than an insult to her routinely pampered palate, but now... Well, now, after all she'd been through, and living in the confines of a place so completely devoid of style and excitement, these things actually meant something.

"Miss Hanson, I will have you sedated if you refuse..." began the doctor.

"I *dare* you!" Delilah squealed. The gloves were off, the games were over, and Delilah was completely swept away in frustration that had been building up inside her since this whole Virus nonsense began. "I *double* dare you!" The words themselves could've been shouted by a child, but the tone and fierce determination that accompanied them were anything but. "That's right, I heard one of the *other* asshole doctors say that you couldn't sedate me again. You need to get this vaccine or whatever from my blood, and if my blood is loaded with a bunch of drugs, then it's no good. You need me, whether you like it or not, and I'm not cooperating one damn bit if I have to sit in a room all day alone with nothing and no one to look at but you and your flunkies. Do you understand me?" Delilah was at fever pitch now. She didn't know if she was helping or hurting her cause, but it didn't even matter anymore. The only thing that mattered was that she had had enough of the 'white treatment' and if life was going to be hell for her, then she would damn well make sure it was the same for the doctor as well.

"And another thing." Delilah continued erratically, "I want to get out of here and see the outside. I don't know how long I've been here, but if you don't let me out of this place for a while, I'm gonna go crazy. And if I go crazy, I'm gonna make damn sure that I take somebody with me. And why the hell can't I get more than one fucking station on the television or the radio? And I want some more clothes! And why the hell can't I call my father?" Delilah was delirious with anger, her arms flailing in every direction and her squeals brought to an ear piercing crescendo. With every protestation, she moved closer to the doctor, so much so that he was actually concerned for his physical safety. Fortunately for him, her outburst exhausted all her energy before she could cause him bodily harm. Now, she stood just before him, her eyes wild and angry, and her delicate breasts heaving for precious breath. It was clear on her face that she had many more angry ultimatums to shower upon the doctor, but not the energy or the breath to demand them. The doctor was again struck dumb. He had expected Delilah to be discontent with his decision to remove her and her newly-acquired things from the room, but he certainly had not expected how spirited that discontent would be.

Meanwhile, the assistants had wisely vacated the room and reported back to Operations, some time ago. Now, one of them returned, and upon entering the room, whispered something into the doctor's ear. The doctor and Delilah were standing in the same position with the same expressions as before, but now, with the assistant whispering in his ear, the doctor's face assumed a series of expressions, something like varying degrees of realization, until at last, a mysterious and mischievous smile alighted on his lips. This smile widened as the assistant continued whispering and, by the time the assistant exited the room again, the doctor's face was completely different. His smile was broad, stretching his lips against his teeth and bunching his cheeks together in deep ridges, the light in his eyes twinkled, and his posture was more relaxed. Much more.

"You know, Miss Hanson," began the doctor, after some contemplation. The mirth with which he uttered Delilah's name warned her that somehow the tides had changed—and not in her favor. "I think you may have a point. Perhaps it *is* time we give you a few more privileges. After all, you *are* vitally important aren't you? And we can't have our VIPs feeling like prisoners can we?" Delilah didn't like the catch in his voice. "So," the doctor continued, "not only can you keep all your things, but I'm going to have one of our mirror trucks summoned immediately, and you're going to get a nice, long, scenic ride out. I'll even see if I can get you out of the compound and into the countryside for a while. How does that sound, Miss Hanson?"

Delilah squinted at the doctor. "And what's the catch?"

"Oh, no catch, Miss Hanson," answered the doctor, as he turned to leave. He turned back just before he reached the door. "Well, perhaps there is one little catch." "You see, Miss Hanson," Dr. Crangler resumed, "according to our findings, we believe we can indeed synthesize a permanent cure for The Virus from your blood, just not your *present* blood. To produce a cure for this unique pandemic, we need a particular type of stem cell, a type of stem cell which your body would only help produce only under certain circumstances...a type of stem cell found in umbilical cord blood."

The look on Dr. Crangler's face suggested that he just said something profound and was expecting a livid response from Delilah, but she had no idea what he was talking about. "I don't understand." She said, shaking her head.

"Miss Hanson," said Dr. Crangler, "in order for us to synthesize a cure, you're going to have to get pregnant."

Chapter 18

The cry Delilah released upon being informed that she was be impregnated and experience the untold horror of child bearing, was excessively loud, long, and intoned. Just as Dr. Crangler had promised, she would briefly be released from her current confines via a scenic ride in the countryside, but it would not be a ride that she could enjoy fully, not with her mind occupied as it was with the information she recently received. This was precisely the doctor's plan. He knew that a former ardent socialite like Delilah would not see pregnancy as the blessing that it was, and that furthermore, it would dampen her spirits no matter what unorthodox privileges she wrangled from him. With Delilah finally understanding the considerable power she wielded, even in this place, this was the doctor's ace in the hole—his *only* ace in the hole—and he was certainly not going to let it go unused.

When it came time for her to leave the compound on the so-called mirror truck, Delilah was like one trapped in a dream. A single word—*pregnant*—dominated her thoughts and rendered everything else somehow unreal. She followed the doctor's two assistants through the maze of corridors until they came to the large entrance hall to exit into the mirror truck waiting just outside. The walls and ceiling were comprised of one way mirrors, giving it its nickname. The outside of the cargo area looked like a huge five-sided mirror. A thin but dark layer of film tinted the outside of the cargo area for obvious reasons and provided an ideal means of transportation where a person could be given a complete view of their surroundings without being seen themselves. Any other time, Delilah may've been brainstorming ways to use this opportunity to escape, but now, she was too consumed in her own thoughts to consider the possibility. One of the assistants sat in the sealed off cargo area of the truck with Delilah and the trip began. She had no way of knowing it, but she had been confined in this secret place for nearly three months, and had she had more wits about her, she would've been looking around to see where she was. As it stood, she just sat with her head down in the back of the mirror truck as it drove about a quarter of a mile, and came to a city street.

Delilah's gaze, not to mention spirits, were still down, until about thirty minutes later, when Dr. Crangler's assistant lightly whispered her name. She was stuck in her own world and didn't respond, so he called her name again. And then again. The third time he called her name, she finally looked up.

"This trip is for you, Miss Hanson." said the assistant, "You might want to, you know…enjoy it." At that, Delilah finally took the opportunity to look around.

She had no idea what city or even state she was in, but wherever it was, it was simply gorgeous. The truck drove down a four lane highway that was surrounded by a dense patch of forest with perhaps a few homes and a convenience store or two interspersed here and there. Apparently, fall was in full bloom, because all the foliage was fantastically colored in varying shades of orange and red. The setting sun cascaded over the horizon and Delilah thought to herself that it was one of the most beautiful scenes she had ever beheld. After seeing nothing but white for months, all these vibrant colors looked like heaven. In her time, Delilah had seen the sparkle of diamonds, the glisten of the most expensive cars, and virtually everything in between, but all of it suddenly seemed to pale in comparison to the gorgeous countryside that was zooming past her now. She looked out of the mirrored truck bed walls, enthralled with the miracle of nature that she had never really noticed before, until one car in particular passed by the truck. The car was no Bentley or Ferrari. In fact, there was absolutely nothing noteworthy about the vehicle at all from Delilah's perspective, except that in the passenger seat of the car sat a woman who was well advanced in her pregnancy. The car was a convertible and the top was down, so Delilah could see quite clearly the woman's belly bulging excessively beneath her thin shirt. From her vantage point, Delilah could not see the smile on the woman's face as she enjoyed the cool breeze outside, but the natural deformation of the woman's body was enough to nullify everything else. Rampant thoughts of her effortlessly-maintained midsection being invaded by some foreign entity plagued her even more from that moment on. She didn't know much about pregnancy—only that she didn't want to be involved with it. In her mind's eye, it may be fine and dandy for the woman in the car as well as the other women of the world (though that was certainly not the case now that The Virus had arrived), but not for her: Definitely not for her. Besides the irreparable damage she was sure it would do to her awesome figure, she was much too young to be shackled with something as consuming and needy as a kid. It made her nauseous just to think of it and had it not been for the fact that there was nowhere to throw up in the truck that she wouldn't have to see and smell until the ride was over, she would've vomited more than once right where she was.

The truck drove for nearly an hour more through equally beautiful and majestic scenic routes, and though the assistant encouraged his charge to enjoy the sights—"Who knows when the next time, if there even is a next time, you'll get this opportunity." the assistant counseled, Delilah was too distracted to fully enjoy anything. She stared out at the virtually limitless panorama of the free world, but the only thing she could see was the hideous stomach bulge of the woman in the convertible. Once the ride was over, she was ushered back to the facility and into her room, in the same despondent state. It would seem as though Dr. Crangler had won this round.

Back in Geoffrey's room, without a television or a radio, things were pretty quiet, but such was not the case in his head. At varying intervals, he faintly heard what he thought were voices. The sounds were too faint for him to be sure, and he knew well that the walls were soundproof, so he wouldn't have heard people talking outside his room even if they were yelling at the top of their lungs, but still, the vague voice-like sounds were there. They would come and go sporadically and he couldn't decipher what was being said (if, in fact, anything was being *said* at all) and before long, Geoffrey began to toy more seriously with the possibility that he was finally coming unglued. Perhaps he was finally going crazy. *After all, isn't hearing phantom voice the first and most recognizable sign of impending dementia or outright insanity?* he mused to himself.

"Well, at least they're not telling me to kill someone." He tried to jest with himself, but found that he was in no mood to laugh at the situation. No one had come after he'd finished his last meal, even though he was certain someone saw him beckoning toward the camera, so he stood up and motioned to the camera again that he had trash that needed to be taken out. He heard the vague voices again and sat back down. "I'm gonna need some interaction. I can't just sit here and go crazy." He advised himself, "A radio, a video game. Hell, I'll even settle for a book."

Just then, the hiss-click of his room door's locking mechanism filled his ears. It was a welcomed sound, not only because it meant that some other human being was coming to break the monotony, but it also assured him that there were still *actual* sounds in the world and not just the phantom voices in his head. He would've been grateful to see any living human being, but he was especially grateful to find that it was the doctor who entered his room.

"Hello, Dr. Crangler." Geoffrey greeted, with obvious eagerness. "Listen, Doc, I need to talk to you about something."

"And what would that be, Son?" The doctor was distracted by the trash on the floor. His tone was equally distracted.

"I need some kind of interaction, I don't know, a radio, a…"

"What is this?" interrupted Dr. Crangler, suddenly intensely alert, as he bent down to pick up the food container on which Geoffrey had scribbled.

"Oh, nothing. It's just trash." answered Geoffrey, looking somewhat confused. He wondered why a simple piece of hole-ridden garbage had attracted the doctor's attention so.

"Did you...d-did you *draw* this?" the doctor asked. Geoffrey was now alarmed as well as confused. The doctor stood silently for a moment and so did Geoffrey. Meanwhile, the voices (or rather, voice) in his head returned. This time, it was distinct enough for him to hear exactly what it was saying.

"Sure, why?" Geoffrey answered, though he was nearly as shaken as the doctor appeared. Though the doctor was speaking to him verbally, the voice in his head was also the doctor's.

"Amazing!" the doctor exclaimed, more musing to himself than in answer to Geoffrey's inquiry. He lifted his gaze from the foam plate and addressed Geoffrey directly. "Geoffrey," said Dr. Crangler, "this is a perfect representation of..."

"Of the aliens you've been studying?" Geoffrey answered in a highly concerned voice. The doctor peered at his patient deeply.

"Yes, Son." he answered, maintaining an unshakeable gaze, "Yes, Son, that's exactly what it is." The doctor licked his lips slowly. "Have...have you seen this...in your head?" he asked cautiously.

"No, I don't think so, Dr. Crangler. I was just doodling…but I can hear you in my head."

The doctor took an involuntary and alarmed step backward. "What do you mean, exactly, Mr. Summons?"

"I can hear you in my head, Doctor…I think I'm hearing what you're thinking."

Chapter 19

Dr. Crangler took a step forward and seated himself in a chair near the door. The frown on his face made the furrowed lines in his forehead prominent. His gaze looked inward and every so often the frown deepened. Geoffrey looked down at the doctor and after about five silent minutes passed, he, too, assumed a seat on the only other place there was to sit—on his bed—three feet or so from the doctor. He needn't ask the doctor what he was thinking—he could hear his thoughts. Meanwhile, Dr. Crangler began wringing his hands—a sign that he was sinking deeper and deeper into whatever weighty musings were plaguing him. What felt like a very long time passed like this with the doctor, wringing his hands and moving his eyes back and forth as his mind raced, uttering only the periodic, "Amazing" as if he could think of no other word to describe what Geoffrey had just told him.

In reality, *amazing* (or perhaps *absolutely* amazing) would be the best description of what Geoffrey had recently proposed to the doctor. *Unfuckingbelievable* may've been an even better description, but it was not likely that a professional like Dr. Crangler would've used the term.

"You said you could hear sounds that you thought may've been voices, earlier, right?" asked Dr. Crangler. He intended to employ a test to see if his patient's telepathic assertion was true. Geoffrey nodded.

"Yeah, here and there, I think." Geoffrey indicated areas of a far wall of his room.

The amazement already in the doctor's face grew a little. "Okay, now, this is very important, Mr. Summons," the doctor leaned in close, "can you remember just how far apart these voices were?"

"Well, you know, Doc, it's not like I have a clock in here…"

"Just do the best you can. Whatever you can remember." The doctor looked and sounded increasingly anxious.

"Well, I'm still not 100 percent sure they were voices, they were *sounds* like voices, but…" and Geoffrey told, as best as he could, when he first started hearing them and how far apart they were. Dr. Crangler heaved a light gasp, and sat down on Geoffrey's bed. Collapsed really. He looked like a man who'd just had the wind knocked out of him.

"It can't be coincidence." The doctor said to himself.

"What can't be?" Geoffrey asked.

"The times when you heard these…voices. They were all remarkably close to the times that my assistants would've been attending to another of my patients. This patient is not far from here and it's likely that my assistants would've been passing by in the hallway on the side of that wall," the doctor pointed at the wall nearest Geoffrey's bed—the very place Geoffrey indicated hearing the voices "but you wouldn't have heard them."

"Why?"

"Because every room in this facility is soundproof." Neither said anything for a moment.

"And another thing too." Geoffrey said after a while. "I get the distinct feeling that I'm being watched by three men in another room."

"There is, and there are." The doctor answered simply. He gazed intently at Geoffrey, then turned away to stare at nothing and do nothing more than wring his hands and whisper "Amazing!" from time to time.

Geoffrey sat, looking on at the doctor for some time in silence. Every now and then, certain expressions crossed his face as if he was engaged in conversation with some unseen person, but other than that, he didn't speak a word. Eventually, he broke the silence. "Who's Delilah Hanson?" Geoffrey asked, abruptly. "There's somebody else like me here?" By 'like me' Geoffrey meant someone else that had been stolen from the outside world, someone who had been used to wearing and living in something other than *white* at some point in time. At these questions, the doctor looked at Geoffrey with alarm etched on his face—he had been so caught up in the implications that came with Geoffrey being able to read his thoughts that he completely forgot that Geoffrey *could* read his thoughts. He was about to rush out of the room as fast as he could, but Geoffrey, being much younger and faster than the doctor, cut him off at the door.

"Look, Dr. Crangler," he said, holding his arms out so the doctor couldn't pass him, "you can't just keep leaving me here alone like this. If there's somebody else here like me, then maybe we can keep each other company. I need something to do besides stare at these damn walls all day, Doc!"

"Yes, sure, Mr. Summons." The doctor answered hastily as he waved behind him toward the corner camera for someone to open the room door...*now*. The locking mechanism unlatched and he shoved Geoffrey aside before nearly running out of the room. Geoffrey certainly didn't like being handled so roughly, but he fully understood the doctor's angst. It wasn't every day that he found out that someone could read his mind, after all. Now, unfortunately, Geoffrey had time to be ushered back to the reality at hand, himself. He had tried to get the doctor to understand that he needed something, anything, to occupy his mind during his many solitary hours—especially now that he had foreign voices in his head—but suddenly, the main concern seemed to be what in the world would happen to him now that he had become the first professionally witnessed and soon to be documented mental telepathy. Just as importantly, what did this mean to Geoffrey himself? He had thought that perhaps he was going insane before, but now that he knew that wasn't the case, he had to decide how *he* felt about his new and unexpected abilities. Right now, he didn't know. It wasn't like he had just found out that he was good at math, he could hear people's thoughts (whether or not he wanted to) for goodness sake. It would definitely take some time for him to process this new reality.

Then a completely unexpected benefit to his freshly-forged telepathy occurred to Geoffrey. With nothing of interest to look at, no one to talk to for long periods of time, and no escape in sight, honing this telepathy thing would definitely give him something to do with his time, and, surrounded by such an interactively sterile environment, it should be like studying for an exam (albeit, a very unique exam) alone in a quiet room. So, he set to the task. Remembering how urgently the doctor had vacated the room, Geoffrey was fairly certain that he wouldn't be seeing him for a while and there was a good chance he wouldn't lay eyes upon his assistants for a while either.

"Well, since there's no one to talk to, maybe I can find someone to *listen* to."

Geoffrey mused as he positioned himself on the far edge of his bed closest to windowless wall that separated him from the neighboring corridor, and, unbeknownst to him at the moment, from Delilah's room. He massaged his temples in an effort to concentrate. He heard nothing. "Well, if I don't have anything else, I have time." He observed, and continued his experiment.

Dr. Crangler watched from the monitors in his office as Geoffrey rubbed his temples and squinted in deliberate concentration. The doctor shuddered to think just what his patient was trying to do, but along with that apprehension was a distinct fascination. Proven telepathy carried with it a number of profound implications. Perhaps Geoffrey could somehow connect with the alien intelligence on its own level and supply the doctor with even more pertinent information than what Geoffrey had written in the notebooks. Geoffrey's new abilities could endow mankind with greater technologies, but more importantly, it could help mankind develop defenses against further alien assaults. Maybe it could even result in the development of advanced weaponry by which mankind could take the offensive against hostile alien intelligences for a change. Either way, it was too promising to leave unstudied, but the doctor had no desire to perform any up-close *study* of his telepathic patient any time soon. It was too unnerving to be around someone who could read every thought and there was nothing he could do about it. Nevertheless, he knew that he would personally have to deal with Geoffrey eventually. This was not something he could leverage upon his aides indefinitely, and furthermore, if his superiors ever got wind of this, he was certain that considerable pressure would be applied to him to document the full extent his patient's ability.

The doctor suddenly felt very tired. He felt like butter that was spread too thin on bread that was too large, but the excitement, excessive though it may be, was not to end just yet, or any time soon for that matter. The doctor decided to take a walk around the outer edges of facility— the farthest away from Geoffrey's room—and try to gather his wits. He had always seen smoking cigarettes as an absurdly heinous practice, but for the first time in his life, he thought he might enjoy a good ole' cancer stick. He roamed the halls in solitude, muttering to himself, until his legs and feet both protested, then headed back to his office. He thought that he felt marginally better until he entered his office and saw on the monitors that Geoffrey was waving at the camera. The doctor felt suddenly tired all over again.

"I know someone's there." Geoffrey said, "I need to use the bathroom." He repeated himself a few times, until a couple of Dr. Crangler's aides knocked on his office door to ask what he wanted done.

The doctor thought for a moment, and then, heaved a deep sigh. "Escort Mr. Summons to the restroom and tell him I'll attend to him shortly." The assistants left to obey the directive and Dr. Crangler buried his face in his hands. It felt like things were closing in on him, suffocating him, but as is usually the case, the most difficult time is also the time when it would be the most dangerous to give up.

Chapter 20

By the time Delilah and the doctor met again, a full week had passed since he had delivered the devastating announcement that she would have to get pregnant. Pregnant! Of all things! The very word inspired loathing, disgust, and outright horror like Delilah had never known before, and she wasn't even considering the real complications of pregnancy. She was thinking more of what it would do to thighs and waistline, and oh God, it would certainly destroy her gorgeous complexion even more than these horrible lights already had. The idea of carrying something foreign, something *living*, in her belly that would make her look like the latest diet fad gone horribly wrong was just too much for her delicate constitution. In fact, her mother had told her more than once that the only reason she had been born was for 'insurance purposes', meaning that Delilah's mother had deemed her father's proclamation of undying love insufficient for her purposes, but marriage and a child…

"Well," quoted her mother on those occasions, "you know what they say about a three-fold chord. And that's exactly what I never intended to be again—broke."

Delilah's current situation was definitely not an endearing one as far as she was concerned, but she began to figure that, like her mother, she could use pregnancy as a way out, not out of poverty, as it was for the late Mrs. Hanson, but out of confinement. Perhaps, if she had this child and saved the world, whatever that meant, she could leave.

It was the first comforting thought Delilah had in what felt like a long time, but still, it was only relatively comforting because the ideas coalescing in her mind of what pregnancy would entail were still ugly and heinous to the very extreme. It was in this limbo that she found herself during the week that she saw nothing of Dr. Crangler, who was being thrown for a loop of his own. He had locked himself in his main office for days. This particular office, which was much larger than the one he normally monitored his two star patients, was equipped with a small sleeping area and a full bathroom, as well as a moderately-sized storage closest. The only thing it lacked was a kitchen because no food was actively prepared in this part of the underground facility for fear of the as yet untested effect it may have on the Cleaning Lights. Other than that, the doctor had virtually everything he needed to remain in his main office indefinitely. Had it not been for the fact that he needed to eat, he may've likely done just that. During that time, he had been faithfully locked behind the thick steel door of his office, poring endlessly over Geoffrey's notebooks, but the subject that occupied his mind most viciously was Geoffrey's newfound telepathy. Its graveness was awesome beyond the doctor's ability to fathom, and though there was much to be gained by this new ability, there was also much to be lost. For instance, if Geoffrey could read his fellow humans' minds, perhaps the aliens could as well, and if that was the case, there was no hope of ever thwarting their assaults. How would humanity defeat an enemy that is fully privy to whatever offensive they may plan against them? Such was the foolishness of Lucifer and the fallen angels, and if such stories are to be believed, then the message is crystal clear.

Then again, perhaps Geoffrey could hone his telepathic ability to actually eavesdrop on the alien intelligence, light years away. It was an extreme stretch of the imagination to be sure, but the things that had taken place already had proven that virtually anything was possible. These and many other musings plagued Dr. Crangler so thoroughly that he went without food, water, or a bath, even though such things were at his fingertips, for three solid days before he at last left the confines of his messy and smelly (thanks to his recently declined hygiene) office. Once he did leave, he roamed the halls on his way to the exit as vacuously as if he wasn't present at all. A blank gaze had replaced the scientific sparkle that once characterized his eyes. His hair was dirty and disheveled, and the thick stubble shadowing his face was in desperate need of attention as well. He shuffled along aimlessly through the hall. If there had been anything in the way, he would've certainly made tripped many times over.

Oddly enough, all this was part of the plan…sort of. Along with his complete lack of rest, he was stretched well beyond his limits, but he realized that Geoffrey may likely be able to read his thoughts even now. Until he could get a grip on himself and figure out what his next move would be, he didn't want that type of intrusion. So, besides the fact that the doctor was genuinely distraught and worn bare, he employed his last remaining mental energies to try to avoid any coherent thought, other than the need for food, to enter his head where Geoffrey may be probing. Somehow and for some reason, (perhaps it was a movie he saw) he believed that his thoughts were safe while he was in his office, protected behind the thick, steel door, but out here in the open…well, hadn't Geoffrey heard what his assistants were thinking while *they* were in the halls? And so, Dr. Crangler was, at the moment, a man doubly lost, lacking the presence of mind to gather his wits, and alternately trying *not* to gather his wits. Dr. Crangler was in a truly wretched predicament indeed, and he certainly looked the part as he cut his slow, lumbering path through the labyrinth of well-lit hallways leading to the ground level exit of the facility. Once he reached the exit and was outside in the open, he was so enthralled with his literally thoughtless tasks that he completely failed to notice the cool, late evening breeze washing in waves across his skin and through his white garb, or the gorgeous sight of the sun's rays making its final retreat beyond the horizon across the way.

It was late evening now and would be completely night very soon. The doctor welcomed the impending darkness, but other than that, all the other privileges of being able to quit his confinement at will—unlike Geoffrey or Delilah—were completely lost upon him in his distraction. There were three identical industrial-sized kitchens that serviced the entire gated and heavily-guarded complex that housed the underground facilities. These kitchens were scattered at strategic places across the premises. Dr. Crangler walked to the nearest one, about fifty feet away, with his head still bowed in anti-thought and his feet shuffling roughly through the cool grass. It would seem that his outing had been as equally ruined as Delilah's. Karma is usually a slow shuffling bitch, but obviously she can keep in quick stride when it suits her fancy. The kitchen that the doctor was approaching, like its sisters scattered across the premises, didn't serve chef quality food, but the grub was hot, edible, and quite tasty once one got used to it. The vast majority of Dr. Crangler's professional career had been spent at this facility, so he had had plenty of time to 'get used' to the food, and by this time, he quite liked it. But not this evening. Once he ordered a plate from the kitchen's buffet style set up and found a seat in a far corner where he could hopefully be alone, he also found that the food was as good as grey matter in his mouth. His mind was overwhelmed and would allow for no rival sensations, including enjoyment. His plate was filled with Salisbury steak, mashed potatoes, and some mixture of steamed vegetables, all piping hot from spending more than ample time beneath abusive heat lamps, but it could've been sawdust-flavored steamed rice cakes and Dr. Crangler wouldn't have noticed the difference. In fact, the only thing that tasted as it should, was the generic bottled water that stood beside the meal tray.

Even so, the doctor forced himself to finish as much as he could tolerate (he didn't want to make another trip out here if he could avoid it), and by the time he reentered the underground facility, he was as despondent as ever. Now, replenished with a hearty meal (even if it was discouragingly tasteless) he managed to bathe and shave. Then, he returned to the notebooks and his own frustrations. Of the many things he had deciphered in his feverish marathon study was that the alien intelligence was, indeed, a global community, a singular consciousness perpetrated among many entities, and that Geoffrey's sudden telepathy was a byproduct of sorts of how this singular consciousness communicated. The doctor rightly surmised that when Mr. Reynolds opened Geoffrey's mind for telepathic communication, he had also opened his mind for communication with other humans as well. The telepathy was one-way at the moment, but perhaps his ability to would spread to others as it had been spread to him. Only time would tell. One thing was for sure, though, this was how the alien intelligence communicated. The notebook indicated that the more the alien consciousness communicated to its host subordinates, the stronger that communication became. One of many things that was eerily unsettling was that the aliens shared many similarities with the human masses of Earth.

Just like us, their bodies were comprised of the same material as their home planet, though that planet was of different material than ours. There were millions of them, but they had infinitely more in common than otherwise. They had already shown that they were intelligent beings, but, the way information was spread was a major difference. The doctor wanted to believe this, but his logical mind advised otherwise. The most abundant amount of information today was spread by light, spanning limitless gulfs via endless miles of ever increasing technologies like fiber optic cables. Also, the doctor remembered learning somewhere that the structure of houses, trees, the very earth itself, everything, absorbed energy, even the energy of speech. Long ago, it had been proven that sounds, music, words; all were comprised of notes that had actual physical properties. One need look no further than the proverbial song-shattered wine glass for proof of physical properties of sound waves. Only fairly recently, someone had discovered that such energy could also be captured in physical objects. With the right instruments, ones, unfortunately, that current technology was insufficient to produce, the words of every human being throughout the ages could be 'recaptured' from tree bark or mountain stones, and every single word ever spoken could be replayed for all to hear.

By the same vein, it was nearly proven among scientists, some of them astronomers like the late Dr. Reynolds, that the origins of the universe could be traced back to actual sound waves. Dr. Crangler mused over this until he finally fell asleep on the simple pull out bed in his office.

A full week after he last visited her room, Dr. Crangler, with an equally haggard look and gait as he had before, went to check on Delilah.

"Wow…you look *horrible!*" She exclaimed to him when he entered. "Man, you really do look…" Delilah's eyes were wide and her mouth was pulled slightly to the side in a grimace as she looked the doctor up and down.

She had been at least as sullen as Dr. Crangler for the last week, but the good doctor really did look awfully…"bad." Even though shooting for something less dramatic, it was the only word Delilah could think of to describe how Dr. Crangler looked at the moment. He looked so bad, in fact, that she was tempted to feel sorry for him, but the temptation was very brief and paled in comparison to her own anxiety. Her spirits had been broken since their last meeting. She had resolved some time ago that though she would go through with this pregnancy—the idea still tied her stomach in knots since it looked like her only hope of escape.

Her lips and jaw muscles were set like her mother would've approved of, her arms were folded in defiance, and her eyes drawn and sparkling with intensity that was anything but affection. She was prepared to concede defeat, but not without inflicting some mortal wounds of her own if at all possible. Still, for all her insolent posture, she and Dr. Crangler were both broken people trying to appear whole. Even though they were both shielded from the plague ravishing the outside world, it was clear that the effects of this alien invasion were taking their toll on them as well, and just as harshly. Meanwhile, Dr. Crangler gazed around Delilah's room. It was, by far, more colorfully stocked than any of the other rooms in the facility, but by the looks of things, not much new had been added since the doctor last visited. It was something of a shock to the doctor because, though he by no means condoned it, he had fully expected Delilah to have summarily converted even his newest assistants into her fretful minions by now.

Just goes to show how utterly discombobulated I've been lately, he thought to himself. Even though he had her, Geoffrey, and virtually every square inch of the facility on his monitors for round the clock observation if he desired, he had been paying no more attention to them than if they were a million miles away. His mind was too occupied with other things, and what's more, he craved freedom from the stress associated with both Geoffrey and Little Miss Obstinate sitting here before him with her arms and legs crossed. He walked around the room, sighing deeply, as he feigned disapproval at the small but new assortment of products, hair care, and makeup vials that populated a dresser and night stand. He feigned disapproval as eloquently as his face would allow, but in reality, he was exhausted, mentally and physically, and he didn't want to be there. If he quit there would be serious disciplinary measures. Years of time and perhaps hundreds of millions, of secretly-allotted taxpayer dollars had been funneled into this facility as well as Dr. Crangler's training.

His entire career, his schooling, his knowledge of highly-classified matters, none of it would ever be allowed to be made public. If he was ousted, he would drop instantly from one of the most preeminent and privileged doctors in the world, to a middle-aged nobody. He would be forced to start from less than scratch. More importantly, he would be ousted from ground zero of one of the most important times in human history. Though Dr. Crangler knew this well and needed nobody to tell him, his superiors had made their position—as well as his own vulnerability—very clear. There was no time for nervous breakdowns, not now, not with everything dangling dangerously in the balance. If he couldn't do his job, then those superiors would damn well recruit someone who could, and he'd pay the price for it for the rest of his life. It was this express truth that encouraged him to leave the messy, musty solitude of his main office and get back to work. Right now, he needed some blood from Delilah and to run some simple tests to verify again that she was healthy.

This constant testing was superfluous really, but again, his superiors wanted to make certain that she wouldn't fall over dead from anything that could've been prevented if it had been detected earlier. After Dr. Crangler displayed his disapproval at Delilah's apparent expertise at rule breaking, he summoned a few of his assistants to draw the necessary blood, measure vital signs, and do whatever other simple tasks needed to be performed. Usually, he would've done this himself, but right now he was thinking about how best to approach the real issue at hand. Before, the subject was a barb that he used to bludgeon Delilah into broken spirited submission, but now, it was just another lengthy and arduous hurdle that he hated to scale nearly as much as she.

"Miss Hanson," the doctor said wearily after his assistants had finished and left the room "I spoke to you last time about…"

"Yeah, yeah, I know *Doctor* Crangler," she hissed, "I need to get pregnant. I *know* you know that I heard you last time." She tried to give the doctor the most fiery gaze possible, "Well, I'll give you what you want," she sounded as if she was bequeathing some dirty, unbecoming favor, "but afterwards, I want the hell out of here, is that understood?" The doctor's gaze temporarily flared. *Who does this…this…spoiled little girl think she is, leveraging demands on me like I'm one of her obedient little servants from back home?* He decided he didn't have the energy for a pissing contest, at least not right now.

"Yeah, yeah, whatever, Miss Hanson. Whatever you say."

"You're damn right, whatever I say." she countered, pressing her perceived advantage, "And another thing, I choose who I get pregnant by. I'm not having just any fool's baby. You won't go out there, wherever you go to, and pick just anybody you want to for me to…Ugh!" She couldn't even finish the thought. It was more than obvious that she would've been a real pain in the ass had she been born when arranged marriages were the accepted norm. "Anyway, I choose the guy."

"I'm sorry, Miss Hanson," the doctor said, though his tone didn't match his assertion, "but I'm afraid it doesn't work like that. You'll be artificially inseminated with…" he paused. He didn't want to risk another outburst. "a specimen from a donor that has been thoroughly tested and is completely free from disease or defect."

"What? You must be crazy. You tell me I have to get pregnant and then you think that I'm gonna let you in…in…"

"Inseminate you, Miss Hanson."

She scoffed. "Whatever. You actually think I'm gonna let you do *that* to me with somebody's sperm," well, so much for the doctor's earlier tact, "that I don't even know." She looked appalled at the idea. "Well, you're highly mistaken. If I do this, *I* choose the person, or I at least get to see who's chosen…" she thought about it for a moment "no, you know what, I choose the guy altogether."

The doctor sighed so deeply that she envisioned him sighing his very spirit from his body. He was more tired than ever. "Okay, Miss Hanson. Whatever you want. We'll have eligible contestants shipped directly to your door in neatly wrapped packages in no time." He threw his hand in the air as if dismissing her from his mind as he turned and stormed out. She could hear him scoffing.

Delilah was just about to shoot back that if he wanted to be sarcastic, he could have this damn baby himself, but she didn't get the opportunity because he was already exiting the room.

"I choose how this happens!" she yelled as he disappeared.

The doctor murmured to himself as he shuffled heavily down the hallway, "Yeah, I wish I could say the same."

Chapter 21

Before his last visit, it had been a full week since Delilah had laid eyes on the doctor, but by the time Geoffrey saw Dr. Crangler again, nearly two weeks had passed, and those two weeks had seemed like an eternity. It was already difficult being deprived of all human interaction except the doctor's and his orderlies, but with every passing day the loneliness grew exponentially. Geoffrey began to feel as if the white walls were closing in on him, as if this was what a hell of eternal nothingness must feel like. It was during this time that the doctor made his unannounced appearance, but, thanks to Geoffrey's new abilities, it was not completely a surprise. Before the locking mechanism unlatched, Geoffrey already knew who was at the door…as well as what he was thinking. Still, when the doctor entered the room, neither man spoke for almost five minutes. Eventually, Dr. Crangler opened his mouth, but it was Geoffrey who first broke the tense silence.

"Yes, Dr. Crangler, I *can* still hear what you're thinking, and yes, I *do* know that you're as worn out as you look, and believe me, you do look extremely worn out."

Upon hearing this, the doctor slumped his shoulders even more than they were already. He didn't want to deal with this, but what could he do? Slowly, tiredly, he tottered nearer to Geoffrey. Geoffrey, meanwhile, gestured for the doctor to have a seat across from him in a simple folding chair that was recently added to the room.

"Yes, I see your room has one or two new…furnishings," he was going to add *that I didn't approve of*, but decided against it. Normally, he was the head guy in charge, the top authority, and took great pains to make sure no one forgot it. These days, though, he was just no longer himself, and he didn't know when, or if, his old self would ever return.

"Well, you would've seen, you *do* have like a thousand monitors right there in that nice main office of yours, except your mind has been pretty…well…*busy* lately. Anyway, it's not much." Geoffrey said,. "Nothing like all the colorful stuff Delilah has in *her* room, per se. But hey, beggars can't be choosers, right?" Geoffrey's tone held no hint of sarcasm or anger. In fact, he sounded as if he was simply making a few unemotional observations.

Dr. Crangler was anything but unemotional. His eyes and mouth were wide open with amazement and even a touch of ill-restrained fear, so much so, that even Geoffrey was startled. He had never seen the doctor, never even imagined that he could look, so unprofessionally *human*.

"You...how...*what*?" the doctor sputtered.

"Why don't you have a seat, Dr. Crangler?" Geoffrey gestured toward the folding chair a second time. The doctor was about to decline the offer yet again, but Geoffrey interrupted. "You might as well sit down, Doctor. I already know what you're thinking, obviously, so there's no need for you to keep up the facade any longer." The doctor's eyes were as large as fifty cent pieces and the tightly stretched lines around his mouth said that he was more apprehensive than ever. "That's right," Geoffrey continued, unabated, "I can now hear you, and everyone else, even in your big office at the end of this maze of hallways...and yes, even behind that thick, steel door of yours." Geoffrey paused to let the statement sink in. "Oh, and by the way, the movie was X-Men." The doctor's eyes narrowed and he canted his head back a little as his angst was replaced by confusion. "The movie you thought you may've seen, the one where you got the idea that the steel door to your office could block telepathy, it was X-Men, the sequel I think, but don't quote me on that, though. Magneto got his hands on a steel helmet to block Professor Xavier's telepathy. It's been years since I've seen that movie, and actually, the only reason I remember it at all is because you were trying *not* to think about it. You know exactly what I'm talking about, Dr. Crangler." Geoffrey said, "And what's more, I'm probably the only person in this whole facility that knows what you're going through. Try to think of it like that, instead of intruding into your thoughts, I mean really know what you're going through, because I can tell how it feels to *you*."

Geoffrey gestured again at the seat, and this time, the doctor obliged. Although reluctantly, he recognized the validity of Geoffrey's argument. He was just too exhausted to 'keep up the facade' as Geoffrey had so eloquently put it. He sat down heavily on the narrow seat of the foldout chair, raised his reddened, weary eyes to Geoffrey's and let out a deep sigh that said more than any combination of words would've ever done. Another lengthy silence ensued, and this time, it was the doctor who finally broke the quiet.

"Well, for what it's worth, you shouldn't feel too bad about your situation, Geoffrey. I'm not in a room like this all day, but, except for my brief outings, mostly to the complex's kitchens, of which you probably already know about, I'd suppose, I'm in this facility for the vast majority of my day…" the doctor mused for a moment, "of my life, actually." He paused, "Which brings me to the fact that, like you, I, too, am being monitored every hour of the day." Dr. Crangler motioned toward the hidden camera. "Which means that, unfortunately, I can't be seen idle talking with you like this for too much longer. The powers that be already think that I'm not fit for the job anymore, and it certainly wouldn't look good for me to be confiding or taking advice from a patient, even if that patient can read minds, and probably especially since that patient can read minds."

"Which brings *me* to something I've been wanting to test out. Something I think may help both our situations. Actually, the more I think about it—and believe me I've had *nothing* but plenty of time to think around here—I think it could be a big help. It may even be the answer, or at least part of it, that could bring everything together. But I should probably warn you, it's going to take some faith on your part, and it at first it's going to be a little…*different* to experience." Dr. Crangler hadn't a clue what to make of Geoffrey's vaguely expressed idea, but at this last admission, he thought he may understand; and he wasn't quite sure he wanted anything to do with it. Even if Geoffrey wasn't able to read Doctor Crangler's mind, he would've still been able to read the newly surfaced trepidation on his face. "Listen, Dr. Crangler, I won't shit you. What you think I'm talking about is what I'm talking about, and it won't be fun at first. In fact, if you're anything like me, it's going to be damn scary at first, but I really think it could help things move along here. In fact, I really can't see any other way."

He looked at the doctor for a moment, hoping that his sincerity was evident, before he continued, "Look, you know I can hear your thoughts, and by that alone, I know something of what you're up against, what happens if you fail. I know what has to happen with Delilah and I think I can help. Besides, what could it hurt to give it a try? It would seem as if we're all on the losing end of a full scale intergalactic war anyway, right?" Geoffrey gave the doctor another silent moment to think it over. "I've experienced it and it didn't hurt me, at least as far as I know. It was definitely a new experience, but it didn't hurt me, and if I'm correct, it won't hurt you either. And if I'm right, it may even change you like it changed me." At this the doctor's ill-restrained look of concern gradually changed to fascination. Before this period in his professional life, he would've never given a moment's consideration to what he knew Geoffrey was proposing, but now, with all that had been weighing him down, it was, at least, an option.

After seeming to consider Geoffrey's as yet unspoken proposition, the doctor abruptly stood, scolded his patient for nearly luring him into his auspices, signed to the camera for the room's door to be electronically opened, and disappeared into the hallway outside. The lock latched back into place noisily behind him. Geoffrey showed no surprise. He turned away from the camera so that the assistants wouldn't see the lack of surprise on his face. He sat like this, turned away from the camera, until the sound of the heavy door's lock again filled the room some time later and Dr. Crangler returned. "If you can still read my mind, then you already know what all that was about."

"Yes, I *can* still read your mind, Doctor, and yes, I *do* know what all that was about." He *could* and *did*, and because of it, he knew even before Dr. Crangler bolted from the folding chair so unceremoniously, that he had just put on an elaborate but necessary show for the spectators watching. If Dr. Crangler's superiors saw him breaking down and taking advice from one of his patients, it certainly wouldn't bode well for him. After he left the room, Dr. Crangler had his assistants temporarily disable the camera, under the pretense that he intended to interrogate Geoffrey in private for his insolence. In another odd turn of events, the doctor's recently highly unusual behavior helped aid his plan more than he could've ever anticipated. When his superiors got word some time later that he had ordered the monitoring of one of his star patients temporarily halted, which was completely unheard of, considering recorded footage of the two patients could yield an invaluable edge in this war against The Virus, they naturally assumed he had taken their ultimatum very seriously and was doing whatever it took to get results. No one, from the assistants to the superiors, suspected that something very different was taking place between Geoffrey and Dr. Crangler.

"Okay, are you ready, Dr. Crangler?" asked Geoffrey, poised as if ready to strike the doctor with a bolt of lightning (which, as the doctor was about to find out, was not far from the truth).

"Y-yes." The Dr. Crangler stammered. He took a deep breath, trying to steady himself.

This was his facility. He had performed procedures not only on humans but also alien life forms that would've aroused the professional envy of just about any other doctor on the face of the planet. As such, his pride would not allow him to show Geoffrey the whimpering, frightened child that was just behind the cool facade that he was struggling desperately to maintain. Geoffrey knew all this, but he also knew that what he was about to do was similar to the childbirth that the doctor was trying to elicit from Delilah. There was no way to truly be prepared for such a monumental event. Besides, Geoffrey knew that if he didn't test this experiment now, the doctor may lose heart later and he would be stuck alone in his damned room for another two weeks before he caught sight of any living human being besides the assistants who took care of him.

"Should we hold hands, I mean, should there be physical contact involved?" Dr. Crangler asked, still trying not to sound like a frightened adolescent.

Geoffrey smiled faintly. "You know, Doctor," he answered, "one of the benefits of being around somebody who can read your mind is that you don't have to fake it like you're not scared. And no, I don't think physical contact has much to do with it. Mr. Reynolds certainly didn't hold my hands. But, whatever, let's get started. Just one piece of advice, though, like I said, it's going to be very *interesting* at first, so just remind yourself of that and try not to panic." Dr. Crangler nodded his head and waited. Geoffrey closed his eyes tight and almost immediately, something like television or radio static filled the doctor's head. Just as Geoffrey had warned, it was, indeed, interesting. The experience of having foreign sound projected into his head, not his ears, but into his very brain, was enough to cause the usually reposed doctor to clasp his head frantically with his hands, just as Geoffrey had back at his first experience. The static sound was not loud, but rather unnervingly clear, since it was not being filtered through physical eardrums. The sound was as clear in the doctor's head as his own thoughts, which made it all the more surreal. It was as if his brain had been hijacked and made to play a tape of unknown origins.

After a few seconds, Geoffrey opened his eyes, and grabbed Dr. Crangler's hands, simultaneously stopping him from assaulting his cranium and halting him from jumping out of his seat in panic. The static sound stopped immediately, and the doctor quickly calmed and refocused his eyes. "I told you it would be new," said Geoffrey, "But take a moment and feel. Are you hurting anywhere?" The doctor took a moment, and found that he wasn't hurting. He thought that he was hurting a moment earlier, having an outside influence penetrate the wiring of his brain must have caused it to send mixed signals to his body, but now, he felt fine: A little shaken, but otherwise, okay.

"All right, we're going to try it again, Dr. Crangler. Hey, you got it good I think. Mr. Reynolds damn sure didn't give me time to get used to it."

"Why does it sound like static in my head?" the doctor interrupted.

"I don't know, really. I'm involved I guess, but I'm not what you call an expert on this thing. It was the same way with me at first, though. I learned from my father that the body's senses work off electrical impulses or something like that. I'm sure you'd know more about that than I would, and so do radios and televisions. I think it's like that, the signal trying to become clear or something." Geoffrey shrugged his shoulders. The doctor nodded during the explanation. Afterward, he watched Geoffrey thoughtfully. He was impressed; Geoffrey's theorem sounded plausible.

"So, you ready to try again, Doctor?"

"No." the doctor answered truthfully, then bowed his head so he could concentrate on staying calm.

Geoffrey didn't close his eyes this time, but the static sound returned to Dr. Crangler's head nonetheless. Now that the doctor was better prepared and much calmer, he noticed that the sound was not quite static, at least, not erratic white noise. It had an organization to it, a vague underlying pattern that was becoming clearer with every passing moment. Gradually, that pattern became like a voice. Then that voice, something like words.

Then a phrase, a repeating phrase—"Cnn ya err e ow...cnn ya err e ow...can ya ear me ow...can you ear me ow...can you hear me now?" The doctor smiled, despite himself.

"Good," the soundless voice answered into his head "Very good. I see that you can understand me. I was skeptical about whether this would work or not."

"Well, it does work." The doctor answered aloud. "But, let's talk the old fashioned way for a moment. I think I'm going to need a little while longer to get used to this."

"Fully understandable. I wish I had had time to acclimate to the situation more thoroughly myself."

Dr. Crangler gave his patient a wry look. The strangely accurate explanation of what the static from earlier may've been, the sudden proficiency of vocabulary, could this transformation actually be making Geoffrey...*smarter*? "I don't know, Doctor." Geoffrey answered the unspoken inquiry. "I certainly have been thinking more, I don't know...clearly, than I usually do lately, but I figured it may just be the stimulus sterile environment. You know, you can learn a little about yourself when this is all you have to look at all day." Geoffrey motioned around him.

"When did this new ability come? As if it weren't phenomenal enough that you can read thoughts, you can *project* them now as well?" the doctor asked. He still looked haggard and worn. Geoffrey's telepathy was amazing, but even it wasn't able to give the doctor another desperately-needed shave and shower. At least the curious glisten of discovery was returning to his weathered eyes.

"Well, it didn't really come to me, per se. I kind of worked on it. It's not like I have much else to do here, you know. And so I focused on hearing what was in my head a little better, and after about a week...I'm assuming it was a week, I don't know how long it was, really...or so, it actually worked. You heard how the words I projected to you became gradually easier to understand? It was like that. Like when you hear a faint, foreign sound in your house, if you sit still and be really quiet, you can hear it better. Well, I guess that's what I've been doing, sitting still—for a really long time—and listening really hard."

Dr. Crangler recalled the image on his monitors of Geoffrey squinting and massaging his temples in concentration. Before he could halt it, the thought crossed his mind of what *else* Geoffrey may be able to do with a little more time to practice, and it sent an involuntary cringe through his body. There were new abilities that stood to be unlocked, myriads of dormant areas of the brain that no longer had to remain unusable. It would usher in a new horizon for the human race, but there was no way to estimate the price that would need to be paid for such a game-changing breakthrough.

"I agree completely." Geoffrey answered, even though the doctor had posed no audible question. "With everyone reading everyone else's minds, all of us speaking the same mental language, what would separate us from the aliens? We'd have a global community…just like they, we'd be able to share all known information instantly…just like they, and then eventually, we wouldn't see any reason not to try to conquer other areas of the universe…just like they."

"Perhaps," the doctor conceded, "but we wouldn't be simply different bodies, hosting a single super brain…like they."

"As you say, perhaps. Only perhaps. If every human on the planet was of the same accord, wouldn't that make us of a single mind, a single great consciousness? Back to the Tower of Babel, and all that sort of thing? And, as I

230

recall, *that* didn't end all that well." Geoffrey watched the doctor as the same old apprehension from before returned. "But we don't have to think about that now. We have a more pressing issue on our hands: This other patient of yours, Delilah. I know she's already told you that the only way she'll cooperate is if she chooses the guy. Well, perhaps, with this special new skill set of mine," he didn't sound as if he was certain he was prepared to assume this kind of responsibility. "maybe, just maybe, I can help persuade her."

The doctor furrowed his brow at Geoffrey for a moment, then his mouth curled up beneath his unshaven growth of mustache, into a faint grin. "I see." He eventually said, "And certainly it wouldn't hurt for you to *persuade* her in your direction, which would be much easier seeing as how you would be able to know everything she's thinking, right?"

Geoffrey chuckled. "And why not? Do you have a better idea? If this girl is anything like you think of her, she could easily make an already complicated situation even more difficult. Unfortunately, you need her to cooperate for this. You can't sedate her and impregnate her because it would affect the process, and you can't keep her sedated even if you could impregnate her because the child would be affected by whatever drugs you put into her system, and you need this baby to be a healthy as possible if you're going to get this cure from its blood. And even that's a maybe."

Dr. Crangler was in better control of himself now, but not so much that he wasn't clearly shocked that Geoffrey could be privy to information so well guarded that even his own assistants didn't know it. All it took was a little thought to remind him that Geoffrey was capable of knowing anything he knew, or at least knowing *that* he knew it. There was no reason to adamantly deny the fact and call the mere assumption utter foolishness, as he would've definitely done had it been any other person addressing him like this. There was no need to deny it, though it stung more than a little for him to feel like he no longer had the upper hand. At least it didn't appear as if Geoffrey was trying to abuse his suddenly-elevated importance. Besides, as much as the doctor hated to admit it, Geoffrey was right about everything including the assumption that there appeared to be no other choice. Dr. Crangler reluctantly agreed to hatch a plan that may finally move mankind's hope for survival along.

"Well, you know what they say, Doc, communication is the key, so the first thing we have to work on is..."

"Yeah, I know." Dr. Crangler interrupted, "Let's just get started so we can get this over with. I'm a doctor so I'm much more comfortable with me working inside people's bodies, than the other way around, so this is going to take some getting used to."

"Yeah, I would think so. But don't think that this is like child's play or something to me either. This is all very new to me too. But, anyway, like you said, let's just get things started so we can get this over with…"

And so they began.

Chapter 22

When the two star patients first met, it was a grand event. Geoffrey was excited because he had not seen a woman or anything colorful for several long months now, and seeing both at the same time was a simply ecstatic moment. Delilah was pleased because she hadn't seen anyone who wasn't a professional in this strange institution. For the moment, they seemed pleased to see how things played out from here.

Dr. Crangler began to introduce Geoffrey, "Delilah, this is…"

"My name is Geoffrey, but most people just call me Geoffrey." The patient interrupted. Dr. Crangler frowned. He didn't know what Geoffrey was doing. He could only hope that the other did. He was the mind reader, after all. It didn't take long before it became evident that Geoffrey knew what he was doing. Though Delilah was elated to see someone who was obviously not one of the professional residents in the facility, she tried not to show it, but with Geoffrey's completely ridiculous introduction, she couldn't help but giggle. It was refreshing to have something to giggle about. Afterward, Geoffrey asked the doctor to leave them alone for a while so they could get acquainted. Unfortunately, though, Dr. Crangler couldn't agree to that idea just yet. Delilah was the personification of a VIP right now, with all hopes of civilization resting upon her well–being. The doctor's superiors may bend on a few things, but they would raise holy hell if the doctor left her alone, unattended, unprotected, with another patient.

Every one of the assistants who had come in contact with Delilah at any time had first been put through a battery of tests themselves for contagious diseases or viruses, as well as a full battery of psychological tests for otherwise dangerous tendencies as well as extensive criminal background checks as a prerequisite to working in this top secret facility. Everyone had been thoroughly checked out before being allowed within a few square miles of Delilah, except for Geoffrey. In all the chaos, no one had exhaustively probed his background and mental conditions. If they found out that the doctor had taken such a risk letting Geoffrey near her, heads would fly, perhaps literally. At the very least, it would allow him to transfer this woman's constant bickering into someone else's corner for a while. Dr. Crangler gathered his assistants in a far corner of the room where he was sure Delilah couldn't hear them, and whispered a directive to them. Both of them looked at him strangely. "Are you sure you want *him*." One of the assistants asked, warily.

"He's been cleared for the facility," another assistant observed, "but I'm not sure he's clear to come in *here*."

"*I'll* clear him." The doctor returned indignantly. He felt as if his two patients were slowly wrangling power from his hands, and he couldn't bear to have his subordinates doing the same. "Now, just go get him. You're here to follow my orders, not question them." He barked. The assistants quickly left the room to complete the errand. By this time, they were well familiar with the doctor's outbursts, especially when what he was commanding was completely out of the question.

"That guy is a real dick and somebody's ass is gonna get chewed, but as long as it's his and not mine, who cares?" One assistant mumbled to the other as they trudged down the hall. Meanwhile, Geoffrey, back in the room, now alone with Delilah and Dr. Crangler, chuckled to himself.

"What's funny?" Delilah asked, assuring Geoffrey with a look that whatever he was laughing at, it better not be about her.

"Nothing, nothing. Dr. Crangler's minions are just thinking about how much they truly like him."

Delilah's face furrowed, "How the hell do you know what they were thinking?"

"All right people," Dr. Crangler broke in quickly, "here's what's going to happen. A colleague of sorts will be here shortly. He's going to sit here with the two of you for a while, while you get acquainted."

"Why?" asked Delilah, with considerable irritation in her own voice. "What are we getting acquainted for?" The heat in her voice rose with every word. Already, she had planted her hands on her hips as she assumed her battle ready posture.

"Well, Miss Hanson," the doctor answered coolly "you were adamant about wanting to choose a specimen donor for yourself."

"You mean that *this*…that *he*…" she shouted.

"What he means," Geoffrey interrupted, yet again, "is that I have been brought here to assist you. I am here to help you in whatever way you see fit. Dr. Crangler's assistants don't really understand what it's like to be kept prisoner here, not able to get your hair done properly, not able to get decent skin treatments, why, I bet your feet haven't been scrubbed and manicured in what, forever?"

"That's right. My poor feet *haven't* been touched in forever." Delilah answered. It was amazing to see such a drastic change take place so quickly with the aid of just a few prudent observations. "And you can get me the things I need?" she asked. Her tone was almost pleading now.

Geoffrey seemed to mull things over for a moment, but in reality, he was listening to unvoiced thoughts. "Well," he said at last "I'm not excessively experienced with pedicures and tanning techniques and such, but I do know how to serve, and I'm sure I could learn the rest if given enough time—and it would seem that time is the one thing we have plenty of, here." He smiled at Delilah sweetly, and though it was highly unorthodox for her, she returned the gesture. She was taking to this stranger pretty well, which was saying a lot considering that she spent the last few days preparing for mortal combat with anyone who would make the unlucky choice of crossing her the wrong way. There was something about this guy, something she couldn't quite place just yet. What he said, how he held himself, the way he looked at her, even the tone of his voice, it was all so mysteriously on point, like there was some connection between them.

"Can the proper arrangements be made Dr. Crangler," asked Geoffrey, turning in that direction, "so I can attend to Miss Hanson here, on a regular basis? That is," he turned back to Delilah now, "that is, if she's willing to give me a shot, of course."

"I'll try you out." She answered politely, then looked abashed as she realized how easily such a statement could misinterpreted. "What I mean is…"

"No worries. I'm the one working on a trial basis here. If there's any embarrassment, it'll be coming from my direction, thank you very much." The same warm smiled followed, but it wasn't returned as quickly as before. Delilah was temporarily offended that she had been interrupted, even if it was in the name of modesty.

"I'm terribly sorry for interrupting, Miss Hanson," Geoffrey answered, "I'm just a little nervous. I haven't seen a pretty woman in quite some time." Delilah smiled broadly. Geoffrey must've said something right.

"Just don't let it happen again." She jested, still smiling.

"So, Dr. Crangler," resumed Geoffrey, turning his attention to the doctor again, "can you arrange it?"

Dr. Crangler, who had been looking on curiously, was speechless. He never imagined this fire-breathing female patient of his could be handled so well. He was convinced that cooperation was not something she was ever acquainted with, but fifteen minutes with a total stranger and she was cooperating in a childlike manner that months and months of stressful interaction with the doctor could never produce. Dr. Crangler looked on at Delilah for a long second, trying to decide if the real Delilah, the one that made his life a living hell every opportunity she got, had somehow been abducted, and replaced with an elaborate clone.

"Dr. Crangler?" Geoffrey beckoned the awestruck doctor.

Dr. Crangler quickly caught himself and thought about the question at hand. All that Geoffrey was proposing, everything he had just told Delilah, was strictly forbidden in this facility, but then again, many of the things she had in her room while the doctor was occupied elsewhere, were likewise prohibited. Besides, Geoffrey seemed to know what he was doing. If nothing else, he was already having a more profound effect on Delilah than the doctor or any of his assistants. What other real choice did he have?

"It may take some time, but I'll see what I can do." He answered. Just then, the sound of the door lock interrupted the procession.

"Well hello, General." Dr. Crangler said to the visitor who was, at that moment, marching through the doorway. He was the largest man Delilah had ever laid eyes on. The man looked like he routinely swallowed normal sized men whole, digesting one at each bicep, another two at each thigh, and two in his neck. He was a mammoth, and though Delilah clearly heard the doctor refer to him as 'General', she was sure he was some kind of steroid-binging football player, or celebrity body guard. As far as the latter assumption went, she was mostly correct, because he was here to guard her. Dr. Crangler introduced Delilah and Lieutenant Dan as the lieutenant general extended his hand. Delilah reluctantly extended her own, mostly because she didn't want this guy to think she was scared of him. Even as frightened as she was, her mother had taught her to bow to no man, especially if there weren't massive amounts of money to be had in the process. Not even the ardent admonition from her dead mother could keep her from wincing in anticipation of the crushing she was sure her hand was about to suffer. Luckily for her, the new stranger apparently knew how to curb his great strength, because he was as gentle with Delilah's delicate and slightly shaking hand as a man a fraction of his size. His grip was much firmer than any other Delilah had experienced, but nothing like what she feared.

She was so relieved to have her hand intact once the shake was over, that she wanted to thank Lieutenant Dan, but thought better of it.

"I will be sitting with you, Miss Hanson, whenever Mr. Summons is present." Lieutenant Dan's voice bellowed, though he tried to lower his voice so he wouldn't startle his young female charge. Delilah nodded that she understood. She was familiar with body guards, though never anyone like him. The lieutenant general marched to a modest wooden chair that Dr. Crangler had set up for him during this brief exchange. The chair was noticeably too small for the lieutenant general, but if he was uncomfortable, neither his face nor posture betrayed it. Palms planted on his upper thighs and elbows tucked tightly to his side, he sat with his back ramrod straight against the chair's slight backing. Once he situated himself, he gazed straight ahead and didn't move a muscle. Delilah wasn't even sure he was breathing.

Wow, this guy is the real thing. He'd definitely put those stuffy-looking guys in Britain or London or wherever, that guard whatever that place is, to shame. She thought. Just as the thought passed her mind, Geoffrey chuckled, then quickly coughed as if something was stuck in his throat. Delilah thought nothing of it until she looked in his direction to ask him something. She noticed a look just leaving his face that looked like he had done or said something that he immediately wished he hadn't. *Must be that nervousness*, she thought, and though she didn't see it, a look of relief crossed Geoffrey's face.

Finally, Delilah asked him the question that was on her mind, "Are you dangerous or something? Is that why this guy is here? Cause if you're dangerous, you should know that I am in no mood to be screwed with." She tried to sound as threatening as possible.

"I assure you, Miss Hanson, I pose you no danger. Lieutenant Dan is here because you're a very important person and a lot of people just want to make sure you're well taken care of." He gave another warm smile, "I'm sure you're used to people being around to make sure you're safe."

"I am," answered Delilah, as if to say, *you'd better believe it, buddy*.

Dr. Crangler was still dumbfounded at Geoffrey's instant progress with his wayward female patient. She even allowed Geoffrey to assume a seat beside her on the leather couch that she was now sitting on.

Now, the doctor finally spoke up. "I will be monitoring you as usual, so if I am needed, you can just summon me from where you are." He said, "Otherwise, the lieutenant general will be here to keep watch over things, and I will return later to escort you back to your room, Geoffrey." With that, the doctor gestured to the room's camera and the heavy room door unlocked and opened. The doctor disappeared down the hall as Delilah looked on. Except for the three occupants, the room was empty now, and everyone sat silently, with Delilah trying to make heads or tails of the tree trunk of man stationed to 'guard' her, as well as the new stranger that she was apparently supposed to make friends with, and Geoffrey probing Delilah's mind in an effort to discern what the next move should be. Lieutenant Dan, as unmoved as ever, looked like a stone sentry that could breathe death upon anyone living at the flick of an eyelash.

Even when Dr. Crangler returned to one of his smaller offices to watch the scene on a monitor, everyone stayed in the same position. "Let's hope you know what you're doing, Geoffrey ole' boy." he whispered to himself. Only time would tell.

Chapter 23

From the first day, Geoffrey's experiment with Delilah promised to be a wild success. He seemed to have a way with the normally-rebellious vixen that no one else could command. Technically, he didn't *command* her; no one, not even a stranger as perfect as this one was, seemed to be able to do that, but if she didn't respect him as a superior, she certainly saw him as the closest thing to an equal, at least in most areas. It didn't escape her notice, however, that every now and then, a certain frown or slight smile graced his lips, and always, suspiciously, after a random thought had just crossed her mind. Other than that, everything went smoothly, and even those incidents waned in time. There did seem to be a connection, however vague, but a correlation nonetheless, between how she felt or what she was thinking, and a corresponding change in Geoffrey's immediate behavior. *It must be all in my head*, she told herself. After all, there was no way for a guy to know what was going on inside her. No, she had simply been in this place way too long and it was beginning to weigh on her senses.

Meanwhile, Dr. Crangler escorted Geoffrey back to his own room late every evening and back to Delilah's room early each morning. It was during these escorts that the doctor grilled his patient on exactly how things were progressing with Delilah.

"Well, she's certainly opening up to me," Geoffrey informed the greatly-concerned doctor, "and she has already made up in her head that she'll go through with this pregnancy thing because she thinks it's her best hope of escape from this place. Other than that, she's a little suspicious at times, about my *abilities*."

"She knows about the telepathy?" Dr. Crangler's eyebrows shot up in surprise. When they came down, he was frowning. Aside from Geoffrey, only the doctor knew of his patient's capabilities, and he wanted very much to keep it that way. If his superiors ever caught wind of what Geoffrey could do, they would certainly want him tested and experimented on until there was nothing left of him but a used shell. Besides the fact that he was a living, breathing human being, and not one of the alien life forms on which the doctor had already experimented on to no avail, he was also Dr. Crangler's only real hope of progress now. As is too often the case, the people in charge who watch from positions of safety and comfort, demand substantial results at every turn as if those results are simple matters. Dr. Crangler and his associates, the ones in the actual thick of things, knew all too well that such results could not be simply concocted like a magic brew in a witch's cauldron. There were variables that had to be worked out before any lasting results could materialize, and if anyone found out that about Geoffrey's telepathy, those variables would instantly increase a hundred fold. If Delilah found out, it would destroy any progress that had been made in that arena, so it was imperative that no one found out Geoffrey's secret.

"Does she know?" Dr. Crangler asked again, a single step away from hysteria now. Geoffrey simply looked on, relishing the doctor's rising angst for a brief moment. How many hours had he spent in his whitened room on the verge and beyond hysteria? How many days was he trapped in this place, away from family, friends, and familiarity, without so much as a hint as to when, if ever, all of this was to come to an end? When Geoffrey saw telepathically in the doctor's panic, he about to give Geoffrey a good shaking and assault the answer out of him, he thought it best to not toy with the doctor any longer, even if it was only fair.

"No, she doesn't know," Geoffrey at last answered, just as the doctor grabbed Geoffrey's shoulders. The relief on Dr. Crangler's face was evident until Geoffrey finished, "at least, not yet, anyway."

"What does *that* mean?" It was difficult for Dr. Crangler to keep his voice at a normal pitch.

"It means that sometimes, not too often, but sometimes, she suspects that something isn't quite…right." Geoffrey answered. Even if Geoffrey couldn't have read the doctor's mind, it would've still been abundantly clear on his face what he was about to ask, "And what does *that* mean?"

Geoffrey answered before the words filled the doctor's mouth, "It means that her mind is not like yours or your assistants', or even mine for that matter. It's like a funhouse of mirrors in that girl's head. Thoughts disappear without warning, other thoughts change instantly for no foreseeable reason. Man, I don't think *she* knows what she's thinking half the time. I remember my father telling me a long time ago that some scientists got together and performed a bunch of research and tests and found out that girls and boys are different. You know, fundamentally different, down to the very neuron organization in their brains. I remember thinking at the time that that was the very personification of stupidity. These were supposed to be the world's most capable minds and they had to spend millions of taxpayer dollars to compile research and run tests to find out that guys and girls are different? It was stupidity, if ever I've seen it. But now, I guess I can see their point, because, trust me Dr.

Crangler, you'll never know just *how* different guys and girls are until you can see into a female's brain. I don't know if every one of them is like that, but that one," he gestured back toward Delilah's room, "her mind is like a very elaborate, changing maze that has no discernible route or exit. Sure, I can read her enough to maybe gain her trust, but to really understand her..." Geoffrey shrugged his shoulders helplessly.

The two had made it back to Geoffrey's room door by this time, but Dr. Crangler didn't lift a gesture to one of the cameras lining the hall for the door to be opened, as he usually did. Instead, he moved closer to Geoffrey. "All right," he whispered, "so you're telepathic *and* a philosopher, but that still doesn't answer my question. What do you mean, she hasn't found out *yet*? And how are you planning to move along with this? I don't think I need to remind you that I need to begin the procedure as soon as possible, or trust *me*, there will be seriously ramifications." Geoffrey saw in the doctor's mind that he meant not only his superiors, but also the ravished world outside. The ravished world outside...it had almost become an afterthought to Geoffrey and Delilah. Shielded as they were behind bunker doors and beneath ever-working Cleaning Lights, they had almost forgotten that countless scores of women around the world were being literally ripped apart by overgrown, unborn children who were not being birthed by nature's usual dictates, and that this was happening every day. What's more, since The Virus saw to it that mother and child (or children) all died even if the child was cut out before the mother's belly, the death toll was now well in the millions. In the coming months, The Virus promised only more casualties, until not a newborn or childbearing woman was left on the entire face of the planet.

Reminded of this truth, Geoffrey chided himself for wasting time having fun at the doctor's expense. "All right, I do have an idea I think will help keep Delilah oblivious to my telepathy and speed up the procedure." Dr. Crangler, or course, was all ears, but it was not his *ears* which Geoffrey had in mind. "But first," Geoffrey continued, "I can see that you don't want to talk in my room because of the camera, but aren't there cameras out here as well?"

Well past shock at his patient's ability to know what was going through his mind, Dr. Crangler answered, "There are, but they're spaced out far from each other and the microphones have a hard time picking up voices at certain places, but all the walls are soundproof, so it's much easier to pick up sounds in closed rooms…" Dr. Crangler thought for moment, "but shouldn't you already know that? Is Delilah's brain really that cluttered, that it's scrambling yours?"

Geoffrey had to chuckle at this, because, though such was not the case, it would've otherwise been quite plausible. "Well, Dr. Crangler, I'll just say this: Any man who thinks or claims that he knows a woman's mind completely, is highly mistaken. *Highly* mistaken. But, no, it's not that. I can read your thoughts, but I can't precisely read your mind per se. What I mean is, I can't hear or see your memories or how you're feeling, only what you're thinking at any given moment. So, since you weren't thinking about the camera in the hall at that moment, I didn't know about them."

"Really?" Dr. Crangler mused aloud. Geoffrey knew what he was thinking; he was happy that at least something in his head was still secret.

"I agree, Doc." Geoffrey answered, though the doctor hadn't said anything. "But let me tell you, this ain't easy for me either. It's exciting sometimes, but other than that, it's scary being able to hear what other people are thinking. It's savage what people think when they know that no one else is listening. I mean, really weird stuff. And I've got enough weird stuff of my own to try to sort through without other people's thoughts filling my head. And then women's minds…that's a whole other story altogether." Geoffrey was trailing off the subject again. "But, more importantly," he resumed "I have another plan. I think we did pretty well with that little experiment of ours, with me projecting my thoughts into your head. I'm not willing to try that on anyone else, but I think we should practice it until we perfect it. If I can communicate with you telepathically, it won't matter where we are, no one else will hear. I can inform you of everything that's going on as it happens and nobody else, including the head guys, will ever find out. And just as importantly, I can tell you what Delilah is thinking and what will help us move things along."

The doctor agreed. "Speaking of which," Geoffrey continued, "I think I'm gonna need a few things right away if we're gonna keep the ole' girl in there happy."

"And what might that be?" Dr. Crangler asked, skeptically.

"Well, for now, a tutorial on how to do pedicures, manicures, and hairstyling, and then a few other things I'll tell you I need when I find out myself."

As Geoffrey listened to the doctor's thoughts, both he and the doctor looked confused. Geoffrey couldn't understand what the doctor was thinking, precisely because the doctor didn't rightly know himself. It would seem that he was flabbergasted by his patient's latest and most outrageous request.

He opened his mouth to speak, but Geoffrey broke in, "Listen, you said that the hall cameras can't pick up our voices, but they can still tape us, correct?" Dr. Crangler nodded. "All right, well maybe we should go ahead into my room and start with the practice. There'll be no way for them to know what we're doing, but I can see that you don't think my request will be too sane, and if we stay out here talking about it much longer, it's going to look suspicious. Once I can project my thoughts into your head more smoothly and establish communication that way, we won't need to talk like this anymore. You can just think what you want me to hear, and I can just project what I want to say into your mind."

"Yes." Dr. Crangler didn't sound overly excited about the prospect "I guess that would be the best way." The doctor gave the signal to the nearest hall camera for Geoffrey's door to be opened. The two entered and began the highly-unorthodox practice of soundless conversation. Meanwhile, topside, thousands, hundreds of thousands, millions more were losing their lives in writhing agony from which there was still no cure. At least half of the these numbers had only experienced life outside the womb for a few brief seconds, but for all involved, it was a slow, mercilessly excruciating demise. Many more would follow this burning path of distress and death, until two men, one a doctor and the other a captive patient, could figure out how to get a young woman, another captive patient with an insatiable thirst for freedom, pregnant with a child whose pure blood would provide the only possible chance of relief to a world in desperate need of it.

No one knew what was taking place on the alien planet from which the hateful Virus originated. Was the alien super-consciousness filling its subordinate bodies with laughter at the sight of so much human carnage being wreaked without it having to do anything? Was it looking on unemotionally, as a human might after crushing an anthill and watching the swarming masses scamper to the surface, the greater number having been already smashed into oblivion, only to be likewise crushed themselves? Maybe the alien entity wasn't watching at all, content to let The Virus do its job, leaving Earth in a matter of a few short years, as far as space time goes, completely devoid of all human life, and ready to be re-inhabited or whatever else the alien consciousness may have in mind. Nothing was for sure, and among the things that were not for sure, was if Geoffrey, in an effort to find companionship in this bleak situation, and at the same time, help thwart an alien assault, was inadvertently becoming more alien himself. If he could spread his telepathic powers on to the doctor, wouldn't that bring the human race to within even closer similarity to the alien intelligence? Wouldn't linking human minds in so intimate a fashion eventually yield something of a singular worldwide consciousness? These were not questions to be entertained just yet— the *real* aliens were the important thing now— but the day would come not too far in the future, when they would have to be answered. But again, not just yet.

Chapter 24

It took about three days of lengthy hours of practice for Geoffrey to become reasonably proficient in, and for Dr. Crangler to become reasonably relaxed with, communication that was completely devoid of audible words. Of course, the doctor couldn't project his thoughts, but Geoffrey could read them, and project his own thoughts, so the communication was sealed. Now, the patient and doctor could talk without ever speaking a word and, especially as Geoffrey's proficiency grew, not even be in the same room to do so. It was directly after this line of communication had been established that the doctor granted Geoffrey a television set and the tutorials he had requested earlier. According to Geoffrey, the best way to keep Delilah cooperative was to keep her happy. He explained to the doctor that the neurological pathways of Delilah's brain were such that if she was not relevantly reminded of certain things, certain luxuries she had been surrounded by her entire life, then her brain would trigger stress hormones to be released cause her to be a certified pain in the ass for anyone who had to deal with her.

When Dr. Crangler asked Geoffrey how he knew of these neurological pathways, considering that he had told the doctor that he simply heard thoughts, Geoffrey looked perturbed. After taking a moment to think, he explained that, as he had said, Delilah's brain was drastically different from the doctor's, any of his assistants', or any man's, for that matter. The best way Geoffrey knew to explain it was when he heard the doctor's thoughts, he saw them as well. However, just as he didn't hear them with his natural senses, he didn't see them by that mechanism either. There was no way to explain what the sound of them or the sight of them was like, but when he saw words, the thoughts of a man's mind, it was as if they were coming off of narrow highways and being continually fed to the mouth, where they would come out as audible speech or dissipate unspoken. Now, in Geoffrey's experience, a man's thoughts materialized from only a few narrow highway paths, but Delilah's thoughts were fed into the forefront of her brain from many, many highway paths, at rapid speeds, and often resulted in massive traffic wrecks. However, when Geoffrey initially mentioned manicures and pedicures to her, and afterward, when they had discussed her life before her capture, it was as if these highway paths ran much more smoothly and without nearly as many jams and wrecks. Geoffrey imagined these many converging highways as neurological pathways, and if that was so, then Delilah's thoughts and thus her cooperation, could only be gained by comforts with which she was familiar.

Dr. Crangler nodded after his explanation. *Interestingly enough, what you've just described in perfect detail is what we think of as the reward system. In most cases, it served as a survival function, during the release of dopamine and endorphins when doing necessary things such as eating, fighting, and exercising. It also breeds drug dependence because they trigger the rapid release of those pleasure chemicals. The thing about neurological pathways is that, like regular highways, they can have grooves worn into them from years of use and the brain permanently associates lasting pleasure with the repeated experience. Just like an addict's brain, if Delilah isn't getting those pleasure chemicals, she could be experiencing symptoms of withdrawal, which would explain why she is being...difficult.*

As Dr. Crangler looked on at his patient, still trying to keep his other thoughts shielded, he recalled Geoffrey's suddenly expanded vocabulary, how he had taken to referring to him as 'doc' lately as if they were lifelong friends, his escalation from mind reader to mind speaker, and now this. Geoffrey's brain was evolving somehow, he was becoming much smarter at a geometric rate. Given enough time, there was no telling what he'd be able to do or figure out…like how to escape. Still, this was a concern that could not be dealt with at the moment. Many such concerns 'that could not be entertained at the moment,' had been piling up as of late and even though Dr. Crangler felt deep in his gut that there was nothing he could do about it, he also knew that these concerns and questions *would* resurface eventually, and when they did, there would be hell to pay.

Dr. Crangler and Geoffrey arrived at Geoffrey's room door. The tutorials Geoffrey had requested were waiting for him. Dr. Crangler gestured to the hall camera and left his patient in his room. The conversation they had just had had been completely unspoken, so even if the hall cameras could record their voices, there were no voices to record. The only audible sound, in fact, was the sound of the doctor mumbling to himself as he trudged down the hall to his office. He didn't even realize he was doing it, but he was musing aloud that time was more of the essence than it had ever been. It wouldn't be long before Geoffrey was completely beyond his control, and with that revelation, he knew Delilah had to be impregnated *now*. The child she would bear was more important than anything else. Everything hinged on it. Dr. Crangler was not a praying man, he relied on scientific evidence, medical procedures, and his own extensive knowledge, but he was closer than he'd ever been in his life to pleading to the high heavens for help.

The next day, he escorted Geoffrey to Delilah's room just as before and retreated to one of his smaller offices to monitor them. Lieutenant Dan looked on as well, positioned in the same absurdly erect posture as before. Besides his initial greeting to the two patients, he didn't open his mouth to speak a word the entire day. Meanwhile, Geoffrey cleaned, clipped, and filed the nails and cuticles on Delilah's hands and feet. Dr. Crangler was not experienced with such pleasantries, but even a novice like he could tell Geoffrey had nearly mastered the tutorials that were given to him, even though he had only had a matter of hours to review and study them. Dr. Crangler managed to secure all the necessary tools for the job and Geoffrey now used those tools with such familiarity, moved from nail to nail and task to task with such smoothness, that it appeared as if he had been doing this for years. Geoffrey spent more than a few hours at his new job as Delilah reclined in her chair, obviously enjoying every moment of her indulgence. At Geoffrey's suggestion, more lavish treatments followed and within a little over a week's time, he had learned to style hair, perform skin treatments, give a full body massage, and nearly every other delicacy that would warm a woman's heart. By the end of that week, Delilah looked nothing like the woman the doctor and his assistants had grown used to.

She had never been ugly, but as she wasted away in this secret facility for months on end without the feminine luxuries and servitudes that filled the bulk of her days before her capture, she had lost much of her carefully-tended luster. Her skin had suffered from lack of natural sunlight, her figure, from lack of appetite, and her teeth color, from the lack of expensive whitening treatments. Now, she was had nearly returned to the old Delilah, the Delilah who knew nothing of hideous skin blemishes, or less-than-perfectly white teeth, or, God forbid, split ends. It would take a little more than a week to return her back to her former glory, but even now she was a sight to see. Her prominent cheek bones seemed to support her newly-sparkling eyes like lightly-bronzed pillars, her hair hung loftily, concealing much of her face, and showering the rest in thin, glistening black strains of elegance. Despite himself, Dr. Crangler was quite amazed as he looked on from his monitor. Even he was forced to admit that this young woman had real beauty.

She even allowed Geoffrey to wax her long legs. Though her thighs and calves were in need of exercise and sunlight, they were still a comely sight, by far better than many other women's legs. Dr. Crangler thought that he may've even seen the lieutenant general flinch as he caught a glimpse of her once Geoffrey had finished. There was still important work to be done, as the doctor implicitly reminded Geoffrey at the week's end.

And 1 wholeheartedly agree. Geoffrey answered soundlessly to the doctor, still in office, after his latest session with Delilah. *And I think it's time. 1 think she's ready.* He continued. *But 1 need one last thing.*

And what would that be, Geoffrey? the doctor asked suspiciously, not willing to concede any further requests until the procedure was at least initiated.

She's already agreed to be impregnated, as she still thinks it will guarantee her release, but 1 just want one day, a single day, that's all, to discuss something with her.

1 ask again, and what would that be, Geoffrey?

There was a brief telepathic silence before Geoffrey continued, *1 just want one day to discuss with her how she is impregnated.*

1 thought that was the case, Geoffrey, ole' boy. 1 thought it all along...but then, I suppose you knew that?

1 did, but can you blame me? You, your assistants, Lieutenant Dan, everyone in this God-forsaken facility has the choice to leave and get a break from this place. Dr. Crangler frowned. *Even if you don't use it. That's your choice.* Geoffrey answered, foreseeing what the doctor was about to say. *But Delilah and 1 don't even have a choice in the matter.* Geoffrey telepathic tone became more serious, *Dr. Crangler, hear me out. I've been down here for what feels like years, I haven't seen or heard from the only family I have, my father. I don't even know if he's alive. And, until now, I haven't even been allowed any human interaction except with you and your assistants, and no offense, but you're not the most lively bunch. I mean, everything has been taken away from me. I had a career and an apartment and a life. Neither it nor the apartment was much of anything, I'll concede, but it was mine, but all of that was stolen from me the moment I set foot on that helicopter. Not to mention all the craziness I've seen right here. I've seen in your thoughts that it's pandemonium all across the world right now, and soon, there may not even be a world to get back to.*

Geoffrey took a moment to let what he was saying sink in. *Now, I've cooperated fully the entire time I've been here. I haven't given you or your staff any real trouble, and now I finally have an opportunity to have at least some kind of relief. I mean, damn, Dr. Crangler, even murderers get conjugal visits. Besides, you've already run all kinds of blood tests on me when I first got here, so you know if I'm clean or not. And if I did check out—which I can see in your thoughts that I did—then why not? Now that I think about it, it would be fitting if I could father the child. I mean besides the fact that I don't deny that I want to do this for the same reason that any other man would. You've seen, Delilah, it's not like she's ugly, look at everything that's been taken from me, including my freedom. Why shouldn't I be the one to father this child? Believe me, children were the absolute last thing on my mind before I came here, but considering that there are millions of guys up there that are watching their kids dies ruthless deaths, I think I'd like someone to carry on my name, now. When Delilah is impregnated, no matter how it happens, I will have helped make it happen, so why shouldn't I be involved in it?*

Geoffrey wanted to say so much more, but he didn't know what, if anything, could be added. He'd been rambling already. Dr. Crangler genuinely sympathized with his patient. He recognized the validity of everything he'd said, and knew Geoffrey was right. He did check out, and according to the same tests that the other specimen donors underwent, he was as good as any for the procedure. In actuality, he may've even been slightly better, since his sperm count would be much higher considering that he hadn't been allowed to engage in any sexual activity at all. He couldn't even masturbate, not with cameras watching his every move, for many long months. Even though the doctor was ready to allow this request as well, it was not because sympathy, but rather fear: Fear of what Geoffrey might do if he was denied. Dr. Crangler had no doubt whatsoever that his patient could use his telepathy for more nefarious means than simple, good old-fashioned sex, and if it wasn't forced on him to find out from experience, then the doctor certainly wouldn't invite it heedlessly.

Just one day. <u>Only</u> one day, and then we begin the procedure. There's no telling if she'll just go along with this, no matter how good you are at these spa treatments of yours. Speaking of which, how do you propose to convince Delilah of this little scheme of yours in the first place?

Well, that's the thing, answered Geoffrey, in the doctor's head, *I haven't had an opportunity, like the one you gave her, to leave the facility for a day. I'd like to have that opportunity and I'd like to use it as a date with her.* The doctor was frowning again. *It's only fair, Doc. How many months have I been here? And how many times have I been allowed a trip in the mirror truck? That's right, zip, none. Look, I'm not trying to escape. I don't like throwing it in your face, but I can read minds. If I really wanted to make a break for it, it's not like I couldn't find a way. I mean, if you or your assistants know the security systems, then <u>I</u> know them. Not to mention the information I get from Lieutenant Dan that he doesn't even know I'm getting.* Dr. Crangler's frown deepened, until he let out an exasperated sigh (the only audible part of this whole conversation), as he knew Geoffrey was right. *No, I'm not trying to escape or usurp your authority or anything like that. I know what's at stake here and I have as* *much to lose from the end of the world as you or anyone else. This is my planet too. I'm just trying to get a few freedoms and not go crazy down here in the process.*

So, what exactly are you asking?

Just a day out in the mirror truck with Delilah, with no guards in the back with us. You can send as many people as you want with us, just have them up front in the cab of the truck. I think things would go a lot better without Lieutenant Dan and his faithful minions around. That's it. Maybe set us up with some food and perhaps a little wine to have while we ride, and that's it. If she doesn't go for it after that, then do whatever you want and I'll provide as much assistance as I can, and I won't ask for anything else.

I'm going to take some time to think about it, Geoffrey. That's all I can tell you right now.

Well, we both know there's not much time. You'll let me know one way or the other by tomorrow?

"Tomorrow." Dr. Crangler conceded aloud and left the room. He had already made up his mind, but he still wanted some privacy to figure out a few things. He left quickly and skirted down the hallway. As much as he didn't want to think about it, he would have to run this past his superiors. He could perhaps get a few things past their ever-prying eyes, but to allow both patients out of the facility and off the premises, especially with the chaos that was ensuing outside, would definitely cost him his head if he didn't ask, and immediately, since things could wait no longer. It would seem as though the unbridled fun would never end for poor ole' Dr. Crangler.

Chapter 25

After enduring hours of exhausting deliberations and questioning, Dr. Crangler finally managed to convince his superiors to allow Geoffrey's and Delilah's little field trip. As the two lucky shut-ins were about to find out, the world outside was very different than what they remembered and because of this, Dr. Crangler's bosses were initially very reluctant to approve of this little outing. In fact, it was only after the doctor had spent nearly all his breath convincing them that Geoffrey and Delilah had formed such a bond that should this request be granted, she promised to render her full cooperation henceforth. Of course, such was not the case, but it was the best argument the doctor could think of on such short notice, and this was only after the commission overseeing the doctor had strictly stipulated that the mirror truck was to be led as well followed by an armed consortium, all headed solely by Lieutenant Dan himself.

When Dr. Crangler arrived at Geoffrey's room the following morning, it was with news that Geoffrey desperately wanted to hear. "But be absolutely assured Geoffrey…" the doctor began seriously.

"Yeah, yeah, I know. I only get this one day, and if things don't go as I planned, then bright and early tomorrow you start the procedure."

"That's absolutely right. No more games."

"I assure you, Dr. Crangler, this has been no game for anyone, especially me, but I do understand...I'll make today count."

With that, Geoffrey and Delilah were ushered to a waiting mirror truck followed and preceded by at least four armored vehicles, and filled with heavily-armed officers operating under the lieutenant general's command. Delilah wasn't nearly as distracted this time as she had been the last, so she got a good look at the grounds under which the secret facility she was being held was housed. It was like a small city. She saw what looked like a small power station and water treatment plant in the distance. A large building with plenty of windows, and a near-constant influx of people, most in uniform, some not, but many holding what appeared to be Styrofoam food containers—an industrial-sized kitchen, perhaps—loomed nearby. She also noticed that directly above the secret underground facility was a large, normal-looking brick building. There were a few other nearly-identical buildings here and there, off in the distance. She wondered to herself if secret facilities—and possibly other captives, who, like her, had been stolen from family, friends, and life as they knew it—likewise sat beneath those buildings.

She and Geoffrey were in the large, vacated cargo area of the mirror truck, alone, with Lieutenant Dan and another man, both heavily-armed and talking into small, black two-way radios, up front in the truck's cabin. A round table had been bolted to the floor nearly in the middle of the space where Geoffrey and Delilah were, and a checkered embroidered cloth covered it. Delilah turned to Geoffrey and was about to ask him what he made of the facility and everything, when she noticed that he was cupping his ears and his eyes were drawn tightly shut. Lieutenant Dan and his man up front were giving orders, but they were barely audible. *What in the world could Geoffrey be hearing*, she thought. "Are you all right?" she asked, with some alarm.

"Huh?" Geoffrey shouted, as if he was forced to yell above the roar of the phantom noise.

"Are you all right?" she asked again, this time much louder.

"Yeah, I'm fine." He didn't sound like it, he was still yelling. "I just haven't been outside in a very long time and I guess I just need to, I don't know, adjust."

This didn't really make sense to Delilah but then again, a lot of things stopped making sense a long time ago, so she just continued to look around her until the truck finally pulled off and out of the facility. As soon as the truck cleared the heavily-barred and guarded triple gates of the complex, Delilah noticed that all she could see of the entire miniature city was a very thick and high concrete embankment that was overgrown into obscurity by an equally thick growth of vines and brush. It took a little closer observation to realize that the growth was not random foliage, but a deliberate ruse to draw attention away from the fact that something very important was hidden just beyond it. She hadn't noticed this formidable barrier before, and as it looked relatively fresh, she thought that maybe it had been recently built. Then again, the last time she was out, her mind had been wholly occupied, so there was no telling if this was one of the many things she had simply failed to notice.

The phantom noise must've dissipated because Geoffrey seemed like his old self again. "Well, you look like you're feeling better." She observed.

"I do. I guess I've finished adjusting."

"Good, cause I don't know how you managed to convince The Warden," of course, she was referring to Dr. Crangler, "to let us out of solitary again. You can't imagine the hell I raised to get out the first time. But, like they told me last time, we should probably enjoy it. No telling when we'll be allowed out of our cells again."

Geoffrey inched closer to Delilah and lit a gentle hand on her own manicured one, "I'm already enjoying it, being out with you."

Delilah turned away demurely, but did not withdraw her hand, "I'm sure you say that to all the pretty girls that are the only ones you've seen in forever." Geoffrey chuckled gaily in a way that was obviously unscripted. It was good, especially considering the proposition that he intended to present a little later. An awkward, but blithely romantic moment of silence ensued, until Delilah again spoke up, "That table was definitely not here the last time. Is it for me? Because Dr. Crangler's little followers didn't bring me my lunch today like they usually do, and they're usually right on schedule. And I'm actually pretty hungry." Now, perhaps a year or so ago, Delilah would've never made an admission like this so blatantly, especially not to someone who she didn't know existed a couple of months ago. It was just not something a sophisticated, privileged, revered socialite such as herself would do, to admit so openly that she was starving. Somehow, after all she'd been through, at least this form of etiquette, if not others, was just not worth maintaining.

"You know what, I'm hungry too," answered Geoffrey, trying to match her zeal. "Let's see what we can do about that. You know, I happen to have a few connections." With that, Geoffrey tapped on the window between the bed and the cab of the truck.

Almost instantly, a booming voice filled the bed of the truck.

"Yes, Mr. Summons, is there a problem?" the voice was so loud and resounding that it felt to Delilah and Geoffrey as if it was vibrating into their bones. It was almost impossible to tell that it was Lieutenant Dan and not God Himself speaking.

"Well, there wasn't," Geoffrey answered, wincing in discomfort "but there is now…would you please turn down whatever speakers you have back here." There was a brief silence before the sound of screeching feedback, even more discomforting that the lieutenant general's godlike voice filled the rear of the mirror truck.

"My apologies, Mr. Summons and Miss Hanson. Is that better?" the voice, speaking at a much more agreeable volume, now asked.

"Yes, *much* better." Geoffrey and Delilah answered nearly in unison.

Geoffrey worked his pinky finger into his ear and yawned his jaw up and down until his ears popped and his normal hearing returned, before he spoke, "Yes, Lieutenant Dan, Dr. Crangler said it had been arranged for us to have something special to eat."

"Yes, Mr. Summons, and a bottle of champagne. Are you ready for those provisions?" It was easy to tell by the words he used that the lieutenant general was a ranking officer, probably more comfortable in a theater of war than surrounded by civilians.

"Yes, I think we are." Geoffrey answered.

The sound of Lieutenant Dan's voice, though not nearly as deafening as before, was still gutturally resonant—no reduction in volume on any speaker could alter that—as he answered, "It has been noted. The provisions will be with us shortly. Is there anything else, Mr. Summons?"

"No, I guess that'll be all." With that, and an audible click of the speaker, the brief conversation ended. Geoffrey watched through the miniature window as Lieutenant Dan said something into his two-way before resuming his gaze on the road ahead. Geoffrey was certain that the lieutenant general demanded the same extreme level of alertness from his comrades in the surrounding armored vehicles. The first legitimate telepath and the potential savior of the world beside him were well protected from danger, that much was for sure. Unfortunately for Delilah's previously-sheltered constitution, they had not protected her from the sights of the chaos that was characterizing the outside world. Shortly after the brief conversation between Geoffrey and Lieutenant Dan, the mirror truck rounded a corner leading into the outskirts of the city nearest to the military complex. Trash, debris, broken glass from the shattered windows and doors of businesses and other buildings, layered the landscape in thick, glistening folds like a heavy, dirty snowfall.

It's highly unlikely that Dr. Crangler would've approved, or Lieutenant Dan would've traversed the scene at all, except that it was the only road leading to where Geoffrey and Delilah were being taken for their scheduled outing. It looked like a war zone. This town, as well as virtually every other town on the planet, had been and still was, suffering the devastating effects of populations of people that gruesome death had darkened their lives and left them with no further reason to remain civilized. Mothers, daughters, granddaughters, sisters, wives, aunts, nieces—women of all walks of life, languages, and hues—had, along with their unborn and newborn children, been tragically and violently snatched from the land of the living by The Virus. Though he didn't realize it, it hadn't been a few months, but a little over a year since Geoffrey last laid eyes on the open world outside and beyond the secret facility where he was confined, and in that time, not only had countless women and children died, but they left behind millions of former boyfriends, fiancés, husbands—all who would've been new fathers—not to mention their own fathers, uncles, brothers, etc., every single one of them left grieving without anyone to turn to for answers.

Nearly overnight, pregnancy became a byword, a certified and unavoidable death sentence, and worse, a ruthlessly slow and violent death sentence. Things had taken an even worse turn when it was soon discovered that even if the fetus was aborted, the change The Virus had inspired in the female body meant that she would still die a slow death from asphyxiation as soon as her body discarded, or the remains of the killed fetus were taken from her preparing womb. As can only be expected, the act of sex itself took on a completely different connotation now. Who, besides the most base and death-craving women, would lay with a man, when it meant that she would be hazarding a slow and agonizing demise? Also, thanks to their Virus-altered biological functions, contraceptives were rendered useless, as none of the specialty medicines seemed to work anymore. Normally, contraceptives worked by manipulating or otherwise obstructing natural processes in a woman's body, but now that those processes had been drastically tainted, no pregnancy preventive treatment worked as it should. Condoms alone still retained their marginal effectiveness, but again, when her life was being risked in a much more real way than ever before, what woman in her right mind would wager upon a thin film of latex?

Members of the feminists federation would've had a field day—after all, weren't filthy minded, degrading, overreaching men, with their overinflated egos and underinflated penises, the very source of pregnancy? They would, were in not for the fact that it was women and their children who were suffering the brunt of The Virus's destructive prowess. In fact, many more women did, in the wake of all that was taking place, join the ranks of the man-hating feminists who desperately wanted to wear the proverbial pants of the world. To the suddenly swelled ranks of this consortium, the male population was demonized outright. Sperm banks were vandalized, burned, and destroyed, and the filthy males who contributed to them (as well as any other non-blood related male in sight) were all but assaulted, though many were indeed assaulted, and some even killed. The logic of these modestly-numbered but ardently-voiced women, was that if they drove away or at least stayed as far away as possible from men and their semen spewing genitalia they could distance themselves from the horrifying effects of The Virus. These women willingly and, in fact, eagerly turned a blind eye to the fact that they, like every other member of their sex, were already infected by The Virus, as could be clearly deduced by their unnaturally flaking skin and yellowed eyes.

Perhaps, if they didn't get pregnant, they wouldn't suffer gruesome deaths like many of their peers, but they, thanks to The Virus, still bore the potential for their demise irrevocably in their body, and would do so for the remainder of their days on the planet. To help them continue to turn a deaf ear and blind eye to this unsettling fact, many of them tried not only to avoid men, but to also avoid themselves as well. Not unlike their feminist counterparts, they were adamantly discontent with the lot that life (or, in this case, an alien consciousness) had chosen for them without their permission, and took every pain to avoid being reminded of it. Many of them buried themselves in bulky pants, long sleeves, and thick scarves to hide their shedding skin, if from no one else, then from themselves, and often wouldn't go near anything capable of casting a reflection that would give them full view of their discolored eyes. From many of the males they harassed as if they were the reason for all this carnage, their group earned the name the 'No More Mirror Movement' for their reluctance to acknowledge what could not be denied—that they, too, were infected. Whether they blamed men for it or not, they would've been laughed at for their childish behavior, except that what was happening to the human race, whether male or female, was no laughing matter.

How news of The Virus had leaked to the public in the first place was anybody's guess, but truthfully, not many people were surprised; with the instantaneousness of 21st century's global communication, there were no true secrets anymore, or if there were, they certainly didn't stay that way indefinitely. Also somehow leaked, was the rumor that the government had known of the alien life form from which The Virus came, for years. They had known and had done absolutely nothing to stop an impending attack. This added fury to the public's already bleak and maddening sadness, so much so that after the towns had been completely destroyed by constituents of all kinds, every government building and agency, no matter the purpose, was set upon next and destroyed. As Geoffrey and Delilah looked on now, wide eyed and mouthed, at what had become of the world they had both once known, they saw the destruction of despondent and confused souls but not the carnage-seeking masses themselves. Not a single person was to be seen anywhere as the mirror truck and its accompanying armed patrol vehicles cut their wide swath through the wreckage-cluttered streets and thoroughfares. They were all, nearly every single man, woman, and child not already claimed by The Virus, either in or headed to, the hearts of towns, setting ablaze police stations, armories, social security buildings, and courthouses, anything that reminded them of the government that failed to protect them.

The savagery was so bad that hostages were taken from some government buildings and tortured mercilessly for a perceived crime with which they had nothing to do. Police, responsible for maintaining safety and peace, were themselves deprived of those very luxuries, as they were pulled from squad cars and beaten to a gory pulp by the insane crowds. Of course, many officers gathered together to wage an offensive, but the public they were facing were not the rational thinking men and women of a former time. These were zombies that only closely resembled living, breathing human beings. In reality, the losses they suffered at the hands of The Virus had rendered them hollow shells, people as bloodthirsty as the undead. When officers were finally forced to open fire with live ammunition, they found that even real bullets were not a deterrent. What was it to a husband of many years to be shot down by an officer's gun when his wife and twins had just died slow, painful deaths, and right in front of his eyes? The firing barrels of shot guns held no discernible meaning for the son who knew that his pregnant sister, the only family he ever had, would soon face the same fate, also in front of his eyes, and there was absolutely nothing he could do about it.

No, firearms and the injuries they promised meant nothing now. In fact, most people welcomed death these days, and to those who didn't welcome death, it didn't matter, it was coming anyway. It was the same everywhere across the country and around the world. Luckily, Delilah and Geoffrey didn't see the roving crowd wreaking havoc at the heart of it, but they did see the bedlam left behind by that crowd, and it was nearly as ugly. The mirror truck continued on to its eventual destination, passing through the fringes of this town, as well as a nearby one, but everywhere, the scene was virtually the same. The specially-adapted cargo truck could've just as well driven around in endless circles and the views of yawning devastation would be no different. Everywhere, as far as the eye could see, buildings were destroyed. The larger ones that were yet standing bore an eerie resemblance to decayed human corpses, the structures eaten away at the fringes and every window completely obliterated, giving full views to interiors blackened beyond repair by the once insatiable flames that had consumed them. Only the largest buildings even survived. The smaller ones were mostly leveled to their very foundations. Stop signs, phone booths, traffic lights, everything that once represented order and civilization, now lay helplessly gnarled in the already-destroyed streets and yards. Some of the lights still flickered weakly as if they were crying out the remainder of their electrical energies; the only tears they could produce for what had happened to mankind.

Cars were everywhere in the wreckage. A rare few were unharmed and left unattended in streets and on sidewalks, doors ajar. It was obvious that the occupants had left in a hurry, but most were destroyed, or crumbled together in what had obviously been heinous and epic car wrecks. As Delilah looked on, aghast, at the sights around her, she was startled nearly to the point of wetting her pants, by a harsh thud and subsequent roar coming from the other side of the mirror truck. She turned instinctively, not knowing what to expect, but what she saw was a strange distortion of what looked like thick heat waves fighting to enter the glass. After a few seconds, her initial panic at the abrupt sound receded enough for her to recognize that what she was seeing was not a mirage, but rather torrents of water bathing the outside of the mirror truck. The torrent passed along the side of the cargo area of the truck as it continued to move on and then was gone. The back doors of the truck were of the same heavy glass as the sides, so Delilah saw clearly as the truck moved along, that a fire hydrant had been broken open and its powerfully dense spray was what assaulted the truck and caused her start.

As if I weren't scared enough, already! she thought to herself.

"I know, right. Sure scared the hell out of me too," answered Geoffrey.

Delilah turned to him, her face contorted in confusion. "What?" she asked.

Geoffrey answered quickly—too quickly, "Oh nothing, I was just thinking out loud." He looked like a young boy who got caught doing something he definitely shouldn't have been before he could catch it. He turned his face away, hopefully in time, and scanned the horizon. "It's gotten pretty bad out here, huh?" he asked, hoping to change the subject.

"Yeah...I guess it has." The brokenness in Delilah's wavering voice at all the atrocity she saw, was so profound, that, even though Geoffrey was relieved that his little slip up hadn't caused more damage, the gravity of the surrounding scene seemed to grow in his eyes as well. In the relatively short time that he had known Delilah, he had never seen her take what was happening to the rest of the world so seriously. Dr. Crangler would've borne out that conclusion as well. There was that fleeting moment of true realization much earlier, when Delilah heard from Doctor Crangler the awesome death that The Virus was inflicting on pregnant women, but other than that, Delilah had been shielded from the full reality at hand, and that, more than by the thick, steel barriers of the underground facility. Her life, her entire life, had been one of ease. Most people would have no way to properly assess such a world altering event as that which was currently happening, but Delilah even less so. As Geoffrey had already seen, the pathways of her brain had been conditioned to luxury and privilege, and there was no way for it to fully sink in that the entire planet, including the portions of it that she had seen in her reign of opulence, was suffering a blow from which it may well never recover. There was no way for that reality to sink in...not until now.

A person can imagine a thing, or read a book, or even see a graphic movie about it, but there was simply no rival to experience, cold, hard, one-on-one, physical experience, on which the mind could feed and the consciousness could absorb. For Delilah, this was that experience. Perhaps, this was the culmination of things destined from the beginning to usher her into a reality other than her own, or maybe her brain had finally had enough of mind-numbing excess. Maybe it was neither of those things, and no more than a coincidental fluke. Whatever it was, a change was being effected in her as she continued to look on at what had become of the world she once knew, a world she would never know again. Suddenly, escape didn't matter, seeing her father again didn't matter; pedicures, manicures, facials, none of it mattered. In fact, nothing mattered. Everything as far as her eyes could see, her mind could think, and her heart could feel, was only wasting destruction and debris. The world had spun off its axis and was careening wildly into the open recesses of space. Unhampered chaos had taken over.

She turned to Geoffrey, who had been looking at her with his head slightly cocked as if he was listening to something. His eye brows furrowed as if he was startled by whatever he was listening to. She buried her face in his shoulder, and did something she hadn't done since she was a very little girl. She cried. Delilah had never been the crying type. Her father would never find her bawling on the floor after a nasty spill, as was the case with most children. Instead, she would look at whatever she had fallen over or into for a while, as if to assess its formidability, then she would likely hit it or throw her hands up as if to ignore it. The sight of her as a toddler striking the floor she had fallen on rather than rolling on it, crying, was something Lenard soon became used to. It was a resilience she had inherited from her mother, and something that, also like her mother, would remain in her very makeup as long as there was warm blood in her veins. At least, that's what Lenard had thought, but if he could see his little girl now, assuming he was even still alive, he likely wouldn't have recognized her, sobbing violently and helplessly in the embraces of a relative stranger. However, this was not the same Delilah. Call it maturity, call it shock, but both the world and Delilah had undergone an irrevocable change. As is always the case with any truly irrevocable change, neither would ever be the same again.

Chapter 26

Delilah had been crying into the Geoffrey's chest so long that a well-defined portion of his shirt from shoulder to pants was now clinging to him, saturated. It didn't appear as if she was ready to finish any time soon. It was as if all the tears her inherited hardiness had not allowed her to shed over the years were finally being released in one long gush. Even though he was being all but drowned in that warm, torrential gush, Geoffrey made no effort to push Delilah away. In fact, he held her tighter as her body shook from uncontrollable sobs. He knew that this was a first for her, and with it, there came a first for him. For the first time since he had managed to scale the initial shock of his telepathic abilities, he tried *not* to hear the secret thoughts of others. In this case, 'others' meant Delilah. Listening to her thoughts while she was enduring such a genuine and profound upheaval just felt wrong to Geoffrey in a way that had never struck him before. He didn't need to listen in on her private thoughts to know that a once in a lifetime paradigm shift was taking place inside her, turning her and everything she held as truth, inside out, upside down, and every other contrary way possible. He felt that to be in her head now without her knowledge, was a violation, and especially at this very complicated and difficult junction in both of their lives, he wanted to leave her private thoughts her own.

As he held her torso against his own, her full breasts pressing against his chest, and being likewise soaked in a flood of tears, an erotic warmth pervaded his body. As he had already stipulated to Dr. Crangler, it had been an incredibly long time since he had seen, not to mention, held, a woman. All that time without interaction with the opposite sex made this experience now all the more potent. Strangely enough, though, another sense accompanied the natural arousal that Geoffrey was feeling, a purer, less sexually oriented sense that lay just beneath the surface. He had been rubbing Delilah's neck and upper back, but now, he took to stroking her thick, shimmering black curls with a gentle caress that was beyond that of simple eroticism. If he was indeed giving vent to something more than merely a year's worth of pent up sexual frustration, then Delilah certainly had more base things in mind, as was apparent when she finally stopped crying and, hesitantly, but nevertheless, resolutely, turned her tear-streaked face up to his. She had a sultry look in her eyes, and an inviting—no, demanding—pursing, was on her lips. With Delilah's makeup streaking dull colors beneath her reddened eyes, over her slightly swollen cheeks, and across her upturned chin, she may've not been completely fit to have a picture taken for one of the many fashion magazines that she had often sought for her daily dose of celebrity gossip, but as far as Geoffrey was concerned, she was as irresistible as he had ever seen her.

Prolonged confinement, especially in a place as devoid of excitement as the secret facility was, can have a profound effect on a person. Just as the cold, steel bars and concrete barriers of a prison facility can change a person in a way that nothing else can, so Delilah's imprisonment had changed her. She was much more receptive to Geoffrey than she had ever been with anyone else in her entire adult life, and though a large part of that cooperation had been inspired by his special abilities, much of it was from just a good old fashioned need for affection and friendship. Like Geoffrey, Delilah craved interaction with someone other than one of her captors, so when this young fellow captive showed up and was more than willing to supply her with all the attention and care she had so desperately missed, it was only natural for her to lower her guard. Still, it wasn't hard for Geoffrey to see the truth in Dr. Crangler's assertion that this young woman was the most difficult patient he had ever dealt with, by a large margin. In fact, just from her secret thoughts and open conversations, Geoffrey could tell that, as far as spoiled went, Delilah was the real thing. A luminary in her own right, and with an insanely wealthy father, Geoffrey could tell that this girl was not the type to take any shit from anyone, and had enough money that she didn't have to offer anything else to get whatever she wanted.

Now, she was offering her most important commodity—herself—and all of herself at that. She was like unspoiled waters to a man who had been roaming the deserts for days, ready at any moment to collapse from exhaustion and thirst. Geoffrey was that roamer, but now that he had found those crystal clear waters, it would seem that they were so awe inspiring that it was improper to just throw his entire head into the stream and dirty it with his lustful lapping as he had planned to do. Instead, and quite to his confusion, he wanted to cradle those waters securely in his outstretched hands and imbibe himself with the relief they promised in something closer to love and further from lust. These were the thoughts that unexpectedly flooded and filled Geoffrey's mind as he gazed down at Delilah's sumptuous lips. They were soft, longing lips, that promised great pleasures to the one granted the opportunity to handle them properly. It was as if her lips were the first pair Geoffrey had ever set eyes on, but for the life of him, Geoffrey could not ravish those lips with his own, as he would've done without a moment's hesitation an hour ago.

Instead, he stared into Delilah's gorgeous face, completely oblivious to the time and space around him, until she finally opened her eyes, wondering why in the world she hadn't been kissed passionately by now. The look on her face as she righted herself in her seat, was what ushered him back into reality. Her brow was knitted, not so much in discontent, as much as in confusion. She knew that, even without the aid of her normally routine beauty treatments, she was still a very attractive women, and she also knew (women just seemed to have an intuition about these things. Perhaps telepathy wasn't so new to the globe after all) that Geoffrey wanted her. Since their very first introduction, she knew that he wanted her, and that to have her was his primary motivation for all he did for her afterward. Not that she was complaining. As with many attractive women, she was used to the dirty desires of men and the benefits that flooded in with just the coy batting of an eyelash or the seductive flourishing of a hip, as a result of those desires.

Considering the circumstances, she had received a certified plethora of worthy benefits from this guy's desires. She had been pampered, appreciated, given skin treatments, hair styling, manicures, pedicures…Why in the hell did this guy seem to be an expert in everything she thought she needed, anyhow? Never mind that, the benefits were well welcomed. As Delilah's mother had taught her, this was one of the easier points of manipulation as far as men were concerned. Most times, that desire, that visual lust, that deep, hot craving to conquer, that infected most men's eyes and genitals, was such that a women need not ever actually give in, to plunder the spoils of courtship. In the right hands, or rather, within view of the right cleavage, most men could be milked completely dry with just a *suggestion* of sex. Again, a warm smile, fluttering eyelashes, a flare of the hips upon exiting—hell, just a relatively short skirt would do it for many men—and a well-trained woman could have the world hand delivered to her door and never have to part her legs to receive it.

"Men are dogs, Sweetheart," Delilah's mother had often said to her daughter, "we're here to take the leashes and make sure they get led and fed properly."

This was why Delilah was confused. She had rung the metaphorical dinner bell loud and long. There should've been an instant and ardent, if not violent, response by now. Was this guy saying that she wasn't good enough? Geoffrey had been looking on as these thoughts ran through Delilah's mind. He was still trying not to listen to her inner musings so he was more than a bit distracted, but as the confusion evident on Delilah's face begin to morph into real apprehension, he understood that, whatever she was thinking, if he didn't act now, his chance with her may be lost forever.

"Oh, I'm so sorry…I mean, I didn't…I wanted to…" Geoffrey stuttered and stammered badly, but, much to his relief, it produced a smile on Delilah's lips where a hard line had been forming. Also, like many attractive women, Delilah couldn't help but enjoy being able to reduce a grown man to a quivering faltering mass at a whim. It was intoxicating to be reminded that, even now, she still had it. Seeing the opportunity, Geoffrey decided not to foil things up with inane babble, and commanded his body to move forward, toward the still-smiling Delilah.

His body moved with much of the same stammer with which his tongue had moved earlier, but it did move. When he was again close enough to feel the heat from Delilah's body, he commanded his lips to approach hers. They too spluttered, but obeyed. When his lips at last made contact with Delilah's, it was not the sensation of a grown man kissing a grown woman, but more akin to the ecstasy of a high schooler's very first kiss, and his very first crush. It felt to Geoffrey like he had discovered feminine lips for the very first time, and it was an explosive experience. Her lips were as soft and warm as a familiar pillow, and it was only after a long while and the boom of Lieutenant Dan's voice, that Geoffrey realized that he had again lost track of space and time. He threw his head back and saw that Delilah, eyes closed in rapture, had been enjoying the exchange immensely as well.

"Please excuse the interruption, Mr. Summons." Lieutenant Dan's voice filled the room a second time.

"Yes?" Geoffrey answered, still gazing at Delilah.

"We are about to reach our destination, and your requested meal will be available shortly."

"Thank you very much." Geoffrey answered without much enthusiasm. A few moments earlier, he would have been grateful for the lieutenant general's interruption, since it would've interrupted a very awkward situation, but now...

Delilah must've sensed this, because she answered almost immediately, "It's okay, I'm really hungry anyway." The smile that had resurfaced on her lips was unmistakable. She had enjoyed the kiss as much as Geoffrey had. After a few moments, though, a question in her mind summoned her attention elsewhere. She looked around the cargo area of the truck where she and Geoffrey were. Of course, there was nothing to see besides the outside world, and *that* was something that Delilah would've liked to put away from her mind for as long as possible. She looked up toward the steel barrier that separated her and Geoffrey from Lieutenant Dan and his driving minion. There was no door, no means of direct physical interaction that she could see, only the small window, and it looked thick and unmovable. She looked at the barrier more carefully before grimacing. "Major Whatever up there says that our food will be ready soon, but how in the world is he going to get it to us?"

Geoffrey didn't need to ask what she meant. Both parties had been dully, adamantly, and, in Delilah's case, repeatedly, informed of a few strict and nonnegotiable mandates from Dr. Crangler that would be unwaveringly enforced by Lieutenant Dan and his men while they were out in the mirror truck. Among these mandates were the instructions that the mirror truck was *never* to make any unscheduled stops for *any* reason, and that the back door to the mirror truck was not to be opened for *any* reason, unless it was back at the heavily-guarded military complex. The mirror truck itself was also well guarded. Besides Lieutenant Dan and the highly-trained security detail at his disposal, the entire mirror truck was fully armored. All surfaces, including the huge one way mirrors themselves, were bulletproof, the tires were self-sealing. The gas tank was sealed against an explosion, the undercarriage was triple reinforced, etc. Dr. Crangler fully intended that Delilah and Geoffrey remain totally behind these safeguards for every second that they were not behind the armed guards back at the facility. In addition, everything about the mirror truck's armor was, just like the underground facility, completely state-of-the-art. Actually, many enhancements were years ahead of their time, since Dr. Crangler had had the opportunity to borrow from alien technology, just as he had with the Cleaning Lights.

Though one could easily understand the prudence in protecting the first permanent and observable telepath, as well as the very last woman on Earth left untouched by The Virus that alone was able to bear a child that may save every other child to come, there was at least one serious drawback to such airtight protection. There was no way to get food into the cargo area to the people who were eagerly awaiting it. Delilah probed the cargo area of the truck more carefully, but still found no indication of how anything might be transferred from the outside without opening the back double doors. The only piece of furniture in the back of the truck besides the bolted sofa that had been secured for its current occupants, was the equally bolted table, so it wasn't as if there were many things to look under or behind, but that didn't stop Delilah from scanning every nook and cranny, and finding, much to her chagrin, that there was no place by which anything could be handed into the truck from the outside.

She returned to her seat beside Geoffrey, exasperated. She didn't have time to be annoyed long, because soon the truck came to a smooth halt. Nearly two hours had passed since the truck had left the base, and now Geoffrey and Delilah found themselves under a medium sized bridge on what looked like an abandoned beach resort. The place where they were parked was only sand and water, but on either side, a little more than a quarter mile away, loomed rows and rows of all manner of eateries, hotels, condominiums, that would strongly suggest this was indeed a tourist area. Or rather, had been. Just as before, the smaller buildings had been mostly leveled and the larger ones were no more than scalded, windowless shells. There was a relatively strong breeze coming in off whatever ocean this beach straddled, and as that breeze blew through what was left of the buildings Delilah saw a few pockets of badly-charred debris and only God knew what else, wafting in the light wind like so much thick, black snow flurries. The larger and heavier remains of the large ruin, the stuff that the breeze could not pick up, but only moved around in eddying swirls, were everywhere. Both Delilah and Geoffrey had enjoyed their brief distraction from the destruction surrounding them on every side, but now that they had stopped, there was no avoiding the dire situation that demanded attention from every horizon.

"Why have we stopped?" Delilah asked to no one in particular. At least that's the way it would appear, because, though her question seemed directed at the only person it could be directed to—her fellow captive—her eyes were tracking something off in the distance. Geoffrey followed her gaze and soon found what she was staring at. The bridge under which the mirror truck was now sitting spanned a small gulf of water that separated the beach in halves. This inlet was about a hundred and fifty feet across, and the bridge that spanned it was about fifty feet further inland on either side. It was toward the other side of the inlet and under the bridge where Delilah, and now Geoffrey, were both staring. Five men, all covered from head to heel in completely camouflaged attire, were huddling near the edge of the inlet, so close that portions of their feet were partially in the water. The men were far enough away on the other side of the inlet that Delilah couldn't discern every detail of their dress, but close enough that she could tell with reasonable clarity most everything else. As such, she could tell that they were heaving something out of the water, but thanks to two of the men who were standing suspiciously between whatever was being dragged out of the water and Delilah's line of sight, she couldn't quite tell what was being recovered.

The camouflaged gear the men were wearing were identical to Lieutenant Dan's and the driver's. She continued to look on, craning her neck to steal any possible glimpse she could. That eagerness paid off, when, every now and then, one of the men moved an arm or a leg and Delilah craned her neck at just the right angle to catch a brief glimpse of what was being dragged. Her first glimpse gave her the impression of a thick, writhing snake, but it was attached to something larger that she could not see. She then caught a glimpse of what it was attached to, a large, misshapen bulk of some kind, but it wasn't good enough to make out what the bulk was either. The men dragged it further out to show thick tendrils that looked like a torn cloth streaming from it into the sand. One of these ripped pieces was longer than the rest and connected to something that was being dragged along separately by another of the men.

It was here that a vague image coalesced in Delilah's mind. It was even more terrifying than the dire destruction she had already beheld. The thought screamed in her mind that she should look away before she caught full view of what she was increasingly certain was being dragged from the water. She wanted to look away, needed to look away, even tried to look away, but simply couldn't. Something stronger than curiosity, stronger than dark fascination, held her gaze hostage. Whatever it was, it was as mysterious as what she was seeing, and just as powerful. Just then, as the men finally finished pulling the thing from the gently-swaying inlet currents, as if by some cosmic coincidence, one of the men who had been blocking Delilah's view, stepped unsteadily to the side, as if he was about to fall, and in the process, shoved the guy next to him to the side as well. The immediate result was that Delilah was given a gruesomely unobstructed view of what all the secrecy had been about. Instantly, she wished she had listened to her better reasoning and looked away before she had been given such a view. Geoffrey, who was even more intent upon the scene, gasped behind her, but she didn't hear it. She was too busy vomiting in the cargo area where they were.

By now, the men across the inlet who had broken formation scurried back into their circle, but of course, it was too late. The sight couldn't be unseen and the damage had been irrevocably done. The 'bulk' that Delilah had seen was actually the torso of a woman. The 'thick writhing snakes' were actually the woman legs, pulverized to jelly by her extended stay in the water. The 'tendrils' were neither that nor cloth, as they appeared. They were thick, torn shreds of human flesh. The longest 'tendril' of all was a still-connected umbilical cord. The unfortunate deceased woman had been pregnant way beyond the normal nine months because the second thing that had been dragged out separately, was a child nearly half the mother's size. It was clear that the mother had tried to cut the grossly overgrown unborn child out of her, and, in the process, had ripped her horribly gorged stomach into literal shreds before ending up in the drink. In fact, if the child's body had not been in the water, it would've certainly been covered in its mother's blood and womb fluid, even now. The worst part was that many millions had already succumbed to much the same horrific fate, and many more would follow.

Chapter 27

Delilah was still vomiting—or at least she would've been if she had had anything left in her stomach to vomit. She hadn't eaten in quite a while and her marathon crying spell from earlier had completely depleted her of fluids, so all she could do was double over on the sofa and heave in dry, violent spasms. She was so appalled by what she had seen that, even when she had initially vomited, she had completely neglected to hold her hair back from the ruinous spew. Luckily, Geoffrey held her long, styled locks carefully behind her downcast head. He had been trying not to listen in on her thoughts but without complete success, and, as such, he knew in advance that she was going to let loose. He also knew that she would've wanted her hair out of the way when she did. Holding her hair back, he was oblivious to the fact that he and she were currently the only two occupants in the mirror truck. Lieutenant Dan and the driver had exited the cab of the truck, and were now situated between the mirror truck and another armored vehicle that Geoffrey hadn't noticed before. Lieutenant Dan was nearest to the mirror truck, looking in every direction, presumably for any threat to the cargo that he had been assigned to protect. He held a very small, oddly shaped mechanism that Geoffrey couldn't see well.

Geoffrey looked at the driver and saw him take a shiny, plastic box that he was being handed from the armored vehicle. They took it in one hand back to the cab of the mirror truck. In the other hand, he, too, gripped a mechanism like the lieutenant general's. After he successfully deposited the plastic box, he returned for another and another. All the while, he maintained a steady grip on the strange weapon. Like Lieutenant Dan, he kept a wary eye upon the horizon. Looking around, Geoffrey was shocked to find many other equally-camouflaged men had flanked the rear of the truck and were watching things as diligently as Lieutenant Dan. Even with the full panoramic view of the mirror truck, Lieutenant Dan's men had moved into position with the stealth of ghosts. They all had similar, if not identical weapons, tightly grasped and ready for action. The armored trucks that had shadowed the truck since it left the base were positioned in a larger and looser circle around them.

For the first time since this whole thing started, Geoffrey felt a little less like a prisoner and vaguely like a head of state. To be certain, he and Delilah were still captives, but obviously very, very important captives. Of course, Dr. Crangler had informed them of this fact many times before, but he never really believed it until now. Once all the mystery boxes were loaded into the cab of the mirror truck, the driver gave a signal, and he and Lieutenant Dan reentered the cab. As soon as they were in, Geoffrey yelled to get the lieutenant general's attention through the small window separating them. "Yes, Mr. Summons?" Lieutenant Dan's deep bass voice answered from the invisible speakers in the rear of the truck. With a small exception, the entire rear of the truck was tinted but otherwise transparent; there was nowhere for speakers of any considerable size to be hidden. Just another derivative of alien technology, Geoffrey thought idly to himself.

Geoffrey answered, "We need some kind of cleanser back here," Delilah was not retching any longer, but she was still bent nearly double as if she could resume at any moment "and quick. Delilah has had an…an accident."

"What kind of accident, exactly, Mr. Summons?" Lieutenant Dan asked. It may've been Geoffrey's imagination, but he thought he heard the slightest hint of concern, possibly fear, in the lieutenant general's voice.

"Well," Geoffrey hesitated "she threw up…and by the looks of things, she may not have finished." He whispered as if he was sharing some dirty secret about Delilah and didn't want her to hear.

There was a brief silence, before Lieutenant Dan finally answered, "Try to stabilize Miss Hanson, Mr. Summons. I will secure some supplies."

"That's great, Lieutenant Dan, but she really needs to get out into the fresh air, and away from…" Geoffrey was in the process of advising, but it didn't matter because the lieutenant general was already out of the cab and headed for one of the armored vehicles surrounding the mirror truck. The lieutenant general spoke into his two-way radio, and apparently whichever subordinate he was speaking to informed him that what he was looking for was in a different armored vehicle than the one he was heading to, because the lieutenant general turned about face and marched toward one of the vehicles in front of the mirror truck.

"What's going on? Is someone coming to clean up this mess?" Delilah asked.

"Lieutenant Dan is on it right now. He's bringing some kind of special sawdust like stuff that'll absorb it and a towel so it can be cleaned up. And he should be here with everything any second."

Geoffrey had barely gotten the words past his lips, before, right on cue, the passenger door of the mirror truck's cab opened and Lieutenant Dan entered with one arm full of everything Geoffrey had just described and the other hand tightly holding his weapon. Thanks to Lieutenant Dan's train thoughts, Geoffrey had also learned the secret of just how anything could be transported to them without the rear doors being opened. Delilah looked on, simultaneously trying not to vomit again as she thought—quite reluctantly—about what she had seen, dealing with the fact that she was in the same room as a rather healthy splattering of vomit already, and trying to figure out what in the world Geoffrey could possibly be doing. He was down on his knees, hovering expectantly over a section of the mirror truck's flooring that looked no different than any other section. Delilah gazed at the spot for a few moments, half expecting something to suddenly pop out of it like a jack in the box. Of course, there was no legitimate reason for her to expect such a thing, as there was nothing out of the ordinary about the spot, just another section of floor, but if that was the case, then Geoffrey was not privy to that information. He continued to look on with anticipation that could not be easily ignored. One would've thought that he knew something that Delilah didn't.

She didn't know if the vomit was saturating the truck with its putrid fumes yet, but in her mind, she was already suffocating. She had never before been forced to endure any situation like this for any length of time, and it was decidedly *un*pleasant. In fact, Delilah had just made up her mind that she was tired of this mysterious hidden piece game, when she opened her mouth to shout at Lieutenant Dan that she still needed someone to clean up the mess she'd made on the floor, but before she could sound off her displeasure, a faint click from Geoffrey's general direction halted her attention. By the time she had turned back to where he was kneeling, the spot that he had been staring at was beginning to move and open. A foot by half foot rectangle of flooring moved into the rest of the flooring, revealing a compartment. Geoffrey lifted out a white Styrofoam container that filled the compartment. The container was relatively square and Delilah thought that it might contain food. Forty-five minutes ago, and that would've been a most welcome reality, but now, after her recent 'spill', not so much so.

When Geoffrey opened the box, it did not contain food, but rather the sawdust material that he had described earlier, and what looked like a thin washcloth.

"Spread the sorbent evenly over the spill site, and use the cloth to reclaim the debris from the affected site. If the cleanup is performed properly, it should leave behind no odor or residue." Lieutenant Dan instructed through the speakers. It was clear that he was not used to speaking in every day conversation. Geoffrey could easily imagine him talking as he just had to a soldier under his command on the battlefield dodging enemy fire, or a subordinate officer, over schematics of rival territory. Meanwhile, Geoffrey followed the lieutenant general's orders as obediently as one of those soldiers or subordinate officers, spreading the 'sorbent', the trademark name for the sawdust mixture, Geoffrey assumed, over the 'spill site', giving it a few moments to absorb, and then, wiping it up carefully with the washcloth. The sorbent had absolutely no smell and, except for the fine grain of it, looked nothing like sawdust. The cloth was abnormal as well. It appeared to be a regular washcloth, though very thin even for a wash cloth, but it felt like a moist chamois. It was so moist in fact, that he was sorely tempted to ring it dry after he had soaked up the sorbent-saturated 'spill' with it, but, it was the very fact that he had just soaked up the sorbent with it, that he resisted.

As he was nearly finished with the necessary but unpleasant task at hand, Geoffrey noticed that he had heard no word from Delilah since he began. He placed the sorbent filled cloth back in the container, careful not to spill any of the mess, and once the container was safely closed, he turned to see whatever had become of his female companion. He turned and saw that her mouth was drawn in a line, and her gaze was unmoving at the horizon, stuck upon the spot where the two lifeless bodies had been earlier. Lieutenant Dan's men had moved the mother and her miniature, though not nearly as *miniature* as it should've been, offspring away some time ago. They had even shuffled the sand trail and imprint that was left behind by the two corpses, so that there was no sign that they had ever even been there at all. Even though the two latest victims of The Virus had been removed, the hideous images of them remained burned in her mind as indelible as if mutilated mother and child were there still in the sand. Every moment she spent staring at the images in her mind, they were engraving themselves upon her psyche as surely as if the bodies were still there on the side of the inlet.

It was likely that Delilah would've remained in this position indefinitely, had Geoffrey not introduced himself and a shining bottle of champagne into her line of sight. He held the bottle up with one hand and with the other, he gave Delilah's knee a gentle but firm squeeze.

"Oh!" she exclaimed softly. She turned away from the horizon and saw the bottle. She looked confused for a moment and the smile that spread across her face looked painfully forced, but it was there. Finally, Delilah shook her head violently. Both she and Geoffrey knew that such realities as they had witnessed could never be shaken completely out of either of their heads, but to occupy their focus elsewhere, at least for the moment, was good too. "Oh." Delilah repeated, but this time with less of a violent start. Once she had reasonably returned to herself, she said, "I guess I was pretty out of it, there, huh?"

"Yeah, you were." He answered, as compassionately as he knew how. "But what else could be expected, especially when you've seen something like…" he was reluctant to even intimate the sight of such an unsettling scene "like, that." He made a vague gesture, indicating the inlet behind him. "I don't think that's something either of us will ever forget."

"Yeah, I think you're right." Delilah answered, in a tone and vacant expression that indicated she was being pulled back into a bottomless chasm. Even though Geoffrey's conversation had been meant to do the exact opposite, it was only reminding Delilah of the images in her mind.

"Right." Geoffrey said, more to himself than to his fellow captive. Then, in a louder and more jubilant voice (which was not easy, under the circumstances) he said, "But look what we have." He raised the bottle higher, where Delilah would be forced to look up and away from the inlet to see it. At the same time, he moved closer and deliberately positioned himself between her and the inlet so that she would have to intentionally move around him to see it.

"Champagne!" she said once she realized what she was looking at. "And, oh my God! Is that…that *can't* be." She tilted her head to the side, "*Cristal*." She reached out quickly to snatch the golden bottle, filled with the shimmering and very expensive liquid. Geoffrey could've easily moved the bottle out of her grasp, but didn't. Once the bottle was secure in her grasp, Delilah coddled the champagne to her chest like a newborn babe.

Just as quickly as Delilah had hugged it, she snatched it away and stared at it in wide-eyed wonder. "Cristal! And it's *cold*, too!" she shouted, excitedly. Holding the frigid bottle nearly at arm's length, she admired the rare luxury for a moment, and then lost no time uncorking it. The cork flew a short distance before finally landing in the exact spot where Delilah had vomited earlier. Geoffrey saw that this was about to happen and had groped at the air-bound cork before it made its landing, but to no avail. It hit the spot with a muffled *thud*. Geoffrey loomed over it, knowing that if he and Delilah didn't finish this entire bottle of champagne, it would go to waste because its cork was not fit to reseal it—not if anyone intended to re drink from it again, that was. Geoffrey didn't bother to pick it up. It was no good now, anyway.

His attention was now drawn to the spot where the cork had initially landed. It was clean, as if nothing had ever been there. In fact, the entire area that Geoffrey had wiped once, twice at the most, with the special cloth as he had simultaneously gathered up the sorbent all but shined as if he had given it a brisk scrub. Geoffrey was tempted to bend down and smell it. It looked so clean that he half expected the area to emit a fresh lavender scent, but he didn't bend over. When he turned back to Delilah to draw her attention to the oddity, she had already drained nearly a quarter of the champagne bottle and would have finished the upturned bottle had Geoffrey not resumed his place beside her and smoothly lowered the bottle from its elevated position. Delilah wiped her mouth with the other hand but didn't try to stop Geoffrey from gently taking the bottle away.

"You know, we do have some very nice champagne glasses." Geoffrey said with a smile, gesturing toward the table where two champagne glasses were sitting atop the table. Delilah turned her head to look. When had those gotten there? It didn't really matter, though, as was clear by her face as she turned back to Geoffrey. He noticed that her eyes were glistening as much as the expensive bottle. She was still trying hard to forget the deceased and ruined mother and child images plaguing her brain, and by the looks of things, that wasn't going so good. The champagne helped, which is why she was trying to dispense with it rather hastily.

"Yeah, I guess this really isn't the time for moderation, huh?" Geoffrey mused aloud, and lifted the bottle to his own lips as well. Once he had drained a little less than a quarter of the contents himself, he passed it back to Delilah who lost no time in re-elevating it. The quarter of the bottle that both Delilah and Geoffrey each had downed, almost instantly took effect and both were satisfactorily woozy.

Even though Delilah raised it back to her lips, her alcohol-affected equilibrium didn't allow her to remain that way for long, nor would her tolerance allow her to overwhelm it so quickly. It was the same with Geoffrey. Both were still drinking straight from the bottle, but much more slowly now, as if they were indeed sipping from the empty glasses on the table not far away.

In time, the golden liquid lessened, and with it, the world around them, until the destruction in every direction, the guards looming everywhere, the gruesome sight from earlier, the very Virus itself, held no meaning. It all flowed together in a dance of unreality not unlike a vague dream that one doesn't even properly remember having. The sun was beginning its descent now and the clouded horizon assumed a hypnotic array of grays, reds, and oranges, just beyond the water's edge. It was simply magical, doubly so for the two VIPs because they hadn't laid eyes on a sunset in over a year. The bottle was empty now, and as the sky's flaming orange jewel made its final peek beyond the horizon, Delilah again lifted her face, no longer streaked with tears and makeup, toward Geoffrey. This time, there was no philosophical meandering holding him back. He lowered his head and kissed her with all the denied passion that had been smoldering beneath the surface. Delilah matched that fervor more than equally, and they kissed for a very long time, tongues and hands both groping

311

wildly in a flaming dance of ecstasy, as the sun drowned itself into the open ocean and darkness covered the destroyed land all around.

Chapter 28

When Geoffrey woke up the next morning, the first thing he noticed, after struggling to piece together a vague memory of what had happened the previous night, was that he didn't have a hangover. He clearly remembered drinking, and he remembered drinking a *lot*. He couldn't recall exactly what it was—only that it was shiny, and that it was *good*—but he knew that it must've been potent because it wiped out most of his memory of it. As more time passed and he had the opportunity to awaken more fully, a clearer picture of the happenings of yesterday trickled into his mind like a leaky faucet. He already remembered one bottle of champagne, but now, he remembered Delilah popping the cork on a second bottle as well. He must've been the one to retrieve the bottle from the hidden compartment in the floor, but he couldn't actually remember doing it. He also didn't remember, as yet, whether more bottles followed, though something inside him whispered to him that there was, indeed, a third. After that, it was useless trying to recall anything; it was lost to the bottles.

Still, his recollections leading up to that first bottle were becoming more recognizable by the moment, but, even then, only in bits and pieces. Geoffrey sat on his bed (exactly how he made it back to his bed was one of the many things lost to the bottles), rubbing his temples and simultaneously trying to organize his mind and clear it of the foreign voices that were growing more intense with each passing week. There was so much going on with him lately that he didn't muse on it much, but now that he was thinking on it deliberately, he noticed that other people's internal thoughts were becoming louder, more profound, and easier to discern from farther distances and with more obstacles in between. By all accounts, his telepathy was strengthening. Though he didn't use it nearly as much, his ability to project thoughts as well as receive them was becoming stronger. He could feel it, just below his skull somehow, bulging against his cranium, becoming stronger and more intense. Consequently, it was more difficult to not use it more and more, but there was a reason he tried not to speak into anyone else's head besides Dr. Crangler's. As the doctor had informed him, this thing was best kept as quiet as possible, and would certainly draw attention, the likes of which Geoffrey would definitely not want. Besides, Geoffrey had spoken telepathically to the doctor, but only after lengthy preparation. Intruding directly into someone else's head could get him killed, or at the least, hurt very badly.

None of this altered the fact that, whether he liked it or not, he was still changing and there was no way to know how far that change would progress. The thought resurfaced that he was becoming more like the alien intelligence and, at this rate, he would have more in common with that alien intelligence than not. If his new ability could be somehow generated in others as it was passed on to him, then the entire human race would eventually become, as he had already prophesied, the newest alien intelligence. Even without telepathy, it wouldn't be long before this new mind reading, singularly-connected breed of humanoids would, like The Virus wielding aliens, want to 'branch out' and conquer those they deemed inferior. Perhaps a planet wouldn't be enough. Perhaps, this single human entity—especially scarred by the millions upon millions death toll inflicted by the merciless Virus—would only find solace in laboring to conquer the entire galaxy. The idea of a Bonaparte contingent spreading out in every direction, leaving little else but ruined, unchartered ecosystems and foreign life forms that had called them home, sent a shudder all through Geoffrey, and made him yet again turn his thoughts elsewhere.

He tried again to think of the happenings of yesterday, but that was a dead end. He had already scoured as much from his Cristal affected brain as it was willing to give. He would do himself no further good beating himself up for clues. He rubbed his temples again. Obviously, the staff were making their rounds because though he saw no one and heard no footsteps, a virtual cacophony of voices filled his mind. As he listened more acutely, he noticed that it was not one or two voices that he was hearing, but rather like a small army of people were all talking at once. The sounds in Geoffrey's head didn't have the confusion of a bunch of people all talking at once, but rather it had a certain ebb and flow to it. It was a decidedly erratic ebb and flow, but an ebb and flow nonetheless. It took Geoffrey a few moments to realize that he was hearing not only the nearest occupants of the underground facility, as was usually the case, but rather he was hearing the cumulative thoughts of the *entire* facility, perhaps the entire complex, though it was too early to assume.

Obviously, being allowed out into the open world, if only for a matter of hours, had had a profound effect on the evolution of Geoffrey's abilities. He didn't know if it was the break from the crippling confinement, or the respite from the ever-present Cleaning Lights, but whatever it was, it had enhanced his extrasensory perception considerably. He fancied that along with foreign thoughts, he was now beginning to receive foreign *feelings* as well. He rubbed his temples yet again, but the sides of his skull protested at the repeated pressure. With a long sigh, he slumped over and tried to figure out his next move. One thing was for certain, he needed to see Delilah and figure out what had taken place the night before. Though he thankfully lacked the migraine and nausea of the expected hangover, he still retained some of the other less savory side effects, like dry mouth and general fatigue. He smacked his lips, as if that alone could return some moisture to his partially dehydrated tongue, and moved his head and arms around to try to work some of the uncomfortable stiffness out of his joints. After he finished and could think of nothing else to do, he returned to his slumped position until an idea finally came to him...

He stood up and lifted his hands as if to press them to his temples again, but instead, let them drop heavily back to his sides. He shut his eyes tightly, and concentrated. Dr. Crangler had been looking on this entire time from one of the monitors in one of his smaller offices, so he could see clearly everything that was going on. What he couldn't see, however—because he distinctly *heard* it—was Geoffrey's voice, booming into his head. The startled doctor gripped his head with his hands, just as he did the first time Geoffrey had spoken into his brain like this. Besides Geoffrey's voice being way too loud in his head, there was a new fortitude, a new dimension...a new *power* to Geoffrey's telepathy that was currently overwhelming the doctor in a way that, even though he was nominally used to Geoffrey's abilities, his brain couldn't tolerate it.

"Stop it!" he screamed. He sounded more like a helpless child than he would've liked. "Stop it, Geoffrey!" and immediately Geoffrey withdrew. The doctor blinked his eyes and rubbed his temples until they, too, were sore in an attempt to regather his wits. As soon as his breathing and heart rate returned to normal, he hastily left his office and headed to Geoffrey's room. He nearly tripped over his own feet as he turned the many facility halls in his rush. Once he finally made it into Geoffrey's room, there was a noticeably discombobulated look about him. He was had shaved and combed his hair but his eyes were wide and his hands were trembling. "What the hell is the matter!" he demanded. Geoffrey's eyes were wide now. He was surprised by the doctor's outburst.

"I'm terribly sorry, Dr. Crangler. Really, I'm terribly sorry…" Geoffrey began, understanding his recently elevated abilities had worked, but had had a very undesirable side effect. "Really…I'm…"

"Yes, Geoffrey, I understand you're terribly sorry, but, again, what the hell is the problem?" Dr. Crangler asked.

"Well, I wanted to know what happened last night. Obviously, something…*different* happened to me."

"I don't understand, Geoffrey." Dr. Crangler answered, now almost completely back to his normal self. "What *happened* was what you asked for. Delilah and you were escorted off the premises for the day so you could implement the plan you presented to me."

"Yeah, well, I guess I'd like to know how that went then, because I don't remember much of it. But also, my telepathy, it's seems to have gotten stronger, somehow. I'm..." Dr. Crangler stopped his patient midsentence with an emphatic shaking of his head, and a nearly imperceptible gesture toward the room's hidden camera. Geoffrey grimaced that he understood and was instantly sorry to have made such a foolish slip. He would've likely assured Dr. Crangler that he was 'terribly sorry' again, except that the doctor spoke this time.

"It would probably be best if..." the doctor said, finishing with another nearly unnoticeably gesture toward his head. Geoffrey understood, but hesitated to give a moment for the doctor to prepare himself first. After this latest incident, Dr. Crangler was clearly not ready for more of Geoffrey's soundless communication, but he wouldn't have suggested it just now except that it was the only way for his superiors to not catch wind of the phenomenal developments that were taking place in one of his star patients. After the brief interval passed, Geoffrey and the doctor commenced with the telepathic conversation.

Had Dr. Crangler's panel of superiors being observing—which they most definitely were—they would've been given no indication that an exchange was continuing to take place, except for a grunt, an answering nod, or something of the sort, that would accompany a normal conversation. Other than that, no words were spoken.

Dr. Crangler was the first to begin. *Before we start with this mindspeech,* he advised sternly, nevertheless smiling to himself at the completely new word he had just coined, *please turn down the volume, because obviously you're right. Something did happen to you out there, because it's more unbearable to endure your telepathy now than it was when we first started. Now, I'd like to think I'd grown rather used to this whole experience, but back there in my office, well, that was just too much.* Dr. Crangler waited for an unspoken response, but none followed. The silence lasted so long, that he was about to open his mouth and ask if something was wrong. Just before he could, though, Geoffrey spoke into his brain in something akin to a mental whisper.

Is this any better? Geoffrey asked tentatively. As Dr. Crangler well knew from his experience with Geoffrey's special gift, mental conversation was nothing like its physical counterpart. Though 'voices in one's head' could potentially drive a person insane (though, many would argue that to have 'voices in one's head' would indicate insanity in the first place), thoughts alone could never be loud enough to literally deafen someone physically. He could scream as loudly as humanly possible in another's head and his physical person would never be affected. So, though Geoffrey was taking great pains to lessen the volume of his telepathic voice, it did no good. It wasn't the 'volume' of Geoffrey's soundless voice that was the problem, it was the increased presence, the sudden elevation in power of that internal voice.

No, it isn't Geoffrey. Dr. Crangler answered truthfully as he forced himself to resist the impulse to clap his hands over his ears. Another lengthy silence followed, longer than the first, but the doctor made no attempt to break this quiet, as it was clear that Geoffrey was musing on something, perhaps some way to mute things back down so he and the doctor could engage in wordless communication as before. By the look on his face, he almost had the answer. Finally, revelation broke upon Geoffrey's face. He put up a finger in intimation that the doctor should wait while he tried something. He laced his hands together at the fingers and twiddled his thumbs around and around each other like someone in deep thought, and shortly afterward Dr. Crangler heard Geoffrey's voice inside his head. This time, something of the static from their initial trials, though relatively faint, had returned, and

Geoffrey's mental voice, though still slightly louder than normal, was much more bearable.

Is this better? Geoffrey asked, twiddling this thumbs faster than ever.

Actually, the doctor took a moment to respond, *it is.* As soon as he had heard the very first indication of foreign sound in his head, he had squeezed his eyes tightly shut in anticipation. He now cautiously opened them. *Now, we may continue.* His relief was evident even in his mental voice.

Good, good. Geoffrey answered soundlessly, still twiddling his thumbs furiously.

But, before we go on, what did you do...how did you tone it down? Dr. Crangler asked, seeing Geoffrey's hand movements, but paying them little mind.

This. Answered Geoffrey, calling attention his hands.

Dr. Crangler's mind said nothing, but his face clearly asked the question.

This. Geoffrey repeated. *I had an idea. You see, being here in this room all day and night with virtually no interaction is terrible for a person's mind...unless he has something to concentrate on. So, that's what I did. You just don't know, Dr. Crangler...actually, that's foolish. Of course you know...how many endless hours I've sat here doing nothing but concentrating, trying to discover if it was possible to hone my abilities.* Dr. Crangler remembered seeing his patient bent over for many hours, rubbing his temples, as if he was indeed in intense concentration. He suddenly wished he had come and given his patient something else with which to focus his attention, but what was done was done. *Well, it was. And 1 did, but nothing like whatever happened to me yesterday. Well, anyway, I could hear other people's thoughts more clearly and, so 1 assumed, from greater distances. Well, the idea came to my mind that maybe 1 could reverse that somehow. See, 1 thought that if 1 did something else, something a little distracting, I couldn't focus solely on mindspeech.* Geoffrey smiled, *with you. If focusing my concentration honed my telepathy, then distracting myself should dull it, at least enough so we can talk. And what's more distracting than twiddling thumbs? 1 wasn't sure it would work, but obviously it has.*

Dr. Crangler began rubbing his temples as he continued to stare at Geoffrey. Not only had Geoffrey's vocabulary benefited greatly from this unmappable expansion, but apparently, his problem solving capabilities were evolving as well. Given enough time, who knows what Geoffrey could be capable of? At any rate, Dr. Crangler admitted to himself that he probably wouldn't have thought of such a simple and therefore ingenious way to handle the problem. The doctor had to resist the urge to exclaim, "Brilliant! but he stifled it as best he could. So, his only response was, "As you say, there we have it, so let's move on."

If Geoffrey noticed Dr. Crangler's momentary angst, he didn't show it on his face or in his reply. *Right, good idea, Doctor.* He returned *Well, I have a few questions. I guess the most important one would be, 'What happened last night?' I remember most of the day, but after the champagne bottles...well, I don't remember much after that. Speaking of which, did you arrange that?*

I did. Dr. Crangler answered simply.

Well, thank you very much...so what happened?

The doctor's right eyebrow rose tenuously, then his lips curled into a faint smile that remained for some time. *So,* resumed Geoffrey, *what happened. Did we...you know?*

Not in the mirror truck, no. Dr. Crangler finally answered, *But from what I understand, you two certainly would have. From the information in Lieutenant Dan's report, Delilah was literally coming out of her clothes and throwing herself at you about midway through the third bottle of champagne.*

So, there was a third bottle. Geoffrey thought to himself, but said nothing to the doctor.

And he specified that the two of you would've certainly...commenced, right there on the mirror truck floor for everyone to see if both of you didn't need to use the bathroom very badly.

Use the bathroom?

Completely consuming three bottles of expensive champagne can have that kind of effect on a body.

Geoffrey nodded. Then, after a moment, he returned to the conversation at hand, but now seemed to be studying his twiddling thumbs more acutely. Even at this angle, Dr. Crangler could see that his face had fallen some. *So…my plan failed, things didn't work out.* It was more a sullen statement than a question.

Actually, it worked perfectly. Answered the doctor, but not immediately. He couldn't truthfully deny that his patient's momentary malaise was heartening, even if it was for all the wrong reasons. Seeing Geoffrey deflated encouraged the doctor that he was still the one wielding the power here, even temporarily.

Geoffrey stopped twiddling his thumbs, and his head (and his spirits too) flew upward. *It did?* Dr. Crangler clapped his hands over his ears as quickly as Geoffrey's head had flown upward. *Oh, sorry Dr. Crangler, sorry. Terribly sorry.* Geoffrey answered, twiddling his thumbs faster than ever.

His sudden excitement had thrown all his attention to the doctor and made his mental voice overwhelming. The doctor's hands were still slapped over his ears, and though Geoffrey apologized another five or six times in a more bearable tone, the doctor showed no sign of relief. Finally, he just sat silently and waited, careful to never cease with the thumb rotations. After what felt like hours Dr. Crangler finally moved his hands away from his ears. Gently, the doctor touched his right hand to the inside of his ear and inspected it for blood. Only then did Geoffrey begin to realize the full extent of his abilities. The doctor stood at strict attention, having leapt up at this latest scare. He slowly returned to the chair, but still he said nothing. Once reseated, the doctor heaved a few deep breaths and finally met Geoffrey's awestruck, confused, and most of all, frightened, gaze. By the way Dr. Crangler was acting, Geoffrey was tempted to check to make sure he hadn't inadvertently given him permanent brain damage.

Dr. Crangler opened his mouth to speak and Geoffrey was so anxious to hear him say that he was okay, that Geoffrey forgot to twiddle his thumbs for a moment. Catching his lapse almost instantly, he resumed with an even more fierce determination, chiding himself internally. Meanwhile, Dr. Crangler, having opened his mouth to say something, yawned deliberately instead. He opened his mouth a second time, again giving every indication that he was about to speak, but only performed the same yawn. At last, with an audible huff, Geoffrey gave up. He stopped twiddling his thumbs, unlaced his hands, and slumped his shoulders. "I think we should give it a break for a while and just talk normally. At least, until I can figure out what's going on." He said. He didn't expect an answer from the obviously ailing doctor and began to turn away, when he heard a whisper.

"I think that would be your best idea yet." Dr. Crangler said so low that it was nearly inaudible.

"What did you say?" Geoffrey asked.

"Just give me a moment to collect myself. That was pretty intense." After a few moments had passed, Dr. Crangler spoke again, in something much closer to his regular voice. "Anyway, what I was saying was that your plan did work. It worked marvelously actually." Dr. Crangler wiggled a finger to his ear again, and checked his finger for blood. "Much better than I expected, to be honest."

Geoffrey face lit up instantly, then, just as instantly, grew more sober. "So I...she...we..."

"Yes you did, and quite successfully."

"What does *that* mean?"

"It means that Delilah Hanson has been successfully impregnated."

Chapter 29

Geoffrey had many questions to be answered, but there was one that stood above the rest. "How can you tell that Delilah is pregnant already? If we did have sex, like you claim, then it would've been, what, just hours ago, right? How can you possibly know something like that so early?"

"I'm sure it seems like a far stretch, Geoffrey, but I assure you we have the technology here to determine the exact moment of conception…and you and Delilah had definitely conceived. Don't look so bewildered, Geoffrey, this is great news. It is the news we were hoping for."

As the conversation continued, Geoffrey found that, thanks to Dr. Crangler and his extensive alien studies, operations, etc., the government, and especially this facility, had been afforded the opportunity to extract and manipulate an insanely large host of futuristic technologies, the majority of which were yet in the experimental stage. They all promised advancements that were, until now, beyond anyone's wildest dreams.

The sorbent, the chamois cloth that came with it, the small weapon Lieutenant Dan and his men were holding—a device, Geoffrey learned, that was able to harness the alien light similar to that in the Cleaning Lights, and focus it to the strength of a million of Earth's strongest lasers; so, for its deceptive size, it was the deadliest weapon mankind had ever had— the mirror truck's invisible speakers, the mirror truck's one way mirror walls; all of that and much, much more was in one way or other the result of alien intelligences. *Just another step closer to us becoming the aliens, and that, in the name of progress,* Geoffrey thought ominously. The Cleaning Lights may've also been, according to Dr. Crangler, the reason Geoffrey had not experienced a hangover. The doctor was surprisingly mum as to any further explanation about this and Geoffrey noticed that he labored much harder than normal to hide his thoughts on this particular matter. *No worries,* Geoffrey told himself. He was just happy for the results, however they had come about. But, as man can walk on the moon and still not eradicate the common cold, so Geoffrey still had a difficult time understanding how a pregnancy test could detect pregnancy at the very moment of conception, even in the light of the many further reaching technologies he had just been made privy to.

This brought the conversation full circle and back to the most pressing situation at hand, upon which Geoffrey found out even more from Dr. Crangler that he hadn't known a couple hours ago. First, though Delilah had literally thrown herself at Geoffrey in the mirror truck, the sex that had certainly been partially inspired by too much champagne had not taken place precisely because of the same thing. Before things had a chance to really heat up, both patients found that their bladders were screaming for release, and Lieutenant Dan, being the war-seasoned lieutenant general that he was, valued the maintenance and following of orders over life itself. As such, he strictly refused both Mr. Summons's and Miss Hanson's ardent pleas to be let out, since it was strictly against the orders of not only Dr. Crangler, but his superiors as well. Even when Delilah finally honored his unwavering obedience with every form of profanity her inebriated brain could conjure, the lieutenant general remained completely immovable. There was no doubt that he would've let both patients fill the rear of the mirror truck to its brim with piss and still not ordered his men to unlatch the doors.

Luckily for them, however, he did speed them back to the military complex before such an undesirable set of circumstances could take place. So, no sex took place on their outing, but that all changed after they were allowed to use their separate bathrooms, and, also thanks to Dr. Crangler's arranging, they were allowed to both go back to Delilah's room—thankfully, without Lieutenant Dan present.

"So, we didn't even make it to your gourmet meals on our date, huh?" asked Geoffrey, in a tone more than slightly downcast.

"I wouldn't worry about that too much." returned the doctor, a faint but uncharacteristically mischievous smile on his lips "Delilah and you enjoyed your dessert." Geoffrey looked up sharply. The realization that if he and Delilah had indeed had sex in the facility, then it would've been recorded by the cameras (as was everything else), which meant that prying eyes watched the entire show, had been one that Geoffrey was trying to avoid thinking about for as long as possible. Now, with the fact thrown squarely in his face, Geoffrey found himself speechless. "Hmm," resumed the doctor. In a whisper nearly as faint as when he and Geoffrey had had their last telepathic communication, "Perhaps, I've acquired a bit of your telepathy, because I bet I know what you're thinking." He rose back up and resumed in his normal voice, "But, again, you needn't worry. I'm a doctor, not a voyeur. I only observed until it was clear that things would progress as had been planned. After that…" he made a gesture like that of turning off a television set. "I have no idea if the same may be said of my superiors." Doctor Crangler made a helpless gesture.

The doctor then informed his patient that if he had any further questions, they would have to be answered another time, because Dr.

Crangler needed to get some important work done now that things were officially set in motion. He gestured to the camera for the door to be opened, and left in noticeable haste. Though the reason he gave for his abrupt departure was a legitimate one, Geoffrey knew that it was not the real one. The real reason the doctor had to leave in such a hurry was because he was still experiencing extreme discomfort from Geoffrey's mental outburst earlier. It was clear that Geoffrey's as yet unexplained surge in mental ability was taking its toll on the doctor. As he mused on this, looking down at his hands, he noticed that it seemed to be taking a toll on him as well. He looked hard at his arms and legs. Were they getting skinnier? He lifted each in its turn, and, though it may've only been his imagination, he was almost certain they were considerably lighter. He thought about the late Mr. Reynolds (oddly, enough, the astronomer had not crossed his mind for some time) and his emaciated frame, but quickly brushed any hint of possible connection from his mind. At least for now. The important thing was that Delilah was pregnant, and if things went well, she would eventually bear the child that would be the herald of hope for the entire world. Not a distant second in terms of importance, as far as Geoffrey was concerned anyway, was that he had been granted the opportunity to form a much needed bond with someone with whom he may well be in love, and in this the most dismal of times. He sat in his room now, uninterested in mental exercises, content to let his mind wander, and waited to see what would happen now.

Sure, he wanted to see Delilah, to hold her in his arms, to stroke her beautiful black locks, to ask her if the sex was good for her—that is, if *she* remembered it—but he knew that she would now be under agonizingly close supervision for the next nine months. He supposed she would be watched more in the first trimester, since the beginning of the pregnancy is usually the most precarious time of all, and especially since this was not just any pregnancy, but the pregnancy to save all pregnancies. No doubt Geoffrey would voice his opinion—repeatedly if necessary—that he not only wanted, but also deserved time with Delilah. However, he thought that just now it may be better to let the doctor, his staff, and the powers that be, do their jobs. Besides, he could certainly use some time to get himself together and try to come to terms with everything that was happening all around him.

After a few solitary days of thinking in the midst of trying to let his telepathy lie dormant and unused—which was a job in and of itself—he decided that he had had enough and wanted to see Delilah.

He had expected Dr. Crangler to remind him of what he already knew—namely, that his once-normally allotted times with Delilah would be greatly discouraged at the very least until later on in the pregnancy when things were more stable—but the crippling aloneness that led him to make the suggestion of him fathering the child in the first place had returned. Now that he wasn't spending time in mental concentration as before, it felt like his loneliness had returned a hundred fold. Besides, if he wasn't going to be allowed to see the soon to be mother of his child for a while, what would it matter if he started the process of wearing the doctor down now? Imagine his surprise when he had barely finished his first request and Dr. Crangler readily agreed.

"But my advice is that you be very careful." The doctor counseled somberly, "Lieutenant Dan has been given direct orders to *disable* you if you even appear to pose a threat."

"Disable? If I pose a threat! What's going on?" he asked.

The doctor gave the same 'it's out of my hands' gesture, before answering, "I'm sure you know…" he began, with a knowing look.

"Actually," Geoffrey interrupted "I *don't* know. After what I did to you, I've been trying not to use…" he gestured toward his head at an angle that he thought the room's camera might not pick up.

"Really?" the doctor seemed skeptical.

"Really."

"Well, these next few months will be touch and go for us as far as the pregnancy is involved. A woman's body is very intricate as far as impregnation is concerned. Any kind of trauma, including emotional, can greatly complicate or even thwart things altogether."

"I understand, Doctor," Geoffrey answered "but does somebody think I'm going to hit her or something?"

Dr. Crangler's gaze steadied in thought, choosing his words carefully. "Delilah's been given some special medication, to help things along. It's very good and poses little to no risk, but its one major side effect is that it makes the patient...*moody*." Geoffrey didn't quite know what to make of what Dr. Crangler was trying to tell him, and though he could've easily listened in on his thoughts, he was genuinely trying to refrain from that until he could be sure he wouldn't cause more damage than it was worth.

"Would you mind doing me a special favor, Doctor? Let me spend some time with Delilah and see what was going on. If you do that for me I promise to be on my best behavior." Geoffrey gestured with his hand as if he were crossing his heart. "I'll be very careful to not pose a threat."

Geoffrey hadn't been in Delilah's room for ten seconds before he was given an example of the 'moodiness' the doctor had cryptically alluded to. When he walked in, Delilah was sitting on the edge of her bed staring at Lieutenant Dan, who was seated stoically in the same little foldable chair and in the same position as always, but when she saw Geoffrey, she leapt up and rushed to him, burying her face in his chest and sobbing pitifully.

After a short time of this, she shoved him away and shouted, "Where have you been?" before again burying her face in his chest and sobbing again. Geoffrey held her and rubbed her back cautiously. He hazarded a glance toward Dr. Crangler and was answered with a raised eyebrow and a facial expression that said clearly, 'this is what I warned you of.' If there was ever a time when Geoffrey felt he needed his mind reading powers, it was now. He didn't know what to say or do, so he wisely said nothing, and continued to hold Delilah while gently rubbing her back.

Fortunately, after several long minutes, she calmed down, and the two of them sat on her bed. Lieutenant Dan looked on like a massive, uniformed stone gargoyle, and Geoffrey tried to make sure that Delilah remained distracted from him as much as possible. Neither spoke for a few moments, and it was she who eventually broke the silence. "I don't know what's going on with me, Geoffrey. I feel so, I don't know, out of whack." She glared at Dr. Crangler, then at Lieutenant Dan. "I'm sure it's the *shit* they've been giving me." Geoffrey saw that things were not progressing in a healthy direction by the way Delilah's face was becoming more distorted the more she thought about the 'shit' that had been administered to her. Still not sure what to say, if anything at all, Geoffrey just pulled Delilah back into his arms and held her. Dr. Crangler eventually left the room, but not without giving Geoffrey a quick nod to remain cautious. Now, only Delilah, Geoffrey, and Lieutenant Dan were left in the room. Seeing that Delilah was unwilling to remain calm with him so close, Geoffrey asked the lieutenant general if he would kindly move to a corner of the room further away, and was answered with a simple head shake. Geoffrey would've tried again, but he knew the extra effort would be futile. The lieutenant general would not be worn down like Dr. Crangler. If he was willing to let the most important woman in the world at the moment piss herself in the back of a cargo truck before he would disobey a direct order, then certainly he wouldn't move an inch now to disobey one.

Instead, Geoffrey led Delilah to the other side of the bed where they sat down with their backs to the general. This seemed to work well for her. "How 'bout we get you cleaned up?" He said, once they were seated, "You know, get that pretty hair of yours done up nicely…not that you need it of course, you're absolutely gorgeous right now." He added quickly, seeing Delilah's head start back and her eyebrows raise in mock offense. After which, her head returned to its former position and her expression smoothed out, much to Geoffrey's relief. She chuckled lightly before laughing outright.

"No, you're right." She said, with genuine mirth, "I do need something done with this." She worried her hair in intimation. Without warning, silent tears began to roll down her cheeks, even though a smile was still on her lips.

"Please, Delilah, I didn't mean it. Really." Geoffrey answered, growing more confused and alarmed.

"No, no. It's not that. Like I said, I'm just not feeling like myself. I don't even know why I'm crying. Really. It's that…that…"

"Okay, okay." Geoffrey interrupted quickly, since any thought of 'that shit' on Delilah's part would certainly mean anti-progress. "Well, would you like a fresh styling?" Delilah made a face, as if thinking the offer over and it didn't sound too appealing. "How about a fresh style *and* a facial?" Geoffrey asked and was met with the same playfully bored expression. "How about a fresh styling, *and* a facial, *and* a foot rub?"

"Now you're talking." Was the jovial reply.

"Well, it might take a little doing, you know," Geoffrey gestured with his head "with King Kangaroo and all over there." Delilah's smile widened even more. "But we'll see what we can do."

He did 'see what he could do', for the rest of the day, in fact, while trying not to let Lieutenant Dan's bulky presence haunt his fellow patient. For the better part of the day at least every other day, he and Delilah were together, but, though their initial meeting had been partially his doing, the current arrangement was all thanks to Delilah. She caused such a fuss for so many days, that to not give her what she wanted was deemed more dangerous to the fetus developing within her by Dr. Crangler's superiors, than the alternative.

As the months passed, things continued on a more or less even keel. Delilah's belly began to bulge noticeably with her growing unborn and Dr. Crangler and his staff's testing and caretaking was as faithful and frequent as ever in an effort to make sure the mother-to-be was as healthy and without defect as absolutely possible. As always, Lieutenant Dan was unnervingly present at his post. More than once, Delilah thought to demand a female guard over the brutish looking lieutenant general (since it was obvious that the powers that be would not allow her to go about her business without some kind of imposing figure always inhabiting her room), but she never put words to the demand. Besides, it would've never been allowed, and for the same reason that it had never been articulated. Delilah was the one and only female on the face of the planet not infected with The Virus. No other female would ever be allowed to be in close proximity of her as she could possibly be infected. There were, in fact, no females even allowed on the entire underground complex. Now, it had already been demonstrated that The Virus changed so radically once it found a host that it could've only been spread from the initial infected fragment, not from person to person, which was precisely why Delilah's newborn's blood could possibly be used as a cure. But, as can only be expected, no one was willing to take that chance, anyway.

Chapter 30

Delilah was in her eighth month of pregnancy now and the world outside was still raging and otherwise continuing its decline into complete anarchy and decay. Those who didn't succumb to the depression of losing so many loved ones to The Virus and committed suicide (which was at an all-time high), burned, pillaged, maimed, and even killed, but still found no reprieve for their anger and hopelessness. Not even the military complex was immune to the chaos. It was so well hidden and bordered by a doubly reinforced and foliage overgrowth that made it difficult to tell that anything was there at all, that it hadn't been stormed yet by the raging masses. However, it wasn't so well hidden that it wasn't stumbled upon by an unfortunate few. In a completely unprecedented move, American civilians were gunned down on American soil for wandering too near the base, then their bodies were carried far away. As unbelievable as it was, such a move had been authorized by the president of the United States, but anyone witnessing the chaos that currently encompassed the globe would've understood why such a drastic move was absolutely necessary.

Had the general public (or what was left of it) discovered that a government installation lay beyond the huge, vine covered embankments outside the city's limits, the angry masses would've certainly fallen against its formidable walls until they stormed it like they had all the other government buildings. Unfortunately, it could not be revealed that that hope even existed as desperate people of all shapes and sizes, family and friends of those now pregnant and yet to perish, would storm the base with equal rapidity, clamoring to secure a cure for their loved ones, even though it was not yet time. The result would be the same; destruction and chaos and the ruin of the world's only possible savior.

Inside the complex, and especially in the underground facility, tensions were high and nerves were stretched to their limit. Besides Delilah's highly-fluctuating mood swings, which were already elevated to maddening proportions by her pregnancy, and then furthered by the medicine administered to aid that pregnancy, things had progressed without any major complications. She was in her 33rd week, three weeks before the baby boy was to be induced into this world. Doctor Crangler wanted to ensure 'fetal viability' so that they would have a healthy baby and a better chance of survival, but then it all changed. She had been moved to a larger room where a small army of special machines could monitor everything from her vital signs, to her blood pressure, to her brain waves, to the humidity of the environment, in an effort to make sure everything was perfect for the impending birth. She had demanded, with undeniable fervor, that Geoffrey be there every day, and so a separate bed had been set for him for that purpose. It was highly unorthodox to have him in the room with her, but with it being so late in the game and the home team so close to the winning goal, everyone wanted to make sure Delilah was as satisfied as she could be. No one could tolerate another of her outbursts, but more importantly, everyone needed her vitals to remain within bounds and not complicate things.

It was mid-day outside the underground facility, and inside, Delilah was sitting nearly upright in a special bed that had been built and fabricated especially for her. It was spacious, lined with ultra-thick Temper material, and completely mechanical. It moved in six sections that could all be adjusted to any degree imaginable. It was more comfortable and luxurious that anything Delilah had experienced, even in her previous life. The Temper material was even lined with special energized nylon strips so the bed itself could be made warm at the touch of a button. Delilah was playing with one of the control units just now. Besides Geoffrey, Dr. Crangler, and Lieutenant Dan (of course), were also in the room. Geoffrey was in a plush chair beside Delilah's mega modern bed.

She insisted that it calmed her to have him near, so the chair had been set up so he could be within arm's reach any time she wanted. He was within arm's reach now, sleeping soundly. His head was strewn back on a cushion and a faint snore was coming from his partially opened mouth.

Though he appeared to be enjoying pleasant dreams, he certainly was not. In his slumbering mind, he was on a strange planet, looking at the same grotesquely distorted figures, that he had absentmindedly sketched on his Styrofoam food tray many months ago. For some reason, he'd been having this same dream ever since he started laboring to not use his telepathy. It was as if not releasing his mounting abilities was causing them to build up inside him and this was the result. The dream was always varying in clarity, much more vague at first, to the point that he could only make out shadows of deformed images, but it became clearer with every passing dream. Now, he could see the aliens clearly. As he continued to stifle his telepathy as best he could, certain other things about the dreams became clearer as well. Soon, he knew that he was on a very different planet than Earth and surrounded by a different stratum of beings than the ones on Earth. He also knew that he wasn't moving. He was always in the same place, but that place was never well defined. It was like he was everywhere and nowhere on the planet at once.

How he *knew* all this was beyond his ability to describe. He knew it, and that was that. As this strange reoccurring dream clearer, he began to hear voices, a trillion voices, all in unison, but also not voices, not even sounds, rather, a *being*. The being—whatever it was—was not talking to him, but *infusing* him with knowledge, common knowledge of some sort, but nothing he could remember once he awoke because it was too foreign to him. He thought little of it: The last two years of his life had been filled with so many strange things that an unusual dream just didn't stand out much. This particular time, it was different.

He woke up with a start and looked around; everyone was there. He gestured to Dr. Crangler, who, at the moment, was administering a final dose of 'that shit' to Delilah. The doctor finished up, ungloved his hands, and came over to see what the problem was.

"We need to talk." Geoffrey whispered, which was completely ineffective. The room was deathly quiet and completely soundproof besides, so his low whisper resonated clearly to everyone in the room. It didn't matter, this was important, as he animatedly assured the doctor when he answered that he was too busy at the moment for a private conversation.

"Geoffrey, I have more tests to…"

"This can't wait." Geoffrey's voice rose, even though he was trying desperately to remain calm. The doctor didn't know it just yet but Geoffrey had just realized that his dreams were not dreams at all, but something akin to out of body experiences, where he would end up on the alien planet from which The Virus had been sent. The 'knowledge' he was receiving, though it was no good to him since he couldn't decipher it yet, was the common knowledge being constantly broadcast to the central alien intelligence's varying housings, like one of the ones the doctor had been working on for some time. It was a major breakthrough, but not one he was willing to discuss with anyone other than the doctor just yet. Of course, if he had just said this, the doctor would've immediately asked Lieutenant Dan to leave the room, or more likely, he would've immediately whisked Geoffrey off somewhere they could talk, but Geoffrey didn't elaborate because he didn't want Lieutenant Dan to hear. Dr. Crangler had already warned him of what would happen to him if his superiors ever got word of Geoffrey's telepathic abilities, and he was not too keen on being experimented upon like the alien that he feared he was becoming.

Unfortunately, the doctor was simply not getting the picture. Right now, all Dr. Crangler was concerned with was Delilah and her unborn baby. Geoffrey's frustrations were mounting. He saw the doctor was about to leave, presumably to get more material for more tests, but Geoffrey needed Lieutenant Dan out of earshot and *now*. Who knows what kind of vitally important information could be gained from these dreams, and furthermore, who knows if Geoffrey would remember what he'd seen and experienced enough to explain it the very next hour? It was, after all, a completely foreign planet with completely foreign beings. He didn't understand it himself, how could he draw any parallels that Dr. Crangler would understand. The doctor was heading for the door now, even against Geoffrey's painfully subdued protests. Then a thought came into Geoffrey's mind of how to possibly rid the room of the ever-present Lieutenant Dan. Then, at least, maybe he could convince the doctor that they needed to talk somewhere beyond camera's view.

Perhaps, he could employ his telepathy this one time, just to give the lieutenant general a brief uncomfortable sensation in his brain. Surely, he would need to leave for a moment to see what was going on with him, and that would give Geoffrey all the time he needed with Dr. Crangler. Dr. Crangler was now at the door, gesturing for it to be opened. Geoffrey had to do something, and quick. He opened the ability that he had stifled for the last nine months, but, in his rush, he opened it too quickly, and it was too powerful. Instead of a slight, uncomfortable sensation, Lieutenant Dan could hear Geoffrey's voice in his brain, filling his skull beyond its capacity, with a power and reverberation that would've instantly driven a lesser man to insanity. As is stood, Lieutenant Dan furiously pounded his head. He didn't know what the hell was going on except that somehow Geoffrey was in his head, and it hurt. *Badly*. It felt like his brain was being blown up like a balloon with fire instead of air.

Geoffrey's telepathy was so resonant in the lieutenant general's brain that it literally affected his sight. It was like having a jet engine blast past so close that a person could not only hear but *see* the sound, except that this jet engine was mental and greater in intensity for that fact. His head felt like it was about to literally burst, and a thin line trickle of blood began to roll down the side of his neck from his ear. He was on his feet now, slamming his head with his hands and yelling to high heaven for relief. Lieutenant Dan had been on the battlefield many times, right in the very thick of things, with bullets flying past his head and explosions all around, but he had never experienced anything even remotely and horrifying as this. Seeing his reaction, Geoffrey immediately stopped his experiment, but it was too late. His powers had become so profound in the absence of use that just the echo—if it could even be called that—of his telepathic voice was enough to inspire madness, if not death. It was only because Lieutenant Dan was a war-seasoned veteran that he had not lost his mind altogether and hurt someone seriously. When his sight began to shake and fade with the sheer force of the power that was ripping his brain apart, the thread of his sanity finally broke.

Now, suddenly, he was back in a violent theater of war but the enemy was not on the battlefield, but *in his head*. Geoffrey was now standing near the doctor, both of them by the door, about twelve to twenty feet from where Lieutenant Dan was raving and beating his cranium. Something broke in the lieutenant general's head and in an instant, he had spanned the entire distance separating him and Geoffrey and was literally on top of him. Geoffrey didn't even know he was sprawled full length on the floor until he looked up and saw one of Lieutenant Dan's huge fists coming down toward his face. Everything went white, whiter than the room already was, and when color returned, it was the color of his own blood on that fist, coming down for another hit. And another. And another. And another... Of course, Geoffrey didn't realize it. He didn't realize anything anymore. Everything, the screams, the haze of pain, the fist pounding his face to pulp; all of it was a single indecipherable blur like the dream in the beginning. The doctor had tried to pull the lieutenant general off the patient and was knocked completely off his feet and into the air. He landed some feet away, unconscious. Meanwhile, Delilah screamed and thrashed, but heavy as she was with child, she could do no more than panic fruitlessly.

Geoffrey soon lost all consciousness, but though his awareness of the world around him ceased, the brutal merciless beating didn't. The lieutenant general's enormous fist continued pounding into his horribly disfigured and broken face like a mallet ramming into a pulverized sand bag. The lieutenant general kept pounding until he locked those killer hands around Geoffrey's limp throat and squeezed until bones cracked beneath the awesome pressure. Five assistants burst through the door as soon as it could be electronically unlatched, each of them armed with a tiny weapon like the one Lieutenant Dan and his men had wielded. The weapons were set to the minimum limits, which, thankfully for the terrified staff members, was more than enough to paralyze the massive and angry lieutenant general. Though, one of the assistants had to fire his weapon twice before the raging lieutenant general was as unconscious as the doctor and the telepathic patient he had just mauled beyond recognition, his gargantuan hands still had to be pried from Geoffrey's flattened neck. Dr. Crangler began to stir painfully back to life. As soon as he had returned to the world around him, he instinctively looked over at Delilah, and not a moment too soon, because she needed him desperately. All the excitement around her, as well as her own ensuing panic, had induced premature labor.

She was no longer thrashing, but she was still screaming, as her body prepared of its own accord to expel the very special baby within her. Dr. Crangler's chest was smarting terribly from the hit he had taken. He shook it off as best he could and leapt into action. Even after the completely unanticipated happenings of the last few minutes, the proper birth of this child was still the most important thing by a vast margin. The umbilical cord blood necessary to synthesize a cure to the The Virus had to be extracted while mother and child were still alive and healthy for it to be viable. Then, that blood had to be maintained under very strict conditions and properly cultured and used within a very limited amount of time for this to work successfully. Dr. Crangler had but a single shot to make all this happen, and that shot was right now. Dr. Crangler instructed his staff member to move both Geoffrey's and Lieutenant Dan's body out in the hall until other staff members could get to them.

More staff members were quickly summoned, while the doctor and the present staff members tended to Delilah. It took four stout men to haul the lieutenant general into the hallway, and Geoffrey went out next, leaving behind a near continuous line of blood in his wake. The doctor yelled at a group of the newly-arrived assistants to clean up the blood, as it would pose a slip hazard for other assistants that the doctor needed. Afterward, Lieutenant Dan and Geoffrey were carted away on gurneys and off for medical attention of their own. The lieutenant general would likely suffer no more damage than a sore body and a throbbing headache when he awoke, but Geoffrey...well, that was another story. His poor brutalized body had lain helplessly and without the urgent attention it needed for over forty minutes. From the beating, he was sure to have suffered brain swelling and a crushed airway at the very least. He was breathing shallowly—very shallowly— as they took him off, but there no was telling how long that miracle would continue.

Chapter 31

"Get that IV over here, *now!*" Dr. Crangler demanded "Where's that clamp? I need it, *now!*" The doctor's elevated voice seemed to fill the entire room to beyond capacity and spill out in thick waves into the hallway every time the door was opened to let a rushing assistant or two out to retrieve something being yelled for *now!* Once a steady flow of panicked and rushing assistants surrounded Delilah's bed with most of what Dr. Crangler demanded, his voice lowered to something like a soft cooing, slightly above a whisper. "Okay, Delilah, I need you to calm down and breathe." The doctor said.

"Fuck you! You calm down and breathe!" was the spirited reply, "This *hurts!*"

Unfazed, Dr. Crangler continued, "It's going to be all right, I'm here." Certainly, Delilah was not soothed by his presence, but it was the most natural thing to say, "Just breathe." Delilah wanted to yell again, but the baby was coming based on the pain that was surging through her. Nearly hyperventilating, she was forced to take the doctor's advice and struggle to take long, deep breaths. Dr. Crangler was seated between her legs now, ready to receive the child. At his command, two assistants—one holding one of Delilah's sweating hands and forearms, and the other gently stroking her sweating forehead—were stationed at the head of Delilah's bed. Five or six other assistants were positioned some feet away, also per the doctor's command, near the door in case he needed anything further. Though his head never turned from the woman before him, the doctor yelled toward the assistants near the door, "Oliver, get over here and get that anesthesia started like I showed you! Get some painkillers in this young woman!" Even in the midst of her great painful distraction and labored breathing Delilah had never wanted to thank the doctor so much after hearing this.

One of the assistants leapt forward toward the IV machine and obeyed the doctor's orders. Even before the medicine was in Delilah's blood stream, her breathing seemed to calm. Just the knowledge that some powerful high-grade pharmaceutical help was on the way was apparently enough to help smooth things some. And things continued to smooth out from that point. Delilah's breathing was still harsh, but much less so, as the doctor continued to talk to her in that cooing voice that would've never been used for anything less important than this. He reassured her the entire time that everything was all right, always reminding her to breath and occasionally to push, and in the process deliberately keeping her distracted as the elongated head, then narrow shoulders, then torso, then purplish discolored legs and feet, of the savior of the world were pushed from her. The desperately needed umbilical cord followed, as did the placenta, and with the baby's first breath and first resonant cry, the birth was said to be a resounding success. Birthing children was not Doctor Crangler's primary profession, but, looking down at this screaming baby boy, and realizing, as if for the very first time, that because this life had taken place, all other newborn lives would be able to take place, stirred something deep within him. In an instant, he saw in this newborn's existence every new life to come: Black babies, white babies, Asian babies, Taiwanese babies, Mexican babies, Middle Eastern babies, and every other baby in between. Every single one of them symbolizing the hope and future of their people, every single one of them gasping would live because this child gasped its first breath. Every one of them would see the light, hear the sounds, and feel the warmth of the world that had been prepared for them, all because of this child.

It nearly brought the great doctor to tears, and likely would have, except this was not the time. Shaking himself back into the reality at hand, the doctor promptly clamped and cut the precious umbilical cord, handed the baby to its mother, instructed his assistants to tend to her and the newborn right away, and disappeared from the room. He raced down the labyrinth of hallways, umbilical cord in a special dish, to the room set up for the purpose, where the blood could be properly cultured and stored, and a cure to the mercilessly destructive Virus synthesized. Meanwhile, back in Delilah's room, she was allowed to hold her son while the machines were quickly taken away and replaced with things more suitable for attending baby and mother such as soft towels, warm water and swaddling clothes. As this was going on, Delilah gazed into her child's eyes for the first time. Until now, the life that had been growing inside her was as foreign as the alien intelligence that made the child necessary. It was not her child, it was a thing she had been forced to have because other people's lives, people she had never cared about other than as paid servants, depended on it.

Now, looking into the small face that resembled her own, she realized that this child would need her, would cherish her, would love her, not because of what she had but because of who she was. She was his mother and he would love and need her for that fact and that fact alone. Tears that she didn't know were there began to stream down her face as she gazed deep into her little boy's eyes—eyes that were gazing back at her with more than equal interest—as it continued to dawn on her that this was not an 'it' but an authentic human life. She couldn't put into words what she felt. It couldn't be described, it could only be experienced. And she was experiencing it now, true love for the very first time in her life, breaking her haughty spirit and rebuilding in its place a more humble and receptive one. It was also only now that it really dawned on her what this child of hers was affording to the world. This child's life would grant that this indescribable experience of love could be enjoyed by countless other mothers and fathers too, throughout the annals of history to come, until time and relationship, the only immutable besides God Himself, were no more. She beamed at the child because the truth filled her mind that even if this child never accomplished a single other thing of worth in its entire existence, it had already, here and now, accomplished more than any other child, save *the* Savior Himself. She pressed the child, her child, to herself, as her warm tears covered both their faces.

Chapter 32

SUCCESS OF THE CENTURY! CURE FOR VIRUS FOUND FROM CHILD WORLD NEVER KNEW EXISTED!

This was the headline of just one major newspaper as news swept the globe like a tidal wave that a viable cure had been synthesized. The Virus had at last met its match. Clinics and hospitals, two of the only institutions or buildings that had not been burned to ruin or leveled completely, were packed. In some places, lines stretched for miles, with people crowding in makeshifts tents to get a dose of the cure. Besides the few lucky women who were yet pregnant but not so far advanced that they would succumb before the cure could be administered, nearly every other woman able to bear seed wanted to be pregnant now. Over half the population of the planet had been wiped clean from existence, many by The Virus itself, but many more by the ensuing chaos. Now, with a cure present, and in the wake of all this, the women of the world wanted to repopulate the planet with a vengeance. A global feeling of rebellion against the faceless alien intelligence that would dare perpetrate such a heinous destruction upon the planet, our planet, had materialized and crystallized and would not be denied. The loved ones that had been lost could never be replaced, true, but new loved ones could certainly be produced, and if the strong, healthy women left in the world had anything to do with it, they damn sure would be.

Without doubt, the devastation and loss would not be undone quickly or forgotten, but even the longest road to recovery begins with a single step, and the first of the those single steps, which is also the most important of the steps, had been granted by 'a child no one knew existed'. As per Dr. Crangler's—now an overnight global celebrity of the highest order—advice, the entire military complex was converted to a facility by which to stockpile the cure in massive quantities. The base's huge number of military vehicles, planes, and helicopters were used to distribute those massive stores to the world's clinics and hospitals. Where there were people who could not get to the cure, hospitals and clinics were set up in what was left of their villages and cities so that that would not stop them from receiving the cure as well. The worst was finally over and the world, though still broken and reeling, was anxious to rebuild.

Lieutenant Dan recovered with no permanent damage, and his brief moment of insanity was never rehashed again. Geoffrey, on the other hand, didn't fare as well. The lieutenant general's thrashing had left him in a coma from which no one knew if he would ever recover, but fortunately (or unfortunately, depending on the things that were to happen next) that was not the end of his story. A strange incident took place with the doctor while he was supervising one of the larger remaining hospitals in what was left of one of the U.S.'s major cities. As was normal since word of the cure had reached the world, the doctor was working around the clock. He was sitting in a special, protected room that had been set up as his personal quarters and had been helping with the overwhelming workload for the last sixteen straight hours, when something like radio static began to fill his head.

He looked around this way and that, and, discovering no possible source of the static, listened more carefully, as an evil foreboding began to settle upon him even before he realized what was going on. As he listened intently, he began to fancy that the static was not static at all, but a meshing of voices...mental voices. "Oh, God!" he shouted, bolting to his feet, but resisting the powerful urge to box his ears because he knew that that would do no good against *these* sounds. "Please, God, no!" Now Dr. Crangler was a professional, a medical professional. He had always prided himself on not believing in fairy tales, even ones as elaborate as 'God', but all that had begun to change the moment he first laid eyes on the child back at the once-secret facility that had helped to usher in this whole global revival. Though he still didn't fancy himself a religious man even now, he could think of no one higher, no one with more authority to call upon to stop what he was sure was happening. "Please, God!" he shouted again, genuinely terrified to the very marrow of his bones. "Don't let us defeat the alien intelligence, only to *become* them!"

Unfortunately for Dr. Ian Crangler, the famed synthesizer of the cure that would save the world's progeny and thus its future, only God Himself knew if that was a prayer He would choose to answer.